LINE OF DISSENT

RAY SCOTT

Publisher: Silverbird Publishing

Ray Scott

website: www.raycwscottwriting.com.au

First published in Australia 2022

This edition published 2022

Copyright © Ray Scott 2022

Cover design, typesetting: WorkingType (www.workingtype.com.au)

Scott, Ray

Line of Dissent

ISBN: 978-0-6456266-3-6

pp262

ABOUT THE AUTHOR

Ray Scott was born in Kent in England and lived and worked for over 30 years in the Midlands near Birmingham. After National service in the Royal Navy he joined the insurance industry and was employed for many years in Birmingham and Wolverhampton. He and his wife Mary and their two boys immigrated to Australia in 1970 and have lived since then near Melbourne where he again joined the insurance industry, while Mary rejoined the nursing profession.

Ray has been writing for many years. This is his fifth venture into publishing, the others being *"The Fifth Identity"*, *"Cut to the Chase"* (also a paperback) *"The Wimmera Shoot"* and *"Double Dutch"*, all thrillers.

www.raycwscottwriting.com.au

To the regrettably late John McCormick, whose wit and intellect I still miss. Years ago, I gave him my finished manuscript for approbation and approval. That was not what I received. He declared it only worthy of consideration as a first draft, then proceeded to show why. This finished book reflects many of his suggestions.

PREAMBLE

Reports in a Melbourne newspaper
15th April and on subsequent days:

Man collapses in Melbourne Hotel

There was an incident in a Melbourne hotel in the city yesterday, when a man collapsed in the bar room. Emergency services were called and he was taken to hospital. It is understood that he may have had a heart attack. As yet he has not been identified.

20th April

Death in Melbourne Bar

A man identified as John Bromyard, at present thought to have been living in the St Kilda area, died in hospital after recently collapsing in a Melbourne hotel in the city. No cause *of death has yet been released. The matter is in the hands of the coroner.*

Mr Bromyard, who is unemployed, is thought to have a wife and child living in Ferntree Gully but is believed to have been living with another woman in St Kilda for the past six months.

22nd April

Police Investigating Mysterious Death in Melbourne bar-room.

Police investigating the recent death of John Bromyard of St Kilda, who collapsed and died in a Melbourne bar last week, as yet have no leads. Detective Sergeant Tyson, of the Criminal Investigation Branch, is in charge of the case, which is now being treated as a murder enquiry.

Mr Bromyard is believed to have been poisoned. Police enquiries are ongoing, they are anxious to hear from anyone who was in the Waverley Hotel, situated on the corner of George and Alexandra Streets on Wednesday 14th April between the hours of 2.00 pm and 3.30 pm. The police have no leads at the present time, and can offer no explanation for the occurrence, which is believed to have been a homicide by a person or persons unknown.

4th May

Mystery Bar-room Death in Melbourne Hotel

Police are still no nearer to resolving the mysterious death of John Bromyard in the Waverley Hotel in the middle of April. Traces of a lethal poison were found in the glass from which Mr Bromyard had been drinking at the time, all bar-room staff members have been interviewed by the Homicide Squad and all have been cleared. Police have interviewed other patrons of the hotel at the time but are no nearer to a solution.

CHAPTER 1

'A fair shot,' Frank Gilmore commented as the ball curved slightly in the air and dropped behind the trees. 'You may be just off the green.'

'Not bad at all,' I thrust my wood into my bag. It was one of those rare occasions when the club hit the ball just right and the ball went exactly as intended. This hole was a difficult one, a dog leg with a clump of trees on the inside of the bend, and a water hazard beyond situated alongside the green.

Gilmore hesitated before he drove off, he seemed undecided whether to emulate my shot over the trees or to go for the safer and more orthodox one-two, a straight hit to the corner of the dog leg, then a straight drive to the green. After some thought he decided on the same option I had selected.

'Here we go, ten dollars if I'm on the green.'

'You're on,' I said absently. I noticed a flash in the trees, possibly a reflection of the sun's rays.

'What's that over...?' I began when something hit the tree

behind us, followed by a high-pitched screaming noise, then the sound of a distant reverberation.

'What the hell...!'

Gilmore was in mid stroke, he faltered and sliced, the ball took off on a low trajectory, headed straight down the fairway then swerved to the right for the trees.

'What the blazes was that...?'

'Christ knows!' We both turned to the left as a shout emanated from one of the groundsmen working on the adjacent green. He was waving angrily at us, then ran towards us.

'What the bloody hell was that? Was that you? What the hell is going on?'

'No idea,' Gilmore's ball had continued its flight, plunged into the trees like a rocket and penetrated the undergrowth, leaving a few fluttering leaves in its wake. We both turned as Jack Lorimer, the groundsman, came pounding up, still waving his arms.

'You can't do that here'

'Do what?' for a moment I thought he was saying we couldn't drive over the tree hazard.

'That was a bloody gun shot. Have you been shooting?'

'Shooting?' I was thunderstruck. 'The hell I have. What would I be doing with a gun in the middle of a round?'

'Well someone's taking pot shots, I know the sound of a ricochet when I hear it.'

Jack Lorimer was elderly, dressed in corduroys, a red check shirt, an old trilby hat. He was wiping copious beads of sweat from his brow. His companion, a younger man armed with a rake, was also heading in our direction. We knew them both by sight, occasionally exchanging greetings with them when we passed them on our weekly round.

'Wait a minute! Who's that?'

We all swung round as Gilmore pointed. Well away in the distance we could see two figures emerge from the trees nestling in the dog leg, they had just come into view as they moved to the right. They both appeared to be carrying something of golf club length under their arms and were in a hurry. One of them looked back at us as they headed in the direction of the water hazard.

'Oy!' Lorimer uttered a stentorian bellow, but the distant figures merely increased their rate of progress as they rounded the water hazard and disappeared over a knoll in the middle of the 14th fairway which ran parallel to ours.

'Stupid bastards!' the groundsman cursed angrily. 'They could have killed someone.'

'Why should anyone be doing any shooting here?' I was perplexed.

'Well, we get occasional duck shooting going on around here, but they're out of season,' Lorimer replied. 'I suggest you gentlemen carry on with your round, I'll report this to the club-secretary.'

He and his young companion, still armed with his rake which he looked capable of using well in an emergency, headed down the slope towards the trees and the club-house. Gilmore looked at me and shrugged.

'Do you reckon somebody really was taking shots?'

'Pigs arse!' I replied. 'Jack's re-living his time in the Vietnam War.'

'Well let's get cracking,' said Gilmore.

We started walking down the slope.

'Getting warm,' commented Gilmore as we approached the trees.

I agreed absently, I was eyeing the trees warily, and could feel the top of my head tingling. Was Jack Lorimer really imagining things? Or could there really be some lunatic taking pot shots? Jack had done some years in Vietnam in his younger days and usually said so at length when he'd had a few, to anyone who cared to listen. I too had served some years in the Australian Army and had spent time on many jungle patrols in what amounted to a war zone. I had not been regularly under fire, but had been on the receiving end of rifle fire from insurgents enough times to have a real idea of what a bullet would sound like when it buzzed overhead. We also had Lorimer's emphatic opinion that it had been a shot. We entered the small copse and began searching for Gilmore's ball. As we foraged around, I noticed a small plume of smoke rising from the bracken.

'What's that?'

'Some bloody fool has thrown down a lighted cigarette,' grunted Gilmore. He reached down with his club head, with which he had been beating the undergrowth, and made as if to crush the nub end with the steel head. Then he bent down and picked it up.

'That's odd, it's still in a cigarette holder.'

'What!' I took it from him, prised it out of the holder and was about to crush it underfoot when I had another look.

'That's funny, it's foreign,' said Gilmore. 'It smells like a French Gauloise.'

'Well, whoever he is, he could have set the whole damned lot on fire, this is the bush fire season.' I said angrily. 'What have you got there...is that your ball?'

'No' Gilmore stooped and picked something up. 'It's a cartridge case.'

'A cart...! It's what?'

'A cartridge case!' Gilmore scratched his head. 'Bugger me, here's another.'

Unmistakably they were just that, two used cartridge cases.

I caught sight of a flash of white as I looked further and found Gilmore's golf ball nearby.

'What the hell is going on?' I said in wonderment. 'Somebody really was shooting, and they weren't shooting duck, not with these.'

'Too right they weren't,' Gilmore looked thoughtful. 'Why should anyone be using a rifle like that here?'

'Maybe a dissatisfied policy holder.'

Gilmore grinned, this was a standard insurance man's joke!

'Maybe they were shooting snakes.'

'If anyone is going to shoot snakes around here it would be the greens staff, in any case it's illegal, isn't it? Don't they have to arrange to have them caught and moved elsewhere? Aren't they a protected species round here?'

Gilmore shrugged.

'I've never really thought about it. Well, let's get on with it. I'll try a shot from here, and see how I go.'

His ball landed on the green. My own ball was sitting on the fairway, after my first shot had cleared the trees and landed there, I promptly made a mess of a promising position. My thoughts were utterly distracted, I was wondering about gunshots and spent cartridges and as a consequence landed in a bunker that possessed a pronounced overhanging lip which cost me a couple of strokes. We finished the round and were approached by Ron Parish, the club secretary, as we were leaving.

'I understand something funny was going on near the 14th, Jack Lorimer has been having words with me,' he said. 'Somebody with a rifle, so he said.'

'Something like that,' agreed Gilmore. 'Jack thought it was us at first. We found a couple of spent cartridges but we decided to leave them at the scene, we assumed the police would prefer that.'

9

'Yes, good thinking, I'll mention it to them in case they miss them but they're pretty thorough. A squad car arrived a few minutes ago and they're searching that wooded area. We've informed the police the shots appeared to come in your direction so they'll want to interview both of you and Jack Lorimer, although I don't think he saw much.'

'None of us did, we heard more than we saw, but one of the shots was bloody close,' Frank Gilmore said. 'If it had been much closer it would have parted my hair.'

Parish nodded.

'Very well, the police have your details, your phone numbers anyway. They'll be in touch.'

After the round we left the club-house and loaded our clubs into our car boots.

'See you next week?' asked Gilmore as we prepared to board. I shook my head.

'No can do,' I replied. 'I have to go to a christening in New South Wales, my sister's first born.'

'I thought you weren't on speaking terms.'

'We weren't, but this came out of the blue,' I replied. 'A good thing really, I guess I've been nursing a grievance long enough, silly really, it was all about very little, storm in a teacup. Just as well if we bury the hatchet.'

'What was it about?'

'Elder sister, younger brother stuff, she seemed to think she had the perpetual right to tell me how to behave and how to dress...maybe she was right when I was a ten-year old, but when you reach middle twenties plus it becomes a bit wearing.'

'How long since you've been in touch?'

'A few years, I hadn't told her when I moved up country and I didn't tell her where either, the invite came via an old buddy of mine in Sydney.'

'What about the police, about today's shooting?' asked Gilmore. 'They'll want to see us pretty soon.'

'Well, I can't do it today, I'm leaving early tomorrow. I'll see them when I get back.'

We exchanged farewell salutes and drove out of the car park. Frank and I were both insurance representatives, not with the same company. We covered much the same territory geographically and came across each other frequently on our travels, at Insurance Institute meetings and Golf Days. We met occasionally on our rounds, in insurance brokers' offices and at Insurance Institute educational seminars. We first crossed swords on a Golf Day when the Tasman Insurance, Gilmore's company, had played the Jupiter, my own employer, in an Insurance Charities Golf Tournament. That had been some years ago, now our golfing days were strictly 'amateur'. We had one afternoon a week on the golf course, same day same time, weather permitting.

As I drove from the club house, the strange event crossed my mind again. What on earth had occurred today? Would anyone shoot at us? Was it us they were shooting at or was it just a trigger-happy idiot with a gun fooling about? If they *were* deliberately shooting at either one of us, clearly it was a case of mistaken identity. Alternatively, it could have been either a duck shooter in the wrong area or a lunatic. Another consideration was that there were some police members of the club. Now I thought about it, one of those could have been a possible target, maybe somebody from the Underworld trying to silence a detective or to even up an old score. I puzzled over the incident afresh but then dismissed it from my mind and headed for the office. I had paperwork to lodge before I left for New South Wales in the morning.

CHAPTER 2

had been christened Philip Samuel Bromyard Meredith when I was born 29 years ago. The last two names had originally been hyphenated, a feature I had noticed on my father's birth certificate when filing details of his death a few years ago. He had never used the hyphenated version, always being known as Roland Meredith, although he had felt sufficiently strongly about the other name to include it not only when he had me christened, but also bestow the name on my sister Mary who was seven years my senior. My father's younger brother Ralph, now in Canada, had also retained the name when naming his own sons and daughters and I had a sneaking suspicion it may have been the name borne by a de facto 'wife' way back in the 1880's on the wrong side of the blanket before the family left England. I had been sufficiently curious once to look it up in Debretts Peerage and also Burkes Landed Gentry, but although Meredith did appear on its own, I couldn't see any connection. Of the surname Bromyard there had been no mention. I had asked my father once, but he shrugged his shoulders and replied 'Heaven knows!' and carried on working out the household accounts.

My sister Mary and I were born in Queensland in some one-horse town where everything went mildewed if it was left unattended for a period of longer than three hours. My father worked in a bank at the time and had followed the possibilities of promotion by working overseas in New Guinea and after five years being transferred to Sydney then back to Queensland and after that south again to Sydney. He was believed to have contracted some tropical disease during his overseas tours and he had died a few years ago.

My sister and I had no other siblings, my parents had, I think, initially decided one child was enough, as my father spent much time overseas. My mother once said my father had celebrated overenthusiastically when his favourite football team had won the premiership seven years later and I was the result.

After I enlisted in, served my time, then left, the Army, I joined an insurance company in Sydney, was transferred to Victoria, then left that company and joined the Jupiter Insurance, the post I now held. This was in country Victoria covering about nine small towns attached to a branch office situated in one of them.

Up to now I had avoided marital status, I had had two false starts and the second time had reached the point of actually fixing a wedding date, but after we had exchanged engagement rings I became increasingly uneasy as my fiancée became more proprietary and her voice became more strident whenever she addressed me after the wedding date had been settled.

I had noticed her mother ruled her father with a rod of iron; she was clearly in charge of the household and collected his wages from him when he brought them in through the door. Their daughter obviously accepted this state of affairs as normal once a man had been snared, the formality of our engagement signalled an abrupt change in her behaviour and manner towards me which became more marked when the wedding date was fixed. This, fortunately, had been several months ahead so consequently when matters finally came to a head no heavy expenditure had been incurred, apart from engagement rings.

I returned her ring, but never got mine back, it probably finished up in a second-hand jewellers in Stawell somewhere. I wasn't that bothered, being merely thankful to have avoided what could have been a terrible mistake and to be off the hook. I was still marvelling that I had become engaged to her in the first place and failed to see her true nature in my first blaze of love but attributed that to love being blind. Nevertheless, I was thankful the said true nature had revealed itself in time.

I had been casually dating a girl, Jane Bergman, in the office now for about three months, we had both been taking it in a somewhat offhand manner, I think she was on the rebound too, although I was becoming aware my adrenalin began to run whenever I saw her, a sure sign I was becoming more 'locked on'. I hoped she was too.

The following morning, I set off and eventually arrived in northern New South Wales. My initial meeting with my sister Mary was not easy as we both experienced embarrassment. I had flounced off in a huff some years before when she had criticised my personal appearance at a formal gathering, which had been the latest in a very long series of criticisms which she believed she had the right to address to her brother seven years her junior. To make matters worse, I hadn't been too keen on her boyfriend at the time, I thought he was the worst type of 'ocker' Aussie and feeling and, acting in a retaliatory mood, had said so, which hadn't improved matters. She subsequently married him and I didn't attend the wedding, although this was not out of pique, I was then serving in the Army and overseas. After I returned to Civvy Street we had drifted further apart, she lived in Sydney and I was in country Victoria.

After the first stilted greetings were over and I had dumped my travelling bag in the room allocated, we met downstairs and began to talk. Over the intervening years she had mellowed and, in addition, I discovered her husband Robert Wayman wasn't such a bad fellow after all. My initial impression had been correct, but there is many an 'ocker' Aussie who realises, when he has a wife and a mortgage, his behaviour pattern has to modify and the pub and racetrack are not the best places to 'invest' your money.

During a conversation on my second day there, the day before the christening that was the main reason for my visit, she did utter one criticism, in this case justified.

'Why didn't you tell me your address when you moved?'

This was a question I found difficult to answer. Some of the proprietary comments she had made to me in past years had still rankled, consequently when I moved up country, she had been low on my priority list of people to be informed and as time drifted on, she had drifted off my radar. I had never thought of telling her, although I may have got around to it eventually.

'Guess I just didn't' I mumbled, our eyes met and she smiled.

'Don't bother to explain, I know why,' she said wryly. 'I was a bitch, wasn't I?'

'Well, maybe,' I decided not to dwell on it. 'But you invited me here, the olive branch eh?'

'Something like that,' she said. 'But I must admit it was sparked off by a phone call from a friend of yours, someone anxious to get in touch, and I was ashamed to admit I didn't know where you were. He didn't believe me, but I couldn't help him.'

'Oh? Who was that?'

'Someone I didn't know,' said Mary. 'I've forgotten already, but I wrote it down, I think it was a Graeme Short,' she turned to her husband who was talking to a mutual friend of ours at the other end of the room. 'Can you bring my diary over here, please Robbie?'

Robert picked up her diary from her desk and handed it over; she thumbed through the pages, flattened it out and handed it to me.

'There he is. Oh...it was Shaw, not Short. I didn't know him at all.'

'Graeme Shaw,' I thought over the past few years and where I'd been. The name didn't ring a bell at all, not from school, my first few workplaces, the Army, nor my recent insurance and golfing past.

'Did he leave a number?' I asked.

'Yes,' Mary shook her head. 'But he said he was in a hotel in Sydney and had to chase other leads, I didn't quite know what he meant by that and he didn't elaborate. He said he would only be there for a couple of days and he'd be in touch again, but he hasn't.'

'How long ago was this?'

'Oh, how long ago was it?' she pondered. 'About three to four weeks. That's when I began to realise that perhaps I'd treated you badly and started looking for you myself. Eddie Callaghan was the first one I thought of, I knew you used to be close with him.'

'Yes, Eddie got in touch and said you were looking for me. So...you've heard nothing more from this Graeme Shaw?'

'No, not as yet. What do I do if he rings again?'

'Just get his number and pass it on to me, you know where I am now. But the name doesn't ring a bell at all.'

The visit and the christening went off well, our relationship seemed to have started afresh and I left with some regret I wasn't staying longer. I backed down their drive into the roadway, waved frantically to Mary and Robert and others who were still there and drove slowly away.

There was only one jarring note. Who the hell was Graeme Shaw?

*

There was a message on my answering machine when I arrived back home, it was Roger Longville, a local detective-constable. I knew him well as I often consulted with him when I was investigating local burglary claims. My usual questions addressed to him were on the lines of...were the claims genuine or not, had they been reported to the police, and did the items reported to us as stolen correspond with those reported to Victoria Police? He was also a member of the golf club and I had played with and against him in tournaments.

His message indicated he wanted to interview me regarding the shooting incident at the 14th hole, he left his number for me to call. When I did, we arranged a time, I called at the police station and he took me to an interview room.

We engaged in a bit of small talk to begin with, mainly about the golf club generally and a hole in one he'd recently made.

'Could have cost me a fortune,' Roger said with a grin. 'But years ago, I took out one of those 'Hole-in-One' policies through Frank Gilmore, the one that repays what you pay at the bar if you do a hole in one. I told Frank he was profiteering, selling policies that would never pay out, and within a month I landed a drive straight in the hole. My drinks bill came to over $100 that day, but the policy paid up.'

I nodded. Frank had sold me one as well, although up to now I'd had no need for it. The Tasman Insurance tended to go for some of the more bizarre type risks it thought might attract further lines of business. In some cases, they were right. Roger reached for his pad.

'Bloody odd, this shooting business,' he shook his head. 'I've been in the police for a few years now, I did a stint in Melbourne and we had occasional shootings especially in the Western suburbs. But since I've been stationed here there's been nothing. Now when we do get one, of all places it happens at the golf club. Unbelievable!'

We talked about the shooting for about twenty minutes before we put pen to paper, I marshalled the facts and sequence of events in my mind and dictated while Roger wrote it down. I couldn't say much of any use to the police. That particular hole was a dog leg, with a thick clump of trees in the 'elbow.' Frank and I usually tried to carry over the trees and land on the fairway beyond, we'd been doing that for some time now and succeeded more often than not. This time Frank had landed his ball right in the trees, mainly because he had been distracted while taking his shot. The first bullet must have come close to me as the police discovered it hit a tree trunk some way behind us, where the second one had finished up was anybody's guess. We had been aware something had whirred past us and then heard the sound of the shot.

'Assuming you or Frank had been the target, you've no idea why anyone should take a pot shot at either of you.'

I shook my head.

'I know this sounds silly,' Roger said wryly. 'But any dissatisfied customers?'

This was something Frank and I had said in jest, but Roger wasn't joking. I shook my head.

'We dug the bullet out of the tree,' said Roger. 'We haven't identified the weapon yet, the bullet was badly damaged, maybe they used an AK 47, but we don't know yet. Those cartridge cases you and Frank found, and the bullet, are still at forensics.'

'Bloody hell!' I said heatedly. 'They could have killed somebody.'

'I think that was their intention,' Roger said dryly. 'They weren't shooting at ducks, and those shots, considering where they were fired from, were very accurate and came very close to you and Frank.'

CHAPTER 3

'Have you any idea how much is missing?'

I propped myself against the counter to make myself more comfortable. It was an old-fashioned shop, with goods on shelves all around the walls, plus a counter, behind which stood the proprietor. The door was half-glazed with four small windows in its top half. Why anybody would waste their time and energy burgling a small grocery/hardware cum old junk shop no self-respecting customer would be seen dead in was beyond me. The crime was either committed by a local drug addicted teenager to whose addled mind the shop assumed the proportions of a profitable supermarket with vast quantities of loose cash, or maybe a passing thief who suffered from boredom and/or short sightedness. There was also the possibility of fraud; the shop didn't look as if it would be too profitable.

'When did you discover the break-in?'

'About four am this morning,' he replied. I ignored the tautology as I completed the question on the claim form. The shopkeeper's name was O'Flynn, a short, squat man, with a round shaped head on top of which sat a ring of black hair. His face was flushed and his eyebrows were a dark pair of crescents above his green eyes.

'Have the police been yet?'

'Er...no,' O'Flynn looked crestfallen. 'They haven't. Not yet'

'When did they say they would get here?'

'Well...er...I haven't actually told them yet, I've been busy cleaning up the mess and ...!'

'They will have to be informed,' I adjusted the form on my clip board. 'Without a Police Report we can't complete or pay any claim, it's a condition of the policy, and you'll find the police won't be too pleased either if there's been a burglary and it hasn't been reported.'

I was beginning to feel less and less happy about the whole business. I could recall having qualms about putting this particular risk on the books in the first place, it had been at the insistence of a local Building Society manager who had lent money to some close connection buying a house in Stawell. This connection had a friend who had a cousin who had a friend who knew a man...etc, etc. I had suggested extra physical protections before we assumed any cover, a bolt here, an extra lock there and bars on the side windows, but had been over-ruled by my local branch manager who didn't want to offend the large building society connection. Now we were reaping the consequences, if this claim was genuine it would wipe out any premiums for the next ten years.

With my worst fears realised, it gave me great satisfaction as I pictured the scene where I would triumphantly report to my manager that my misgivings had been justified.

'You mean I have to inform the police?'

'I'm afraid you do, Mr O'Flynn,' I replied. 'You'll have to give the local police station a ring, ask for either Constable Berwick or Constable Longville, the sooner the better. And I'd suggest you stop doing any more tidying up, the police will consider this a crime scene and will want things left as they are.'

'All right,' he didn't look happy. He opened his mouth to say something, I bet myself a dollar to five-cents he was going to ask me to bend the rules for him but he finally said nothing.

'Well if you can sign here, Mr O'Flynn,' I pushed the clip board holding the claim form under his nose. 'But I'll have to hang fire on this until I get details from you and the police.'

'Details?'

'The name of the constable to whom you've reported it,' I put the form in my brief case. 'We'll need to see the Police Report. I can do nothing until I hear from you, OK?'

*

I wasn't so sure, as far as O'Flynn was concerned, that it *was* OK! I drove away from the small settlement at a fast rate as I had another call in Ararat that morning, then I was meeting a friend of mine, Bill Otway, for lunch. I reached the 'T' junction where the road joined the Western Highway, after taking the turn I accelerated away fast. I had half an hour to meet my deadline for the appointment, a small broker in Ararat, and estimated I could leave his office and reach the local hotel at noon. With part of the road now a new freeway I should make it on time.

My mind persistently drifted back to the incident on the golf course with Frank Gilmore. I was still puzzled and even more so that Frank and I could have been spied on, quite apart from being shot at. Why was a marksman in those trees? That shot could only have been fired in our direction. A disenchanted policy holder maybe! One who had been upset by one of us? Could it be another O'Flynn? I smiled at the thought, then thought of the rifle shot that missed us both by a whisker, at which point I stopped smiling. I glanced at my watch, pressed my foot down and the car bounded forward. It had certainly been an odd experience.

For some time I had been watching a car in the distance behind me which slowly became larger and larger in the mirror.

'He must be travelling,' I mused as it came closer. 'Oh bloody hell!'

I drew into the side of the road in response to the flashing lights and the wave, one policeman remained with the vehicle while the driver climbed out and advanced towards me. He wrote down my registration as he passed in front of my car and cocked his eye at my registration plate.

'You were timed between two half kilometre posts, making one kilometre in distance, and the time taken was 30 seconds. You then attained a speed and maintained it, of about 110 kilometres per hour. The speed limit on this road is 100 kilometres per hour at all times, therefore you exceeded the speed limit by 10 kilometres per hour. Can you give me any reason why you were travelling in excess of the speed limit?'

'No!' I said sullenly.

'Then you can find no reason why you should not pay the statutory fine…?' I didn't listen to the rest, I'd heard it all before, a few months previously. He was busily writing the ticket, with evident enjoyment and pursing his lips firmly. I knew him slightly as I had come across him occasionally at Rotary Club luncheons when he had been a visiting speaker and also when I had called at local police stations when investigating burglaries and stolen motor vehicles. He was also well-known for being a dry, humourless, dictatorial bastard.

'You have 28 days in which to pay the fine. If you wish to challenge the circumstances and the speeding fine you will have to attend court. All right?'

'All right' I answered sourly but it wasn't bloody all right. This would cost me about $150, which I could ill afford, and result in demerit points which I could afford even less. I couldn't see the point of spending vast sums of money on freeways and then imposing a speed limit of 100 kph, exactly the same as it had been on the road it had replaced. I was tempted to pursue this point with Sergeant Ramsey, but thought better of it.

'Where are you driving to?' he asked as he tucked his ticket book into his pocket.

'Ararat' I answered shortly. If the bastard was trying to be chatty, he could find two could be bloody minded.

'Then drive there safely and observe the speed limits,' he said coldly and turned on his heel. He climbed into the car, revved up, described a 'U' turn, traversed the central reservation and headed back the way we had both come.

'You bastard!' I ground out furiously as the police car disappeared at a fast rate. I was late now and stabbed my foot viciously on the accelerator. It was lucky Ramsey didn't see me on the remainder of my journey but I worked on the assumption he was probably the only police car on that particular stretch of road and it was unlikely I'd come across another. I was right, if one had seen me, I doubt it would have caught me.

*

'One hundred and fifty dollars!' Bill Otway was incredulous. 'That's a fair whack!'

'You can say that again,' I intoned sourly.

'Who was it?'

'That bastard Ramsey!'

Bill laughed and I even found myself grinning.

'He's a sour sod,' said Otway. 'Anyway, let's talk of something else.'

'Agreed,' I said. 'Anything else will do'

'Have you fixed up that hole in your tent yet?'

I nodded agreement. Bill and I were planning to take a couple of weeks leave starting in ten days. We had originally met in the Army, both of us having been undecided what to do when leaving school, and decided to join up. We both served in East Timor, the Solomons and other Pacific trouble spots where Australia had been involved in what were more or less police duties. We were also both members of the local rifle club.

After leaving the Army Bill's life in Civvy Street was fairly ordinary, guess mine was too. He worked in a bank at Ararat, but every year we had the urge, familiar to many ex-servicemen who have served in conflict or police situations in the Armed Services, to relive our days roughing it in the outback, or just outdoors. For some years, both being single and unattached, we had taken leave and camped in the bush, sleeping in tents, maybe in the open if the weather was kind and cooking our food over a camp fire.

Bill had been stepping out and living with a young woman he had recently met named Marlene. From comments she had made during my brief acquaintance with her, I had the feeling this camping saga of ours would likely be coming to an end, I could understand that no young woman would approve of her man disappearing off on some Boy Scout jaunt every 12 months without her for a couple of weeks. From conversations I'd had with Jane Bergman, with whom I was fast becoming involved in a more than friendly relationship, it was clear Jane wasn't too enamoured of it either. Nevertheless, Marlene had acquiesced with our proposed forthcoming camp, but it was clear that now their relationship was cementing into something more serious it would more than likely be our last. Marlene was a resilient girl, in the few months they had been an item and decided to try living together, she had put up with his wildness, but had worn him down until nowadays he hardly drank at all during the week with only the occasional beer at weekends. He looked better for it too, the beer pot belly he had nurtured with great success in earlier days had begun to subside. As I watched him ordering a fresh round from the bar, today would be one of his rare mid-week drinking occasions, and observed his thinner waistline, I had to admit she had been good for him.

We drank in silence. I was calculating how I would find another $150 from my long-suffering bank account, courtesy of Sergeant Ramsey, while Bill was clearly wondering whether he could find an excuse for another beer after this one. As he had an afternoon's work ahead of him in the bank, and I had a prospective afternoon on the road, I decided not to accommodate him.

'I hope the rain stops before we head off.' he said.

'Too right,' I agreed. The climate had been one of the wettest for the last ten years, the winter had been so wet there had been fears the undergrowth would grow to be so lush before the summer heat it could turn to tinder and cause a horrific bush fire season. This year we were intending to make the Mount William Range between Stawell and Hamilton our main stamping ground, we would be fairly high up and well out of the vicinity of any water inundated ground, as long as we kept away from any cascading watercourses that could make life difficult.

'Time I was getting back,' he wiped his mouth with the back of his hand. 'See you next week?'

'I'll give you a ring anyway,' I said as we prepared to leave. 'Let me know if you think of anything else we might need.'

'Good enough. See you, Phil.'

*

I drove back to Stawell from Ararat without incurring any further wrath from Sergeant Ramsey, had he seen me he would probably have nodded with grim approval because, being deep in thought, I never reached the 100 kph speed limit. I was thinking of the coming two weeks camp with Bill Otway and, again, the odd happenings on the golf links with Frank Gilmore. I also thought of Jane Bergman, my current girl-friend, who worked on the Accident Underwriting department of our office at Horsham. The branch office wasn't large, we had twelve staff which had five sale reps attached to it. Between us we covered a wide area.

The Branch Manager was Doug Hollister, a genial, easy going type who was ideally suited for a quiet country branch. He had not long to go before retirement, some said he had been retired for years, but he was a gentleman and loved administering his country branch. He tended to be overawed by top brass from Melbourne Head Office, but visits from there were rare.

I became aware of a car in my mirror and slowed down although I was already under the speed limit. The car behind me did so too, it was still behind me by some distance when I reached the apartment block where I lived. I drove into the parking area and parked in my car port. As I disembarked, I noticed the other car had drawn into the kerb a few metres down the road. As I peered at it over the top of the brick boundary fence it revved up and drove off.

CHAPTER 4

'Hi, Phil,' I was greeted by Doug Hollister as I entered the office the following Monday. I responded in kind.

He waved his hand cheerily and entered his office. I looked quickly around the office and caught Jane Bergman's eye. She was chatting to Jack Stanley on the Accounts section. Our eyes locked for a few seconds and she treated me to a beaming smile. She was about 25, I had not ascertained her exact age...yet. She was about 5' 7', dark haired, slim and easy on the eye. She had been working at the Jupiter for about six months and three weeks ago I had plucked up the courage to ask her out for dinner at one of the local restaurants. I had uttered the invitation fearfully, sure I could get a rebuff and be summarily dismissed, but she had accepted. Since then we had established a rapport. I was chatting to Ken McGowan, the underwriter, about O'Flynn's claim but I was anxious to get away from him and talk to Jane.

I finished my conversation with Ken, like me he thought the

claim was shonky and said he would check with the police to see if it had been reported. I strolled over to Jane's desk.

'Would you like to buy a raffle ticket?' she asked.

I nodded in reply, resisting the temptation to offer to buy the whole book. I offered her a ten dollar note to prolong the transaction and we wandered over to the cashier to change it.

'Are you going to the barbecue?' she asked.

'Barbecue?' I was perplexed until I remembered it had been the subject of the latest office social club broadsheet recently circulated. My normal instinct was to avoid like the plague anything to do with internal office functions. I could still remember a Christmas office party one December evening at an insurance branch office in Sydney years before that got completely out of hand. A junior employee had surreptitiously entered the Chief Clerk's office during the latter stages of the evening, probably with the intention of writing some insult on his superior's message pad, and had surprised the Chief Clerk and one of the typists locked in a tight embrace which bore signs of moving onto another plane. The Chief Clerk had omitted to lock the door!

Ken McGowan had a predilection for organising this type of function, he was rumoured to have an unsatisfactory home life which may have accounted for his desire for office social functions. Maybe he too hoped one day he could come to a mutual agreement and lay a secretary across his desk, although no doubt even he would draw the line at Miss Gunter, the dragon who was head of the trio of keyboard operators. In addition, any social functions we organised were often graced by members of staff of other insurance companies in the town to boost the numbers.

'On Saturday.'

'Yes, I remember now,' I said. 'Will you be there?'

*

Saturday dawned bright and clear, the temperature forecast was 33 degrees, it was already in the high twenties when I left my apartment about 8.30 and ambled slowly down the road to the main street. intending to buy a bottle of wine for the barbecue, and a set of golf balls.

Afterwards I recalled I did register the white car parked near the gateway of the block of units where I lived. The man at the wheel was reading a newspaper and another man was in the passenger seat. I don't normally register such details but was obliged to cast my eye at the car in question as I wished to cross the street, so I kept my eye on it for a few seconds in case it became mobile. Then I forgot it.

I turned the corner and entered the main street which was still fairly clear and made my way to the sports shop where I selected a pack of golf balls which I laid on the counter. I also selected a copy of 'The Golfer' and, as an afterthought, purchased a packet of golf tees; I had broken four on my last round with Frank Gilmore. I spent a few minutes passing the time of day with Andrew Foley, the sports shop proprietor, who was also an insurance client in addition to being a middling golfer with whom I played the occasional round.

'Looks like a hot one.' Andrew commented as I gathered my purchases and prepared to take my leave.

'It already is,' I commented dryly.' See you later, Andrew.'

It was still early, not many people were up and about. Many shops had not yet opened up; Andrew Foley's was an exception, he always planned to catch early risers like anglers, golfers and junior cricketers. I cast a cursory glance up and down the street and began to cross.

It was good observation, and sexual awareness that saved me.

As I moved across the street, I was looking through the return window of the milk bar opposite, a window at 45 degrees to the building line. Being a regular customer at the milk bar I knew the young woman in her early thirties who served behind the bar. She was the joint owner of the milk bar with her husband, but her slim, well-shaped frame and magnificent bust customarily attracted the attention of and excited many passing males from teenagers to old age pensioners. It was said the seat on the pavement over the street was customarily occupied by the old men of the town who spent their days eyeing the scenery on the other side of the milk bar window. I cast my eye through the angled window to see if she was there, one of my little pleasures that enabled my world to go round. I had just noted that she was nowhere to be seen when my eye registered the reflected scene, the road to my left. What I made out was a white car approaching at high speed.

I had heard nothing but it was a large six-cylinder car and must have purred up to roughly 80-90 kilometres per hour from an almost standing start. I swivelled to my left and realised it was heading for me at a phenomenal rate of knots. My response was purely instinctive, I jumped and rolled, my magazine and golf balls scattered in all directions onto the roadway.

'Bloody Hell!'

The car veered to its left as if following me. As I took in this aspect I rolled again. I felt something hit the back of my right hand and the instep of my left shoe. I had an impression of black tyres, a white painted vehicle, with an elbow and face looking out of the passenger window. Dust spattered in my face and over my shirt before my head hit against the number plate of a parked vehicle, which was also my saviour since it acted as a protective barrier. There was a screaming of rubber as the car swerved around the corner, a blaring of horns as a Mini and a Holden took avoiding action, then the white car was gone.

'Jeez' said a voice. 'Bloody lunatic! Are you all right mate?'

Rough hands assisted me to my feet, a stout man wearing an open neck shirt that exhibited a hairy chest brushed me down, his face alive with anger.

'Did you see that?' he asked another passer-by, who nodded vigorously. 'Did you get its number?'

Nobody had, it all happened far too quickly. A young lad materialised before me carrying my golfing magazine, miraculously undamaged, as he did so he said he thought the number plate had been blacked over. Foley came rushing out of his shop, having heard the commotion.

'What happened?'

'I was nearly spread all over the road,' I said sourly, still shaking with shock and fearing I was going to pass out. The back of my hand was bleeding and my left foot felt sore while there was a score mark across the shoe. My right elbow also hurt where I had landed on it and so did the side of my head where it had come into contact with the parked car's number plate.

'I saw it go past, thought you were a goner,' said Foley as he turned and waved to a young lad a short distance away. 'Pick up those golf balls, there's a good lad.'

They recovered the golf balls, apart from a flattened corner of the packing the balls didn't appear to be damaged, they would suffer far worse damage on the golf course. The golf tees were further up the street, the car had run over them and some were broken.

The stout hairy man was talking to the milk bar proprietor who had come out to see what was going on. I looked to see if his wife was in the vicinity. She wasn't.

'Didn't even put his brakes on, just kept going and nearly knocked this fellow for six.'

'Could have killed you, mate!'

'Do something for that hand if I were you.'

'Someone ought to tell the police. Never 'ere when they're wanted.'

By now a small crowd had gathered, including the drivers of the Mini and the Holden who were comparing margins by how much the offending vehicle had missed them. Andrew Foley took my right hand in his and pursed his lips.

'You ought to do something about that'

'I'll do it,' a white coat appeared from the back of the crowd, 'Come into the shop, Phil.'

Harry Singleton, the local pharmacist and another golf club member, appeared at my elbow. I obediently followed him into his pharmacy and sat on a chair, ignoring the curious looks of two other customers.

'What happened?'

I told him as best I could while he cleansed the wound and applied iodine. It looked worse than it actually was until the blood and dust had been cleaned off. He put a plaster on it.

'Did you get the number?'

'Not a hope,' I shook my head. 'All I could say is, it was white, probably a six-cylinder model, with black tyres.'

'Hmmm!' Singleton applied the finishing touches to the plaster. 'That probably narrows the field down to about 400,000!'

'He must be one of the worst drivers in the world,' this from the stout man who had followed us into the pharmacy. 'He could have killed you.'

I was beginning to dislike this man, he seemed unwilling to let me out of his sight, maybe my accident was his event of the week, or even his year, and he didn't want to lose any kudos. I wondered if he was a member of or had connections to the local press. If he hadn't, he seemed determined to be in the picture somewhere if or when any local journalist arrived on the scene.

'Yes, it's all over now,' I said. 'Thanks, Harry. I'll see you at the club-house. This will be worth a beer or two.'

I clapped Singleton on the shoulder and made a graceful exit, taking care not to limp as I didn't want the stout man to offer me further assistance. I headed for home.

It was at this juncture I recalled having seen the same white car outside the block of flats as I emerged that morning, now that my mind was thinking on those lines I thought this was probably the car that had hesitated outside my apartment block the previous evening.

I mentioned this aspect to Ken McGowan when I arrived at the barbecue after he asked me what I had done to my hand.

'Sounds odd,' he said. 'Have you got any enemies?'

McGowan was normally a jocular type, but this time he didn't appear to be joking.

'No,' I replied.

'Are you...have you...? Have you got on the wrong side of anyone, somebody's wife...?' he said hesitantly. This was the sort of comment one usually made jokingly, but this time McGowan was serious.

'No,' I shook my head firmly. 'I have not.'

'It couldn't have been O'Flynn, could it?' We both laughed at that, we were still chuckling when a female voice asked us: 'Could what have been O'Flynn?'

Jane was dressed in black slacks that seemed to be glued to her, and a tight white top with a 'U' neck. I swallowed and felt my mouth go dry. I gave her a résumé of the events of that morning, taking my time about it for her presence and her apparel did tend to paralyse my conversational powers.

'Did you get the car's registration number?'

'Not a chance,' I replied. 'The only numbers I got a good look at were the manufacturers' on the sides of the tyres.'

'Could it have been anyone you knew?'

'I didn't see them at all, it all happened too quickly.'

'How strange. Have you told the police?'

I hadn't thought seriously about the police, bearing in mind the local incumbent was Sergeant bloody Ramsey I had no wish to renew the acquaintance.

'No,' I said. 'It's hardly worth it.'

'Well you should. He might kill the next one'

'I suppose so,' I admitted. 'All right, I'll report it, but I've nothing concrete to go on and no definite information. I didn't even get the number and I don't think anyone else did.'

'Maybe it was an angry husband.'

I cast my eyes over her, then hastily returned my gaze to her eyes, which seemed fully aware of the other areas my own had been investigating.

'I doubt it,' I said. 'I'm sort of attached at the moment…!'

She dropped her eyes and began fiddling with her belt buckle.

'Do you want a drink?' she asked.

'That will do for starters.'

CHAPTER 5

I had the road to myself as I headed towards Hamilton from Ararat. It was early morning, I had made a quick stop in Ararat to view an intersection where one of our insureds had had a violent meeting with another motorist, causing severe damage to both vehicles and to the pride of the two drivers. They had been sufficiently physically uninjured to have a furious altercation after the collision. I had taken photographs of the intersection with the office camera, a piece of equipment we used for occasions such as this when pictures were worth more than 1,000 words.

It was a beautiful morning, made even more so as the office phone had been answered by Jane and we had a conversation ten minutes longer than was absolutely necessary. I was exceeding the speed limit, but there wasn't much likelihood of Sergeant Ramsey or his cohorts being on this stretch of road. He always waited at the entrance to small towns where the speed limit dropped from 100 kph to 60 kph. Even experienced drivers could be tardy in dropping to a lower speed and although they were obeying the spirit of the law by decreasing to the required 60, their rate of slowing was often not prompt enough, which enabled an astute Ramsey to place his speed camera just inside a lower limit area and reap a rich harvest.

A speck appeared on the horizon in my mirror on the road behind me that had previously been empty. It grew larger, I calculated it was travelling fast, but then it slackened and remained at a point about a half a kilometre in the rear. I kept a wary eye on it as this could be a police car checking my speed, so I slackened back to the speed limit of 100 kph. I still didn't feel easy about matters after the running down incident the other day so when I reached Maroona I decided to fill up with petrol.

'Mornin'' grunted the petrol station man as I climbed out.

'G'day' I replied, and eyed the road behind as we engaged in desultory conversation. I heard the approach of a vehicle and a green Holden appeared. There were three men in it, which struck me as being unusual, I saw all three faces turn in my direction before the car passed on through the township and out of sight.

'They were in a hurry.'

'What? Who? Oh, I suppose they were,' I hadn't registered or noticed their rate of progress but now he mentioned it I supposed they had been burning it up.

I drove off again and put my foot down, the petrol delay had cost me some time and I had an appointment in Hamilton at 10 am. When I was further down the road between Calvert and Willaura I realised the green Holden was in my mirror again. I must have given a classic double take as I registered them again and my foot automatically depressed the accelerator for a few more kilometres per hour. They were coming closer so once more I increased speed but despite that they remained static in the mirror. The speed increases I had made appeared to be matched by them and I could feel adrenalin coursing through my system. I began to analyse why their presence should be having such an effect on me, was I guilty of watching too much television?

They started to creep up, again I added a few more engine revolutions but they continued to come closer. I decided to let them overtake, having decided my fears had gone far enough, but as I rounded the next bend, I nearly ran into a herd of cattle blocking the highway. I slowly coasted to a halt, passed the outer fringe of cattle and found myself in the middle of the herd. They were being marshalled by a man on horseback, another man armed with a stick and on foot was accompanied by a cattle dog.

The horseman came over and raised an arm in salute. It was Dick Pascoe, who farmed acres near Staveley. I'd met him a few times at meetings of a local farmers association when I had been running question and answer sessions for the Jupiter Insurance, who transacted a considerable portfolio of farmers business. I had once had a long argument with Pascoe on the subject of livestock insurance and what constituted a valid claim, we had eventually resolved our differences over some local ale.

As his colleague made efforts to clear a way for me, assisted by the dog and the stick, Pascoe negotiated a couple of cows that were proving obstreperous, and halted by my window.

'Hi there, Phil, sorry about this. Hope you're not in a hurry.'

'G' Day, Dick,' I answered. 'I hope they're insured!'

He grinned and leant forward over his horse's neck.

'Would it make any difference? You never pay out anyway!' he retorted. 'Where you heading, Hamilton?'

'Yes, I'm due there by 10.'

'Well watch it, my lad's just come in from there, says there's a police trap just inside the town boundary. Apparently, they've set it up just after the 60 sign, so make sure you slow down well before you reach it. '

We chatted in like vein for a few minutes until there was a gap in the herd, exchanged farewells and I eased forward. As I drove off, I raised my hand in salute and he responded, sitting upright on his mount in the middle of the road. As his horse reduced in size in my mirror, I realised I had forgotten the car that had been on my tail. I couldn't see further than Pascoe as he and his horse were in the middle of the road with the cattle still milling around behind him, fewer in number now as they entered a neighbouring paddock. Then Pascoe followed the herd through the gate. Behind him the road was empty.

As I reached Hamilton I was perplexed, as far as I could remember there was no turn off from the point where I had seen the vehicle behind me and where I had been held up by Dick Pascoe. I puzzled over it until I made my first call, then dismissed it.

*

After that first call, I had a busy day, I investigated a small fire claim where a stove had caught fire, completed a life proposal and called on a firm of brokers in the town. The fire claim was interesting if only to illustrate how a moment's carelessness or inattention could have devastating results. The lady of the house had been frying hamburgers, during the flipping over of a hamburger some oil spilled onto a neighbouring gas jet and caused a small ignition on the stove top. Instead of merely lifting the pan off and either extinguishing the flame, or waiting for it to subside as the minimal amount of oil burnt itself out, she had panicked, given a cry of alarm and wrenched the pan violently away. This had ejected a large quantity of its contents onto the existing small fire and over the timber facia of the wall behind the stove. The resultant flare up had climbed up the wall, set fire to some washing, hanging overhead to dry from the heat of the stove, ignited a curtain and a window frame, then roared up an inch gap between two wall cupboards that had acted as a flue.

By the time the Fire Brigade arrived the fire was burning nicely, the one wall's wood panelling was blazing and flames were shooting through a vent into the roof space. A bucket of water she had thrown onto the blaze had promptly spread burning oil all over the working top and into the cupboards below, it merely sat on top of the water and gave it an express run to wherever the water and the force of gravity took it.

I allayed her fears that the company would disclaim liability because carelessness was to blame, and painstakingly explained the difference between accident and arson. I paid a quick visit to the Country Fire Brigade to assure them there was insurance coverage, and that their costs would be met. I then went to a nearby pub for lunch. I met a man I knew from the New South Wales Fire Office in the licensed premises and we traded a few insults at the bar before we found a table and had lunch.

After lunch we chatted for about ten minutes in the car park, exchanged farewells and made our way to our respective vehicles. As I pulled out into the street another car pulled away from the side of the road and followed me as I drove up the main street. I felt the hair on the back of my head prickle as it stayed half a kilometre astern as I left the town behind.

'What the hell is going on?' I asked myself as I viewed the vehicle in the mirror. I increased speed, but after about ten minutes it remained the same distance behind. I had a couple of calls to make in Mortlake and reached there about 3 pm. I parked in the main street and waited; the other car roared into town, passed by me and took the road out the other side.

After making both calls, one was an outstanding account and the other related to completing a new standing order form as the insured had changed banks, I stood by the car and debated what to do. I had intended to head back to Stawell but decided against it. There was a call I had to make in Heywood, and three more in Casterton. I pondered for a few more minutes, then decided to do the call in Heywood, stay overnight in a motel and proceed on to Casterton the following morning. Having made the decision I rang the office to tell them what I was doing and the motel I intended to use. I hoped Jane would answer the phone but it was Ken McGowan. I also had a quick talk with Doug Hollister, and then asked to speak to Jane.

'Any news on your hit and run driver?' she asked.

'No, I haven't done anything about it yet.'

'Well you should,' she said. 'He might kill you or somebody else the next time.'

I shuddered. After the spasmodic tailing by the other vehicle today, I wondered if there would be somebody else, or would it be me again?

'Are you still there?'

'Yes, I'm here.' I replied, 'Maybe I'll do it tomorrow.'

'Shall I see you Saturday?' she asked.

We arranged to meet outside a coffee shop in Stawell on Saturday morning, I told her I was staying overnight in the area and rang off.

I reached Heywood without further incident. I seemed to have lost my tail, although I kept a careful lookout in the mirror there was no sign of the green Holden. I had a good look at a Mitsubishi that approached me at a very fast rate, but it swept past without incident. I booked in at the motel and then made the call, which was at an outlying farm. I returned to the motel, had an evening meal, turned in and slept like a log.

Next morning, I rose early and after breakfast filled up at a local petrol station. We had the usual desultory conversation about the weather and the political situation, then I set off for Casterton. All the way I checked the mirror, but saw nothing untoward. I was overtaken a few times but in each case it was by cars that carried only the driver, from a quick assessment they all looked like commercial travellers.

I investigated the burglary claim, a petty theft from a house standing in its own grounds when the owners had been absent for a few days. It looked like the work of local youngsters to me, a forced lock to a drink cabinet, a few bottles missing, and a small camera and a cigarette box. This last item turned up in the bushes when the lady of the house was showing me the offenders' route of entry via rhododendron bushes, it was lying under one of the bushes.

'They didn't realise its value,' she commented as I picked it up.

'They may have done,' I turned it over in my hands. 'It was useless to them, if they'd tried to hock it in the town the police would have been informed straight away. I'd say they just took out the cigarettes then dumped it.'

'There weren't any cigarettes in it,' she said, 'It was my father's and we only keep it as an ornament. I suppose that will reduce the claim, won't it?'

'Not necessarily,' I turned it over in my hands. 'It's rained since they threw it away and it's stained the wood on the outside. I'll get a quotation from a French polisher; I think there's one in the High Street.'

We filled in the claim forms and I left her one of my cards in case her husband wanted to contact me. She seemed impressed

I hadn't immediately removed the cigarette box from the claim list, but I explained it now came under burglary damage and we would try to fix it if we could. Without trying to sound too altruistic, it was vital, with all claims, justice had to be seen to be done. It was bad management to have decades of endeavour and good publicity in the insurance field besmirched by one afternoon's bad publicity in a local newspaper that could trot out all the old anti-insurance clichés.

For the rest of the week I wandered around the various local towns, making calls and keeping a watchful eye on the mirror. On the Thursday I made my way to the Golf Club and hailed Frank Gilmore as he swept up to an empty spot and spurted gravel over the garden beds alongside. He clambered out and introduced me to a young man in the passenger seat.

'This is John Stringer,' he said airily. 'He's an old buddy of my brother. He fancies himself a bit; he's a professional from New South Wales.'

'Really' I proffered my hand. 'We should be able to give you a few pointers about the game then.'

'Something like that,' grinned Stringer. 'I'm always ready to learn from experts.'

He was a man of medium height, very thin and looked almost fragile. He had a mop of blonde hair and wore sunglasses. He looked as if he wouldn't have the strength to pick up a golf club, let alone rely on hitting a ball long distances for a living. He and Frank extracted their clubs from the boot of the car, we walked to the club-house and booked in. It was hardly necessary as we seemed to be the only ones there. We could see a quartet on the third in the distance, but nobody on the first or second fairways.

'Goodoh!' commented Frank. 'Shall we go?'

In deference to Stringer's status we let him go first, he looked almost as thin as the club he was wielding and likely unable to hit it 50 metres, but he soon disproved that. He nearly hit it out of sight.

'Shit!' was Frank's comment, mine was equally short but more polite..

It was an education to watch the man, he had never seen the course before and occasionally fell for traps laid by the wily course architect. We refrained from warning him so it would even up the odds a little. He went round in 70, his approach shots were a treat to watch and when he landed in bunkers, they were little more than irritants and he actually holed out from the sand on the 14th. Frank and I took more strokes, but I was so inspired by watching Stringer's work that I went around in 79, my best round for months.

I had something of a warm glow in the changing room afterwards; completing a round with an outstanding player is always a good experience as some of his play rubs off on yours.

'You'd be a better player, Phil...' said Stringer, '... if you weren't so anxious to see where the ball was going after you've hit it. Several of your drives, and some of your approach shots too, didn't travel far enough because you lifted your head too soon, as a consequence you lifted your club head a fraction as you hit the ball. What did you go round in?'

'Seventy-nine,' I said.

'That was good, what's your normal round?'

'About eighty-six or more.'

'Well you had a good day today, but maybe you could have lopped about six shots off that if you hadn't been so keen to follow the flight of the ball too soon.'

'You may be right,' I thought back over some of the shots I'd made. I could certainly recall five had kept a low trajectory and not made enough distance. 'I'll work on it.'

CHAPTER 6

The following day was a Friday, I set off as usual and after a few kilometres became aware of a blue car in the rear-view mirror. I thought little of it at first, but as the morning progressed and it was still there in the distance, I began to feel uneasy. The other car was not too obtrusive and if I hadn't had the previous experience of feeling I was being stalked I probably wouldn't have given it a thought. It kept well to the rear and frequently allowed other vehicles to intercede between us. After I had made a couple of calls and it was still there as lunch-time approached, I decided to try and lose it.

I was approaching Avoca and sped up so I was well ahead when I entered the main street. I turned to the left, turned left again, then right into a tree lined track next to a large shop. I bumped my way over the surface, swung right through the trees and then bumped my way onto the road to Maryborough. After that I took another track that led to Homebush, passed Lower Homebush and then went north to Archdale before hitting the secondary road to St Arnaud. I checked the mirror, I was alone. I completed my week with no further incident.

I met Jane in the main street as arranged that Saturday. We went for coffee at the local coffee shop and I found myself looking nervously over my shoulder. We sat down at a table near the window and I spent much of the time scanning the street for blue cars, white cars or thick set men. As the coffee arrived Jane looked at me quizzically.

'What's wrong, you seem preoccupied?' she turned her head to look up and down the street, then eyed me again.

My first reaction was to indignantly deny it, but common sense prevailed. I was becoming worried about the whole business and it would do me good to confide in someone else.

After a brief hesitation, I told her all that had occurred, starting from the attempted hit and run on the main street the previous week, and the various times I considered I had been tailed.

'Are you sure?' her blue eyes widened as the import of my message sank in.

'I don't know,' I replied.' I'm not even sure if I *am* sure any more.'

'If they were following you, why should they?'

'I don't know,' I spread out my arms and knocked over the sugar. 'Damn and blast! I have no idea at all.'

'Well you should do something about it,' she insisted as she scooped up sugar from the table and placed it back in the bowl. 'Tell the police or something.'

'Hmmm! I don't know about that, what do I tell them?'

'What you've told me.'

Her blue eyes bored into me, she nodded at me and I found myself nodding back.

'All right,' I said. 'I'll see the police, but when I see myself trying to explain matters to them it all seems to be so vague.'

'Good,' she said. 'Now what are we doing tonight?'

*

The following Tuesday morning, I extracted a golf club from the boot of the car and trudged up the side of the hill to the paddock on the top of the slope. I hadn't fixed up any calls until 3 o'clock with the deliberate intention of having a few practice shots. There was a large paddock on the road from Horsham to Hamilton, at a point where I frequently stopped and ate my sandwiches. There was a slope upwards from the road and the paddock was on a plateau, sufficiently long to take a five-iron shot without overshooting and losing any balls, as long as they were hit reasonably straight. A thick belt of trees on the side of the hill rose up on the left, a very thick belt which totally covered the hillside. There was a field of wheat in front of me well in the distance. The road, where I left the car, ran to my right and behind me was a steep hill, also thickly wooded almost up to the summit. I carried a five iron, some tees and five balls.

Last Saturday night had been very satisfying, Jane and I had gone to see a film about First World War fliers and afterwards had gone back to her flat. This was the first time I had really been alone with her without any chance of being disturbed, and we both took advantage of it. I was astonished at her intensity when we both realised we had the same idea in mind. I stayed overnight and was quite startled at her versatility. I still had a warm glow as I thought back over that night's activities.

I placed the five golf balls in a line and lined up on the poplar tree at the far end of my 'fairway' that was, to me, the flag. I had often wondered how that solitary poplar tree had arrived there, it stood in solitary state near the edge of the plateau, about twenty metres before the land sloped away downwards towards the wheat field. On my left was the heavily wooded slope, I had lost a few balls in there occasionally when I hooked a shot. I had tended to carry out only half-hearted searches for them as it was the sort of undergrowth where I considered snakes could thrive. A spur of trees jutted into my fairway but these had never presented a problem.

I carefully addressed all five balls and despatched them, four appeared to land within the vicinity of the poplar tree but the last one curled behind the spur of trees. It was, I hoped, still on my fairway on their far side. I shouldered my club and ambled towards the poplar tree at the other end of the plateau.

I could still hear traffic on the roadway where my car was parked, which ran slightly below the level of my practice fairway strip, the occasional truck lumbered past but it was mainly cars and vans. I thought I heard a car slowing up, then it revved up again and passed somewhere below me and headed towards Horsham. An aeroplane passed high overhead, while flies buzzed around me, making attacks on my nostrils and ears.

The first ball had fallen well short of the poplar, I remembered it had been slightly topped but it had still made good progress along the ground. I soon found it, pocketed it and headed for the next one nearer to the tree. As I stooped to retrieve it something hit the trunk of the tree with a loud crack followed by a shrill screaming noise.

'What the hell...!'

I swung around in astonishment and no small measure of indignation. Really some of these shooters were the limit, letting off at any bird or rabbit without any regard for anyone who could be in the line of fire. I saw two heads sticking up out from the bank at the top of the slope that led down to where my car was parked, they were near my tee, the point where I had hit off the balls. A second shot rang out and the bullet ploughed into the ground about ten feet away and scattered small stones and wood splinters over me. At this point I realised not only was I in the line of fire, I *was* the line of fire.

'Look where you're shooting, you bloody fool!' I waved my club up and down to attract attention. They stood upright, although they were over 120 metres away they didn't look very apologetic as they headed slowly towards me, one holding a rifle at the ready. He was the taller of the two, dressed in a dark suit and a hat, which seemed out of place in this part of the country on a hot day. The other wore a soft white hat, similar to those loved by Test cricketers these days, plus a highly-coloured shirt and denim trousers.

As they advanced purposefully in my direction, I felt my entrails curl. Were they shooting at me? Christ, they bloody well were! Those shots had been too close to be accidental, one I could excuse but not two. Then wasn't it a bit stupid to let them come any closer? But wouldn't I look foolish if there was a perfectly simple explanation and I ran off? On the other hand, if they *were* shooting at me wouldn't I look even more bloody stupid if I stood still and allowed them to come in point blank range? If they were shooting at me it was clearly a case of mistaken identity...wasn't it? But what if they put a bullet into me before they found out? And hadn't I been shot at less than a week ago?

They were still about 100 metres away when my Army instincts took over. I reached the poplar in a standing jump, ducked behind it and ran down the fall of the land behind it, trying to keep the tree in line with the two men. If I had any doubts or feelings of embarrassment they were promptly dispelled as two more shots were fired. One I never saw at all, the other hit the ground at the top of the rise and ricocheted off a stone or something solid.

As the brow of the slope hid me from their view, I struck off to

the left and headed for the tree belt on the side of the hill. Once
in there I had some cover, snakes or no snakes. I sprinted as I
had never sprinted before; if they had any woodcraft or military
training, they would surely guess my intentions and move to
head me off. I was still about 20 metres from the trees when I
heard a shout from the top of the rise by the poplar tree.

'Bromyard's over there.'

I risked turning my head and saw the man in the coloured
shirt was gesticulating furiously to his companion who was
somewhere behind him and presumably nearer the roadway.
He must have calculated I would run for my car, not an
unreasonable assumption. The suited rifleman appeared
at the top of the rise, about 30 metres further away towards
the road, knelt down and took aim. I whimpered with sheer
fright, jinked furiously in a zig zag and then dived head first
into the bushes, suffering a multitude of scratches and setting
every bird on the wing within a ten-metre radius. Two bullets
followed me but, luckily, I was in a slight depression and they
passed over me as I lay prone. Such was my fear of my pursuers,
the thought of snakes never entered my head, I grimly wriggled,
or snaked, over the lip of the small depression, down the other
side and plunged into another bush before I rose to my feet. I
had some cover and started running half left so I was making
my way back towards my tee but at an angle away from it and
up the slope, instinctively heading for higher ground. I didn't
hurry, I didn't want to give my direction away by frightening
too many birds, making too much noise or causing a flurry
of movement in the undergrowth. I picked my way with care,
with a prickling between my shoulder blades where I fancied
the next bullet might strike. I kept my ears well cocked so I
could hear any signs of pursuit but heard none.

I stopped to listen, then decided to try to see what was

happening. There was an outcrop of rock in front of me, I knew from previous visits there the view from the top of the rock was a good one, I had a tendency to hook and had actually had a few in past months that went off at a tangent and landed below this outcrop, after abortive searches for balls there it had been but a short climb to go up and admire the view. I clambered onto it and cast my eyes down onto my fairway, about twenty metres below and 100 metres away. I could see the rifleman standing near the poplar tree, there was no sign of his shirted companion. Then I saw a flash of colour near the edge of the bushes, he seemed to be peering through the undergrowth but was hesitant about entering. I watched for a few more minutes and wondered if I could reach my car, or was it safer to stay where I was? I considered the problem and then nearly fell off the outcrop as a bullet hit a tree near me.

'Shit!'

That rifleman must have good eyesight. I cursed as I slipped off the rock, headed off to the left and climbed higher. I ran, realising to my shame I had panicked. I could hear crashing in the undergrowth below and behind me and ran faster, until saner counsels prevailed. If I sprained or broke an ankle now, I'd be a sitting duck.

'Take a grip on yourself, you idiot,' I muttered angrily to myself. Again, I stopped and listened; but could hear nothing. They must have stopped to listen for me. I decided to try and mislead them, and laid down my club . . .Good God! Was I still carrying my club? I picked up a stone, weighed it carefully in my hand and then threw it with all my strength over to the left and down the wooded slope. I heard a voice snap something and then crashing started in the direction where the stone had landed. I headed in the opposite direction, still clambering upwards. I stopped for a quick recce, realised I was nearly level with my driving off tee, the rise and the tree belt swung around to the left here and nearly reached the road where my car was parked.

I paused to consider my next move, should I head in the direction of my car or were they banking on me trying to do just that? One's natural instinct is to head for security and in this day and age the motor car was everyman's second home.

My car would be to my left, and maybe level or possibly slightly behind me. It would be to their left and ahead of them, but what if they had a third man available either to catch their panicked quarry or be ready for a quick getaway...or both. Why the hell were they after me?

Any doubts I had on the issue were now completely dispelled, the bullets had been far too close for comfort or for them to be shooting at anything else. It was clearly me they were after, and the accuracy of the shooting indicated it was not because I just happened to be in the vicinity of a bird shooter's line of fire. Three or four shots passing or landing very close to me was far too many. The other puzzling feature was the shirted man had used the name Bromyard, by which he had described me, although it was a name I rarely used unless signing legal documents.

I swung my club thoughtfully in my hand while I pondered my next move. I could stay in the trees, I could head for the car and risk a possible third man, or I could head for clear ground at the far end of the tree belt. That course would be...Bloody Hell!

The shot was so close it nearly parted my hair, it hit a small branch about two metres away and snapped it clean off.

That rifleman must have eyes like a cat to have seen me, but see me he had, the following shot made that abundantly clear. It was less accurate than the last but still unpleasantly close. How the hell had he seen me and where was he firing from? I tried to gauge the position of the marksman from the snapped twig and the position over my head where it had just missed me, it seemed he was roughly in the position where I had last seen him, but how the hell had he pinpointed me so accurately?

I could hear movement in the undergrowth, were they coming in to finish me off? I felt the hair rise on my scalp. I moved off in roughly what I considered to be the Horsham direction, once more attracting a bullet that came unpleasantly close. Then, as I looked down to avoid any pitfalls the answer came to me, the reason why the shooting was so accurate. The sun flashed back at me from the shaft of my 5 iron as I moved across any shafts or speckles of sunlight shining through the trees. It was acting like a beacon.

I was about to hurl it from me but then had a better idea. I tore off my tie, tied it around the club head, then suspended the club from an overhanging branch where the sun came through aplenty. I stood between sun and club as I affixed it, then set it swinging like a pendulum as I flung myself flat on the ground. That my hunch was correct was promptly vindicated, three more shots were fired into the tree trunk and nearby branches. I headed for the undergrowth and went off at a crouching run, I bade my 5 iron farewell and hoped nothing would befall it. I was fond of that club.

I headed round the trees until I had finally worked myself behind my driving off tee and was overlooking the road. My car, and theirs, was to my left, the road had a slight righthand bend at this point and I was about 10 metres above road level. My blood ran cold as I looked down at the other car. It was hauling a trailer and on the trailer was a box that looked like a carpenter's work box...or coffin! It was about 2 metres long and 40 centimetres wide, and the same in height. Further, there *was* a third man. He was leaning nonchalantly against the side of the car looking, to any passing motorist, as if he was admiring the view. He was some distance away, but looked an ugly customer. I had entertained some wild plan of creeping up on him and assaulting him, but this idea was nullified by the open country and lack of cover down below...plus his muscular build. In any case, I observed the rifleman and his colourful companion were now clambering back down the slope towards the car.

They had a brief consultation, pointed up in the direction from which they had arrived, and then the car custodian looked up and pointed in my direction. I froze with horror, but he subsequently pointed further over in the direction from which I had travelled and appeared to be indicating an estimate of the course I could have taken, the possible area I could be in and proposing a plan of campaign. He seemed to have a good idea which route I would have covered...blast him! He ran his pointed finger in a wide sweep that effectively covered the direction I had taken from the poplar tree, which I could see well over to my left, a surprisingly accurate assessment, even though he couldn't see the tree line, from where he was, because of the slope down to the road.

They opened my car door, had a look inside and searched my jacket. Whatever they found didn't interest them very much and they tossed everything, including my jacket and the brief case, into the rear seat. I tapped my hip pocket, I still had some bank notes in there, I rarely carried a wallet as it tended to pull my jackets out of shape and I disliked saggy suits. I looked down at my trousers; if I ever got out of this my first trip would be to the dry cleaners.

The rifle went into the boot of their car which caused me to emit a sigh of relief. But the feeling of relief was premature, they helped themselves to hand guns and struck off in three different directions up the bank, one heading for the poplar tree, another for my tee, and the car attendant started off in my direction.

I nearly panicked there and then, but once again my former Army training came to the fore. I had been in similar positions to this in the Army, I could remember during a sortie in East Timor when a patrol of Indonesian militiamen had passed within ten feet of us as we lay doggo in the undergrowth, sublimely unaware of our presence. We had all been dog tired and nearly out of ammunition. Our sergeant knew when to look for trouble and when to keep out of it and that time we let them pass. The Australian reputation as fighting men came out of that campaign untarnished, we had been altogether more businesslike than some of the American forces in Vietnam in the 1970's who could be pinpointed by the sound of their transistor radios and the smell of their toothpaste. The best tactic, when not shooting, was to be unobtrusive and keep quiet.

If I went down the reverse slope towards the road there was a good chance I would be seen, the trees thinned out which meant there was little cover. Up here the trees were more mature and the trunks wider, there were clumps of undergrowth, mainly blackberry bushes. Behind me the land inclined upwards into a high hill, the one that overlooked the fairway from behind my driving off tee, there were trees on that and more undergrowth. I remembered the road ran around this hill in a semi-circle, if I could clamber over the top of it and down the other side without being seen, or shot at, I may be able to try my hand at thumbing a lift.

I cast my eye over the man climbing towards me. I began to move away from the crest and made my way towards the hill, keeping as many trees as I could between me and where I thought he would appear. The trees were natural growth, not planted in regimental lines like so many man-made forests. I flitted from tree to tree, also keeping a watchful eye over my fairway, to avoid concealing myself from one direction and exposing myself in another. I reckoned I was safe enough from being shot at, I would be well out of hand gun range, but there was a danger of being chased by one and running into another, apart from the risk of twisting an ankle.

There was a shout when I was half-way up the hill, I looked around in alarm. I found myself looking straight down the hill to the back of my driving tee through a gap in the trees and the man with the highly coloured shirt was standing in the distance pointing up at me. I cursed myself angrily for my carelessness, despite all my precautions I had done just what I had determined not to do, left myself exposed to one while I watched another.

I heard the sound of a shot, but that didn't worry me, even if they had the range, accuracy was doubtful at this distance. But it acted as a spur, I flogged myself to the hill summit, not bothering to shelter behind trees now they knew where I was. My main aim was to put as much distance between me and them as I could.

Reaching the summit nearly finished me, I had panicked and run as fast as I could and nearly exhausted my store of energy. I leaned weakly against a tree and looked for my pursuers. Then I went cold. One of them had headed for their car and was reversing it around He was going to head round the outlying neck of the woods, past where I had been overlooking the road, round the bend and towards the other side of the hill, where I was heading. If I continued with my plan, he would be there waiting for me, all he would have to do was pull the trigger. I looked to the right, the woods were thicker there, but the road swung away at that point.

No time to waste, I headed in that direction. Luckily, I was going downhill so I found that part of it much easier. It seemed I had little option but to head back alongside my fairway, at a much higher level than I had been before and eventually make a landfall alongside the poplar, again looking down on it from the top of the hillside. I didn't think I had been seen this time, not yet, the terrain levelled off and I ran along the side of the hillside. I caught a momentary glimpse of irregular flashing below me, which could be my 5-iron swinging in the slight breeze.

I cautiously threaded my way through my three pursuers, making sure this time I didn't leave myself exposed to one or the other. Progress was easier since I was travelling on the level. It seemed I had little option but to head for a point level with the poplar tree. I found a gap with a rock on the edge of a steep fall, stopped behind it and peered round it. I was still overlooking my fairway; I peered around the rock and took advantage of some branches as cover. I caught a glimpse of a coloured shirt making its way up the hill about 100 metres behind me. Of the others there was no sign, but if one was in the car or climbing up the reverse slope of the hill, I could hardly expect to see anyone.

I forced my way through the undergrowth and it occurred to me that for a long time I hadn't given the idea of snakes any consideration. I dodged from tree to tree, crept around bushes and maintained a watchful eye in case the former rifleman had doubled back to catch me out.

I hit the road, at a point where it forked, and I came out on one of the forks. I was still trying to work out what to do when a truck came around the bend and began to slow down for the road junction. Without thinking I gave him a wave and a broad grin and he slowed to a stop.

'What's the trouble mate?'

'I've...I've...!' I was about to say I'd broken down further along the road, but with most truckies being good amateur mechanics there was a danger he'd offer to look for the trouble, and my pursuers could arrive while he was looking for the fictitious trouble. I also considered that the presence of a third party wouldn't deter these bastards, they could dispose of two bodies as easily as one.

'I've had my car stolen, I stopped for a toilet break and when I came back it had gone. Can you give me a lift into Horsham?'

He was young, well-built and sunburnt, wearing a check shirt and a wide brimmed hat. He nodded, grunted and leant over to open the passenger door and I clambered in.

'Funny sort of day,' he remarked conversationally and I certainly didn't disagree with that. We went slowly into the road junction, and commenced running parallel to my fairway, passing the poplar tree first. We passed my car, which was still where I had left it.

'Is that it?' he asked.

'Er...no!' I replied. I had been tempted to say it was, jump into it and roar off. But they may have disabled it, if they had I could have jumped out of the frying pan into the fire. It looked forlorn as we drove slowly past it, I decided to collect it the next morning, if it was still there, accompanied by a detachment of police and a battalion of marines. We followed the road slightly round to the left, it circumvented the outcrop where I had recently been looking out over the road when my pursuers had had their council of war, and then swung around to the right around the hill where I had previously been, that rose up behind my tee.

We passed the car with the trailer parked on the left-hand side of the road. I looked up the hill and saw two men halfway up it, there were large gaps in the trees on that side. Further away to the right I caught sight of a coloured shirt.

'What are those blokes doing?'

'What blokes?' I asked innocently.

'Those fellas up there,' the driver craned his neck and for one awful moment I thought he was going to stop and get out with the intention of passing the time of day with them.

'Maybe they're doing some shooting,' I commented brightly.

'Yeh! Yeh! Maybe,' he nodded. 'Not the right time of year, ducks are out of season. But I suppose if they look hard enough up there, they'll find something to shoot!'

I could only agree! I shuddered and made affirmative noises. The driver blew his horn at a dog trying to cross the road, which caused me to curl up with fear, fearful he might attract their attention.

'I guess some people will shoot at anything!'

I merely nodded. I didn't feel the urge to disagree.

CHAPTER 7

'You say they referred to you as Bromyard?'

'Yes!' I answered sulkily. Matters were not proceeding as I thought they would. As a law-abiding citizen who had been chased all over the countryside by heavily armed gangsters, I had expected a more positive reaction from the guardians of the law. I had assumed I would be greeted with a furore of excitement, coupled with a return to the scene escorted by a van full of armed police with sirens wailing, but this was not happening.

I was kept waiting in a queue in the police station, behind two small boys who'd been raiding an apple orchard, a shoplifter who looked to be in the advanced stages of alcoholism, and a man who had been apprehended as he peered inside a ladies' toilets in a park. When the desk sergeant finally summoned me to the long counter, I bitterly reflected that by this time half the population of the town could have been wiped out by gunmen armed with AK47 rifles and rocket launchers. It being Sergeant Bloody Ramsey didn't improve my temper.

I hastily stated my story, after all there was still a faint chance, even with the delays experienced, the miscreants could still be arrested this side of the South Australian border, but Ramsey slapped me down and began to fill a form, starting with my name and address.

After these seemingly vital preliminaries had been disposed of, Ramsey condescended to hear my story. He clearly suspected I was going to appeal against my speeding fine, for he raised an eyebrow as I described the shooting, and the use of my middle name by one of the gunmen.

'Why should they call you that?'

'Because it happens to be my name,' I answered coldly.

He jerked upright, pulled a keyboard towards him and hit some of the keys. He looked at what he had on the screen and eyed me suspiciously.

'I thought you said your name was Meredith.'

'I did...it is!'

'You just said that Bromyard...!' Ramsey referred to the screen, then pulled a file from a compartment facing him on his desk and riffled through it. 'You gave your name as Meredith last week when I booked you on the highway. Are you saying you gave a false...?'

'Jesus Chr...!' I bit off the exclamation, realising I could lay myself open to charges of obscene language or blasphemy if he was going to be pedantic and his weekly quota of indictable offences was below par. 'My name is Philip Samuel Bromyard-Meredith,' I said through gritted teeth.

'Down here I've got Philip Samuel Meredith,' said Ramsey.

'Yes, I know,' I pressed my fingers against my temple, really how obtuse could the bloody man get? This man's sense of the trivial verged on the extreme, he seemed to sense offenders and perjurers behind every nook and cranny, in the meantime an armed gang was probably running riot in his area of responsibility shooting at more unarmed citizens. 'I rarely use the name Bromyard, I've found that three is enough, it's a double-barrelled name and to avoid confusion I don't use it. Look, I've just told you ...!"

'So we should have the name Bromyard down here then?'

'What? Yes, I suppose so...look, I've just been shot at...!"

'So...it should have been on the ticket I issued last week.'

'Yes, I suppose so, what the hell difference does it make? Now can we...!"

'It could make a difference if you choose to send back any Summons and claim it wasn't properly addressed. It could be interpreted as a manoeuvre to evade the course of Justice.'

'Good God Almighty! Look, I've already paid that bloody fine, it was about a week ago...and I've more important things to discuss than the correct order of my names or a missing double-barrelled hyphen. I tell you I've been shot at by three armed men, and it was me they were after because they used my name and they chased me for about three miles. Are you going to do anything about it or not?'

In my exasperation my voice was raised angrily, heads turned in our direction, the drunken shoplifter paused whilst still protesting his innocence and the Peeping Tom halted his long explanation about hearing a plea for help. Ramsey compressed his lips, then lifted the hatch in the counter.

'Come into the office,' he said.

*

'Is this your car?'

'Yes' I replied sulkily. I didn't feel disposed to be conversational, although matters had improved after the completion of the interview in the police station interview room. When I finally managed to get through to him that I wasn't trying to evade a speeding fine because of a difference in nomenclature but had been shot at by three gunmen, he didn't waste much time. I noticed when he and a burly constable climbed into a police car, with me in the back seat, they both had guns on their hips.

Ramsey and the constable got out to examine my car, after some hesitation I did the same as my fear of being left alone was greater than the fear of a sniper. I was fairly sure my erstwhile pursuers would be well away by now as there had been no sign of their car along the road.

'And you went onto the paddock over the top of this rise?'

'Yes.'

'For what purpose did you go in there?'

'To practice golf shots?'

'You have the permission of the owner?'

'You...! What! Good God no!' I felt myself going muzzy headed. 'Look, I've told you, I've been shot at by three men...!'

'You didn't have the permission of the owner?'

'No, I didn't!' I snapped. Great Balls of Fire! Never in my life had I met a man so obsessed with the irrelevancies of life, who was so easily diverted from matters of importance by trivialities. I envisioned my rap sheet getting longer and longer with the addition of fresh charges of giving a false name and trespassing on a country property.

'Hmmm!' Ramsey pursed his lips, while the police constable made a note in his note book. Ramsey nodded as the constable finished then walked again to my car.

'Does everything appear to be there?'

I took hold of my jacket and rummaged through the pockets. My wallet, which I usually kept in the glove box, had been emptied but most of its contents were lying over the passenger seat, even the money. Everything seemed intact, the glove box had also been examined but as far as I could see everything was still there, although scattered on seat and floor.

'Brief case?' asked Ramsey.

'I think everything is there.'

'You think?'

I gritted my teeth, bit back an angry comment and searched through it. I used the brief case mainly for proposal forms, company literature and prospectuses. I checked through, found my Golf magazine was still there and some golf club papers. My morning newspaper was still on the back seat.

'Shall we check the boot?' said Ramsey.

We checked it, I hung back nervously and let Ramsey open it, I had a sudden fear there could be a bomb primed to explode when the boot lid was raised. There wasn't! My clubs were still intact as was my buggy, with the exception of the 5-iron, presumably still dangling from a tree branch somewhere on the nearby hill.

We walked over the top of the rise and I indicated the point where I teed off and the distant poplar tree that was my landmark, or 'green'.

'About 180 yards,' commented Ramsey, the constable made another note. I really failed to see how that was relevant, but I held my peace. 'And you drove off from here?'

'Yes.'

Ramsey inspected the ground, there were one or two divot marks on the turf. He went down on his knees to inspect them.

'Hmmm!' he said.

'Don't worry,' I said sarcastically. 'I'll recompense the owner for any damage!'

I intended to continue and say he could add that to my charge sheet but on reflection I thought better of it. He rose to his feet and our eyes met.

'Very good of you to offer, sir,' he said. 'Shall we go over to the poplar tree?'

It was more of a command than a suggestion, we walked over slowly and I peered nervously over my shoulder back up the hill behind the tee. There were no signs of life, but I couldn't rid myself of that prickling between my shoulder blades. We reached the tree and Ramsey subjected it to a close inspection.

'You say something hit the tree?'

'That was my impression,' I said shortly and couldn't resist adding. 'When you hear a crack and a ricochet, splinters fly and you're standing by a tree, it's not unreasonable to assume a bullet may have hit it!'

'You may be right, sir,' he said evenly, but I saw his lips compress and knew I had scored a hit. The constable raised his hand to his face and turned away to hide a smile, Ramsey saw it and it clearly got under his skin.

'Well look around, Broadley,' he snapped. 'Do you expect me to do all the work?'

'No Sarge... er... yes Sarge.'

Broadley hastily moved to the tree and began wandering around it. I could picture the thoughts running through his mind 'The bloody sergeant gets chewed up by a bloody civvy, so he turns round and chews me up...bastard!'

'Well...did you find anything?'

'Two golf balls.'

'Eh! Well bring them here.'

Broadley produced two golf balls, a Hot Dot 5 and a Rocket 7.

'Are these yours?'

'Yes' I answered.

He handed them to me, which surprised me as I thought he'd want to retain them as evidence in the forthcoming court case of The Owner of the Land vs Bromyard-Meredith. I nearly uttered a sarcastic rejoinder on those lines, but suppressed it.

'There's a gash in the tree here, Sarge.'

'Where?' Ramsey jerked around.

'Here.'

We peered up to where the constable was pointing. There was a definite gash that could have been caused by a bullet. We tramped round the tree and Broadley found some splinters. Ramsey picked them up and examined them.

'Hmmm!' he gave a passable imitation of Sherlock Holmes. He peered at them closely, extracted a plastic envelope from his pocket and placed the pieces in it. 'What happened next?'

I pointed out my route, indicated score marks in the turf where my heels had torn out divots in my panic as I headed for the trees. We walked over leisurely, I kept modestly in the rear as I still had the fear a gun barrel might be pointing in my direction from any one of hundreds of trees and bushes. We reached the bushes and picked our way up the slope.

'How long were you in here?' asked Ramsey, and I quelled an angry rejoinder with an effort. I considered he had asked the question with an unbelieving undertone in his voice, or maybe I was becoming paranoid and was finding offence at trivialities.

'I didn't time it.' I answered shortly, I didn't resort to sarcasm, but it being phrased as it was, I didn't need to. I kept it laconic and sharp, I saw the constable turn away and smile again.

'Very well, where did you go after that?'

'I headed for a rock that juts out, it's about ten foot high.'

'I know it,' Ramsey headed in its direction.

'You do?' I was surprised but he was not forthcoming. I should have known Ramsey would have every stick and stone in his patch ticketed and tabbed...woe betide anything that fell out of line. We clambered up to the 'summit' of the rock and looked over my fairway.

'And you were shot at when you stood here?'

'Yes.'

'How do you know it was you they were shooting at?'

'Christ Almighty!' My temper was already on a short fuse and all my good intentions of remaining calm and not offending the man evaporated. 'What a bloody silly question? How the hell do you think I fucking well knew! That bloody bullet nearly parted my hair...!'

'All right...all right!' Ramsey broke in, for once he sounded placatory. 'I phrased that badly. What I meant was, why did you think they saw you and it wasn't just a random shot, fired anywhere into the bush just to scare you?'

'Because it came too close for comfort,' I retorted.' Look, I've done time in the Australian Army, I was in Timor and know when I'm the target. It hit that tree over there.'

We inspected the tree and Broadley began to attack it with his knife. As he did so I indicated a branch that had been snapped off.

'Hmmm!' said Sherlock Holmes. 'What's that?'

Broadley came over with a piece of lead in his hand.

'Where was that?'

'Up there, in that trunk.'

Ramsey stood on the top of the rock and gauged the position where the bullet had struck home. He nodded at me, snapped the gash with his phone, and we climbed down off the rock.

'Where did you go after that?'

I led the way as we threaded through the undergrowth, we reached my No.5 iron, which miraculously was still where I had left it. I gave it a nudge so it swung from side to side like a pendulum. Ramsey looked at it, looked hard at the constable who hastily reached for his mobile phone, photographed the swinging club and made a note. I undid my tie, both club and tie appeared to be unaffected by their experience. I ran my hand over the shaft and felt the club head with my finger nail. It was undamaged.

We proceeded up the slope and worked our way to the left as we passed behind my tee and onto the promontory that overlooked the bend in the road. We found ourselves looking at my car and the police car as they stood together on the roadside below.

'Then they had a conference and they struck off in three different directions.' I said. 'One went over there, one onto the...er...fairway and the third man started to climb up here.'

'Did he see you?'

'No, at least not immediately, I climbed up there. My idea was to go down the other side of the hill and possibly hitch a lift, or cut across the paddock on the other side... assuming I could find the owner and get his permission of course.'

I shouldn't have said that, although the constable appreciated it. So, oddly, did Ramsey, a wry smile flickered for a moment across his features.

'A wise precaution.' he said dryly. 'And then what?'

'I had nearly reached the top without being seen, but I forgot the man down there, he saw me when I was near the top.'

'Then what?'

'I cut back along the way we came just now.'

'Why change your plan and direction?'

I nearly said it was because I couldn't find anyone whose permission I could obtain to cross the next paddock, but bit it back. There was no point in going out of my way to further antagonise the man; our relationship was bad enough as it was.

'Because the third man got into the car and drove back along the road,' I replied. 'So I struck off to the right and then made my way back through the trees, heading back roughly along the same route I covered on the way up.'

'Were you fired on again?'

'I don't think so,' I thought deeply, then shook my head. 'When I was heading along there, I saw them all on the hill back here.'

'Hmmm!' Sherlock Holmes scrubbed his chin. 'And what did you do then?'

'I headed round behind that poplar tree, past that wheat field and down onto the road,' I answered. 'I thumbed a lift off a truck coming from Wartook, he gave me a lift to Horsham...I checked he was insured to carry passengers.'

That was a mistake, it just fell out, but the memory of my speeding ticket was beginning to rankle again and combined with memories of all the comments made in the Police Station and subsequently about the landowner's permission I was near to flash point again.

He ignored it but I saw him grit his teeth and knew I had scored.

'We'll walk down to the poplar tree again then, shall we?'

The trip back to the poplar tree was probably unnecessary, I was beginning to get hungry by this time and I think Ramsey knew that. He dawdled down to the tree and peered down at the road from Wartook where I had been picked up by the truck.

'So you hitched a lift here, you must have passed the gunmen further up the road?'

'Yes, we went straight past them,' I noted his description of my tormentors as 'gunmen', indicating there appeared to be acceptance my story could have some credence.

'Good. Well we'd better get back to the station house. You

can give us more detail about your movements and describe your attackers.' He stooped and produced another golf ball from a tuft of grass. 'Is that one of yours as well?'

I nodded. He dropped it and held out his hand for the 5 iron. I handed it over, assuming he required it as evidence and was startled when he adopted a golfing stance and began to address the ball. He finally swung and there was a clean, crisp crack. The ball took off like a rocket, curved out over the road and then swung back on line with my tee. It cleared the tee and landed on the slope behind it, running uphill for a metre or two before it slowly rolled back. He threw the club back to me without comment and started walking towards my tee. I caught Broadley's eye as we followed him back. Broadley grimaced, then we turned to where the ball had landed.

It had been a fair hit. I reckoned he must have hit the ball over 130 metres. I eyed his receding back with interest and an element of respect, maybe the bastard was human after all.

CHAPTER 8

As Jane sat opposite me in the restaurant, I felt distinctly uneasy. For the first time I began to entertain serious doubts about the advisability of this two week 'camp' with Bill Otway, and whether we should put the idea of sleeping out in the wild permanently behind us and forget reliving our Army days, especially as Bill was now living with Marlene, a relationship which could become permanent.

'How long did you say you were going for?'

'Two weeks, more or less, mainly less, probably ten days.' I answered. 'We camp in the bush, live rough and move around a little, finding suitable camping sites.'

She winced and I hastily tried to water down what I had said. I knew she despised the 'ocker' type Australian, from odd comments she had made from time to time I gathered two of her former boyfriends had been dropped when they displayed tendencies of unmannerly behaviour and a propensity for making a virtue of hard drinking and chauvinistic behaviour.

'What I mean is...we camp and try to live off the land.' I said.' You know Bill Otway, we were overseas in the Army together, and I suppose we're just...er... reliving what it was like then, although without people shooting at you.'

'I've never met him,' she said and I felt the temperature drop. I realised she never had, which was a pity, Bill was hardly an 'ocker' type, not now anyway.

'Well, we go into the Grampians, it's not too far away,' I said soothingly. 'It's only for two weeks, in fact a few days less than that. We find ten days is more than enough these days. Perhaps we're getting old and appreciate creature comforts.'

She permitted herself a quirk of the mouth that could just... maybe just...be categorised as a smile. She was about to say something, changed her mind, then went off on another tack.

'Have you had any further strange incidents?'

'Strange incidents?'

'Like people following you.'

'Oh!' I considered the question. I hadn't heard from Sergeant Ramsey, although to be fair it had only been two days since he had hit a ball the length of my golfing fairway. I hadn't mentioned that shooting incident to Jane as I didn't want to alarm her unduly, but at least I'd done what she'd asked me to do after the previous incident...informed the police. After consideration, I shook my head.

'No' I replied.

'Liar!' she responded.

'Why do you...how do you know?'

'I can tell,' she said shortly. 'What's been happening?'

I hesitated, not sure whether to tell her the whole story or not. After two days of normality it was a story that sounded highly improbable and I had not seen any report of it in the local papers nor the Melbourne dailies. Knowing journalists had their police contacts, the fact they hadn't got hold of the story indicated either the slow reactions of journalists in the country areas or else it could be too unbelievable even for the tabloids. The more I thought about the events of two days before, I had difficulty believing it myself. But she was looking at me questioningly and I couldn't hold out.

'All right!' I went through the whole story from the moment I had climbed out of my car armed with golf balls and the 5-iron, the interview and examination of the site with Ramsey, down to his straight drive from the poplar tree. I didn't try to hide the fact I'd been frightened stiff; I knew I couldn't pass it off lightly.

'But that's frightful, what have they done?'

'Nothing yet, at least I've heard nothing from them.'

'What did the sergeant say to you at the time?'

That was a difficult question to answer. We had spent so much time bickering, sniping at each other and scoring points I couldn't in all honesty remember what he *had* said that could have been relevant or comforting. All I could remember was my smugness when I had made droll witticisms and pointed barbs about the impending case between The Owner of The Land vs Bromyard-Meredith, and in her present mood I didn't think she'd appreciate me trotting out examples of my wit.

'I...I think they took it seriously' I said lamely.

'You think!' she snapped. 'I should hope they did.'

'They hadn't much to go on,' I said. 'My description of the three men was not good. I spent most of my time running like hell with my back to them.'

'And you are still persisting with this ten-day trip into the bush?'

'Yes.'

'Isn't it asking for trouble?'

'No,' I answered. 'I'd feel safer in the bush than anywhere else, I'd know if anyone was within 40 metres of us, or maybe a half a kilometre. As it is, in so called civilisation, people with ill-intentions can approach within a short distance of you, be difficult to challenge and able to act before you can react. In the bush, it's different, people tend to avoid each other, but if there's anyone else around you, you often see or sense them before they see you.'

I was speaking the truth, being quite confident of my bushcraft. My confidence shone through so much I think I convinced her. She smiled at me and I felt my heart leap. Her aggression was, I knew, mainly based on fear and anxiety for me, an emotion that made me feel good.

*

I went to Bill Otway's place for dinner the following night. We worked out the final details, both of us aware that Marlene, who was also present, was not over impressed with what we were contemplating. There wasn't much new from previous years, we usually went to the same place which made a mockery of 'roughing it'. At the bottom of the hill, easily reached by Bill's Land Rover, was the local milk bar where we could purchase most of our needs, and some neighbouring shops.

The bush came up very close to the township and was very thick. Being in The Grampians the ground was liable to slope sharply upwards but we used many camping sites where the slope wasn't too pronounced. We had two tents with two camp beds, cooking utensils, spirit stove, meat safe and an 'esky'. We checked over all the gear, the rope and the tackle, eating utensils, plates, mugs etc while Bill had his Land Rover serviced so there should be no mechanical complications.

'We should be about right now,' Bill commented as he rummaged around in his haversack. That statement had a jarring effect on me, I still felt somewhat alarmist but had no intentions of communicating my fears. Not only had I not heard from Sergeant Ramsey, but there had still been no mention of my experience in the local papers. I was a little perplexed at this, I had no doubt most police stations had personnel who tended to leak to the press, and I thought any country news hawk would have jumped at the story. Nevertheless, I wasn't too upset. I didn't want my life complicated by hordes of newspapermen.

'What about tea and coffee?' asked Marlene.

'We have enough...,' said Bill, '...if we run out, we always have the shop.'

'True enough, and we have the pub down the road.'

'You're really living rough, aren't you?' Marlene commented and we both chuckled. Then she added sarcastically. 'Have you packed your golf clubs?'

'Of course I have,' I said scornfully. 'The clubs are ideal for killing snakes.'

'Oh of course,' Marlene nodded sagely. 'A No 7 iron for killing tiger snakes...!'

'She's getting it at last,' grinned Bill. 'Plus a pitching wedge for the black snakes, and a No 1 wood for a python.'

'There aren't any pythons in Australia,' Marlene objected.

'Agreed, so it proves how successful a No. 1 wood has been in the past!' whereupon we all three cackled with laughter. It was an old joke, but one of our stock ones.

Everything seemed in order. I arranged to come over in a few days, the arrangement was for me to leave my car in Bill's drive and we'd use the Land Rover, being a more suitable vehicle for the rougher terrain if we ever had to leave the road.

If we paused to think about it, we didn't cover much rough terrain in the vehicle. Once we reached our destination, we seemed to use it mainly for running to and from the shops, which in recent years had become more common for us which tended to belie any aspect of "roughing it". Yet the idea of a four-wheel drive Land Rover added something to the aura of 'living rough', and I think it also had the look of a semi-military vehicle which also appealed to us. After all, one couldn't go camping in a sedan car...could one?

I had been thinking about the events on the country meadow, or golf tee shoot, as I had begun to think of it in my mind. I hadn't mentioned it to Bill, nor the possible hit and run attempt some days earlier. Looking at the affair in the cold light of day it was becoming increasingly more and more difficult to believe, in fact there were moments when I had almost convinced myself the last incident could have been farmers shooting cockatoos on their land. Almost was the operative word, more considered thought of the events of that day soon quashed that. Then I would have more nagging doubts, was it me they had been after? If it was, then they had clearly made a mistake, since I wasn't rich nor involved in politics. And yet... they had used my name, or one of them, one I rarely used and which in itself was sufficiently rare as a surname to confirm it *was* me they were shooting at. But why?

I scratched my head as my thoughts brought me around again in a full circle.

'Anything wrong, old son?'

'No!' I said shortly. 'Is there any more coffee?'

'Sure,' Bill passed the coffee pot over. 'Well, that seems to be everything.'

'There *is* something wrong, isn't there, Phil?'

Damn and blast the woman, with the uncanny flair of her

sex for reading people's body language and minds Marlene had locked accurately on target.

'No. Nothing more than usual.'

'Are you sure?'

'Sure as I'll ever be. Although I think I may have a cold coming on.'

*

'There *is* something bothering you, isn't there?' Bill said later. We were standing by my car as I prepared to depart.

'Look, can't I feel a little off colour without people...!'

'It's more than that,' said Bill. 'You've had a shadow over yourself for some time now, and I've noticed it tonight more than usual. If there *is* anything wrong, I'd like to know before we commit ourselves to ten days in the Grampians.'

He stroked his moustache, knowing him as I did, I knew that meant he wanted an answer, an honest one and not bullshit. I saw the futility of trying to hide matters from him, and, as he said, he did have a right to know if something was wrong.

'I think someone is trying to kill me,' I said and instantly realised how melodramatic it sounded, like a phrase out of a television series.

'You what?'

His response was gratifying to say the least, I repeated it.

'What? How?'

I told him of the various episodes, the hit and run, the two men skulking in the bushes when I had been playing golf with Frank Gilmore and what we thought had been a shot, and the shooting incident on my golf fairway in the country. The motor cars I was sure had been following me through country roads, especially the vehicle behind me when I had been forced to stop by Dick Pascoe's livestock, which had vanished when Pascoe had cleared the road, a road with no turn offs.

'But this is fantastic, have you told the police?'

'Yes.' I answered. 'I told Sergeant Ramsey.'

'Oh him! Bloody hell! What did he do...or say?'

'He seemed to be more concerned about my trespassing on private land and the rights of the owner if I dug up divots,' I said bitterly.

'Well that sounds in character anyway,' said Bill. 'Silly sod!'

'So that's it,' I finished.

Bill pursed his lips and considered at length.

'And are you sure it's you they're after?'

'Hell's Bells, Bill,' I slapped my thigh with exasperation. 'I've asked myself that question time after time, and daft as it seems, it appears to be so. The incidents have been too personalised, so far as my travel routine is concerned, to be meant for anyone else. They've even shouted my name to each other, or part of it when they've been on my track...they called me Bromyard. It would be like referring to you with your second name of Talbot. I never use it. I don't think anyone in my circle knows it'.

'That's bloody peculiar,' commented Bill.

'Yet when it comes to asking why, I have no answer. I have no political affiliations, I'm not tied up with any religious sect or grouping, I've never said anything blasphemous that could upset any fanatics. I've never killed or maimed anyone on the roads that might cause a vendetta, I'm pure Anglo-Saxon stock with no Italian blood so it can't be the Mafia or any Balkan feud or faction.'

'Perhaps it's someone you beat in a golf tournament.'

Despite the tension in my soul I did find that funny, and we chortled for a few seconds. Yet that thought had occurred to me, not so much the golf tournament aspect but certainly the possibility of a dissatisfied policy holder. But apart from O'Flynn, I hadn't had any disagreements over claims settlements to cause anyone to go so far as to take pot shots at me. And if I did take O'Flynn seriously as a suspect, the argument over his claim had taken place after the incident on the golf course with Frank Gilmore.

'If you want to call it off, I'll understand.' I said.

'To hell with that, I'd say you'd be safer in the bush than walking the streets. If they came within half a mile of us in the bush, we'd know about it.'

There was much truth in that, I had previously come to that conclusion myself and had said as much to Jane, although I wasn't sure whether she believed it.

'We're still on then?'

'Yes,' Bill nodded vigorously. 'Ring me tomorrow.'

'I'll do that,' I said as I opened my car door, 'Until tomorrow then.'

CHAPTER 9

We passed through the township, and made our way to one of our usual camping sites. The road forked to the right and went up the side of the hill which was steeply wooded. The road had a bitumen surface most of the way, which degenerated into a dust track further up with deep ruts where the rain ran its course during the wet season.

I was feeling exhilarated; I was away from the office and the phone and for the first time in weeks I didn't have to peer over my shoulder. Once again, I'd reached the point where the shooting had reached the state of the unbelievable, I think Bill had too. It's amazing how a life of normality can process out anything off beat or something one doesn't wish to believe. I suppose this was the strength of most religious organisations and political parties, anything that conflicts with the dogma is dismissed as irrelevant...or irreverent!

Bill swung the Land Rover into the trees and we bumped along a rough track, the site was as we had left it the previous week when we had made a preliminary reconnaissance. Bill had left some provisions there in a cache, mainly tinned food he'd buried under one of the bushes. A quite unnecessary aspect, but nevertheless it was something that added to the military mystique. We checked as soon as we disembarked, everything was still there.

'OK, let's get cracking!' he commented and we started to erect the two tents and the awning. We always used two tents, there was less chance of small tents being blown away, if one was blown away the occupant did have another refuge into which he could crawl. We had also heard of friends who had upset stoves and set the tent alight which had wrecked their holiday and nearly themselves. With two tents a similar mishap would only destroy half the available accommodation. We had a third tent, which stayed rolled up, but it was there as a reserve in case we needed it.

I went into the trees and hung the meat safe from a branch. I hunted round and gathered firewood which I dragged into the clearing. The local ranger was friendly with us and knew us well, he was quite happy if we cleared undergrowth of dead and dying twigs and branches, however small the quantity, which could act as tinder during the hot dry season. I also strung up a clothes line to hang the tea towels on, and unloaded the large tub we used as a washtub. We busied ourselves getting everything shipshape, Bill lit a fire while I dug a trench round it to prevent the spread of flames into the main clearing.

We started to unload the Land Rover, which did bring to light a complication. Bill and I, and Frank Gilmore, were members of the local Rifle club, and we spent many a week end at the butts with our .22 rifles. We had all three been down there the previous week, and usually left our artillery at the rifle club, it wasn't compulsory but we all felt better with them safely under lock and key at the rifle club establishment.

Bill had recently updated his rifle, and traded in his existing gun but after returning from the gun shop, had decided to take his new gun home to take it apart, clean it and become generally conversant with it. When we had packed the Land Rover, he had momentarily forgotten his new rifle was stowed in the back of the vehicle and consequently had omitted to remove it when we set off on our trek. It came to light as we unloaded our gear at our camp site.

'Expecting trouble?' I asked cynically.

'Bugger it!' he responded. "I'll stow it in the cab where it can be locked in, it should be OK.'

We unloaded the bedding from the Land Rover and stowed it in the tents before we took a trip into the township. I drove it down the hill and we parked in the main street which possessed a milk bar, a hotel, a small chapel and a few other assorted shops selling camping gear, souvenirs, a plant nursery and an antique shop selling bric-a-brac and works of art. The Post Office was in the milk bar, where the proprietor doubled as the local postmaster and confectionary vendor.

'Hello Tom.' I greeted him as we entered the shop and he nodded gravely. In all the years we had camped here we had never seen him smile. Yet he possessed a dry sense of humour and was capable of uttering the most pointed witty ripostes without so much as a quirk of the lips.

He was over 60 and had been in the shop for years. There was a faded regimental photograph on the back wall, in past years I had squinted at it trying to find out where he was on the photo and what regiment it was, it looked as though he was the second seated on the left. He was a widower and during the summer months was assisted by his son and daughter-in-law.

'Weather doesn't look too bright,' he grunted, but we weren't alarmed by this as he made the same opening gambit every year.

'No, we could have some rain on the way, 'I replied, which was much the same response I made to his opening observation every year.

Bill and I bought some odds and ends. I needed torch batteries and Bill wanted matches. We chatted with Tom for some minutes before we went out into the street.

It looked as though Tom may have uttered some words of truth, there was a mist spreading over the top of the high ground that could only herald rain.

'We'd better get back to camp,' said Bill.

*

For the next couple of days, we played ourselves in and fell back into our normal camping routine. Any leftovers we buried at once and about a foot deep, we had no desire to attract scavengers. We went to the top of the tor one morning and felt exhilarated when we looked over the brink onto the valley below. We made our way down again, drawing clean air into our lungs, smelling the aromas one associates with wet earth and leaves, and listening to the cries of various birds.

We took a trip in the Land Rover to the other side of the mountain and took the third tent with us. We parked for the night and cooked a meal before turning in. It was a cold night but none the less enjoyable for that, there was a tang in the air and the clean air in our lungs made us feel like kings. We could hear the birds, magpies in particular as they too bedded down for the night.

In the middle of the night, I awoke with a full bladder, as I relieved myself against a nearby tree, I looked up at the night sky and all the stars were crystal clear. As I returned to the tent, I could see Mars and Jupiter, plus another unwinking celestial body that I assumed could only be Saturn. As I looked upwards and felt the cold, crisp air on my face I felt a quietude I had not experienced for weeks. For the first time for months I could not hear the sound of traffic, the sound of pop music nor the honking of motor horns.

I could recall reading a book where the writer, Laurens Van Der Post, advanced a theory that primitive peoples could hear the music of the spheres, he was writing about the Bushmen in Southern Africa. As I stood there in the semi-darkness, I could understand that primitive people could still experience so much we civilised beings missed with the self-imposed blinkers civilisation and logic placed upon us. Perhaps the word `primitive' was an erroneous description, maybe the aborigine and the bushman possessed an ability of real value we had lost long ago.

I found my way back to the tent and turned in.

'What's up,' Bill mumbled.

'Nothing, I just watered the horse.'

Bill cursed, rolled himself upwards and crawled to the door of the tent.

'If I'd known where you were going, I'd have asked you to have one for me,' he grumbled, and made his way outside. I heard him on the other side of the clearing as he watered one of the trees. I advanced to the door of the tent and looked skywards again. The stars and planets were still twinkling and shining, I fell back on my bed feeling a wave of contentment. The next morning, we packed everything and returned to our first camping site.

*

The first week passed uneventfully and we began to forget the trials and tribulations of civilisation. We did make one concession; a trip into the neighbouring settlement that boasted a laundrette and did some washing. There was no suitable stream in the vicinity for clothes washing, although there was a spring we used for drinking, after boiling it. I entered the pharmacy cum general stores and used the public phone in the shop to ring Jane. In this area there was no reception on my mobile phone

'Jane?'

'Hiya,' she said. 'How's Tarzan?'

I asked how things were at the office, I wasn't that interested but it was a useful opener. There had been a couple of haystack fires outside the town the previous week and apparently police suspected an arsonist was on the loose. Our company had insured one of the ricks and a farm shed that also went up in smoke. We chatted for a few minutes before I rang off with the promise to contact her again within a couple of days. Bill was still watching the washing go round and round in the laundrette dryer when I joined him again.

'This is better than television,' he observed brusquely. 'How is she?'

'All right,' I answered.

'Do we need anything?' asked Bill. The dryer ceased its cycle and he started to unload it. I considered for a moment then nodded.

'Kerosene and probably some candles,' I answered.

'OK. We'll drop in at Tom's on the way back.'

We were stuck behind a tractor for some of the way, there were a few farms in the vicinity but these were some distance away and it was unusual to see a tractor on the road. When we finally found an overtaking spot, we saw it was our friend the ranger at the wheel. He gave us a cheery wave as we accelerated past. As we pulled away a large black car came up fast from the other direction, roared past and showered us with small stones.

'Bloody hell!' Bill muttered. 'Some people have no consideration.'

We turned off opposite Tom's shop and clambered out. I stretched, yawned and felt my jaw creak. We entered the store where Tom was serving two girls dressed in hiking gear. Bill's eyes rolled in my direction and he leered at me whereupon I played my part and responded in kind. Even Tom seemed amused at Bill's reaction for the faintest of smiles creased his countenance. One of the girls became aware of us and turned around but by this time Bill was carefully studying magazines on the rack by the window with great interest.

'You'll be all right on the mountain tonight,' grunted Tom after the girls had left the store and were out of earshot. 'No need for hot water bottles tonight, eh?'

'My oath!'

We completed our purchases and Bill made one small concession to civilisation; he bought a Swiss roll. We watched the girls make their way to a nearby vehicle, which brought forth some repartee between us and Tom as they climbed aboard and drove off. As we were about to leave Tom called us back.

'Have you brought anyone else with you?' he asked.

'No. More's the pity,' said Bill as the girls' vehicle disappeared round the bend.

'No, what I mean is, is there anyone else with you or is it just the two of you?'

'Just the two of us,' I answered. 'Why?'

'I had two blokes in here about twenty minutes ago, they were asking if I knew of any campers on the hill, I said there was only you two as far as I knew.'

'No. There's nobody with us,' Bill said as we turned for the door. I opened it and Bill passed through onto the pavement outside.

'See you next time, Tom...wait a minute!' I swung around and re-entered the shop. 'What did these two blokes look like?'

'I didn't take to them much, shifty customers, I thought. One of them was fairly tall, much taller than the other. Oh! The short one wore one of those white hats. They had a big car, a black one they parked outside.'

I began to feel my adrenalin run.

'What then?'

'They asked if I knew your names, I clammed up then. I wasn't sure if you wanted to see them or not.' He looked at me quizzically. 'Did I do the right thing? Do you know them?'

'Not sure, and yes, you did the right thing,' I answered. I turned as Bill came back in. 'Two blokes have been asking about campers. They must have been driving that damned car that nearly ran us off the road.'

'Not looking for us, were they?' Bill eyed Tom enquiringly.

'Don't know if they were for sure,' Tom scratched his head. 'They were talking between themselves as they went out. I heard them mention a name as they went out. Neither of you is named Bromyard are you?'

CHAPTER 10

We came the nearest we'd ever been to having a row on the way back to camp. In the end I prevailed and Bill submitted with bad grace. We finally decided to move from where we were, we struck camp and loaded everything into the Land Rover.

'How can you be sure it's the same people?'

'How many times do you hear the name Bromyard?'

'How can you be sure they mean you harm?'

'I'm not! I just believe in taking no chances, that's all.'

After being nearly run down in a main street and suspecting I'd been shot at more than once his questions and my response ranked as understatements of the year. As we completed loading the Land Rover we carried on in much the same vein. Bill muttered to himself most of the time but didn't seem unduly slow moving as we packed our gear.

'Up to the Windy Site?' he asked as we completed the loading.

'Yes!' I answered laconically. The nomenclature referred to a point at the top of the hill where on windy days it could blow a gale. This wasn't the season for strong winds and another point in its favour was that the site gave a good view in all directions and all routes to it were upwards. Bill started the Land Rover and we bumped our way off the site we had been occupying and onto the track.

Bill had recovered some of his equanimity by the time we reached the Windy Site, he was humming to himself as we unpacked and set up the tents. It was late in the day before we finished our labours then realised we'd left the meat safe behind, with that night's meal inside it plus a few eggs.

'Bugger it!'

'Leave it until morning.'

'No! I'll go and get it now. I'll walk down, it will be just as quick and more direct.'

I rummaged in the tool-box of the Land Rover and selected some secateurs.

'What are you doing with those?'

'Just in case I see a rabbit.'

'You what?'

'Just joking...I secured the meat safe with some wire, I may need them to free it.'

He seemed to accept that, although that wasn't the only reason I had armed myself with something reasonably heavy that could substitute as a weapon. I thought again of two strangers asking questions and mentioning that damned name Bromyard.

Come to that, why go down to the former camping site at this time? Why not wait until morning? A fair question partly answered by the presence of bacon and eggs in that safe which I had been savouring all day, and I found it difficult to draw back after I had started heading downwards especially when I thought of those eggs and bacon.

I paused, wondering whether to take the secateurs back, after all they were something extra to carry and I would have to carry the meat safe all the way back. I decided to keep them with me, logic being what it is and still with the memory of the name Bromyard being overheard in Tom's shop and, after all, I had secured that safe with quite thick wire. The realisation hit me I was probably being damned silly, I hesitated and almost decided to return, then realised I was over half way there and might as well continue.

The setting sun cast long shadows across the top of the hill, as I looked down into the valley below nestling in the mountain's shadow, I saw it was already night down there. I could see headlamps threading their way along the roads, rather like insects. The small township was lit up, mainly by the windows of various buildings and a few cars were meandering up and down the main street.

The lower camp was further than I anticipated, although not as far as the journey we had already made in the opposite direction in the Land Rover via the rough track, I headed for it in a straight line where the rough track took a very circuitous route. I forced my way through bushes, brambles and gorse bushes. The stars were beginning to appear and the planet Venus was prominent in the eastern sky. I could feel the cold damp air on my brow as I headed downwards and used a tall wattle tree as my marker. We had paused by that tree for a rest many a time.

I could hear magpies calling in the dusk, and the alarm note of some smaller bird that fluttered in a bush in front of me. It kept just ahead of me and I deduced there was a nest somewhere near at hand and it was trying to lure me away from it. I could hear car horns below in the depths of the valley and the sound of an engine nearby as another vehicle chugged up the hill, presumably to have a night view of the valley from the Hill Lookout situated a kilometre from our Windy Site camp.

I stepped over a tree root as I entered the trees which became thicker at this point and momentarily lost sight of the moving and winking blob of light across the sky that was a passing aeroplane. I threaded through the tree trunks, the secateurs dangling from my hand.

The sun had now vanished behind another hill on the other side of the valley, leaving a dull glow on the horizon, while darkness set in with a vengeance. The shadow had brought all the area I was traversing into darkness. I paused briefly to take my bearings, then struck off once more and travelled another hundred metres or so before pausing again. I reckoned I should not be far off our former camp site now. I peered around me and moved off again, but had only travelled another fifty metres before I temporarily lost my bearings again and had to pause once more. It was this last pause that saved me.

'That you, Bert?'

I froze, all my nerve endings screaming. Believing I was the only person within a wide radius I was quite incapable of movement or saying anything, so complete was my surprise and temporary paralysis. No doubt James Bond, with 007 coolness, would have responded to the challenge, then materialised at the other side of the clearing at the ready. By the time I had reached the point where the tingling and numbness in my system was dissipating the challenger had made up his mind. A torch flashed across the clearing from a distance of about fifteen metres and illuminated me from head to toe.

'Bert? ...Christ, it's him!'

'What's up, Paul?'

'Bert... it's him! He's here!'

At last my limbs began to respond to commands from my brain. As a dark shape moved in my direction, I tried to back away but was forestalled by a tree trunk. In the light of the torch, about three metres distant, I could see that my nearer antagonist was holding something that looked like a handgun.

I couldn't back off, as he came nearer, I heard a clicking noise, which could have been a gun being cocked. That decided me, no point in asking damned silly questions, act first and ask afterwards. I jumped forward and swung viciously with the secateurs, I must have struck him across the cheek bone, he cursed and staggered to one side, and his weapon, yes it was a gun, discharged, I knew not where. Strangely, that came as a relief, I knew then I hadn't mistakenly committed an act of violence on an ordinary, law-abiding citizen.

I turned and darted back in the direction from which I had come and promptly ran into another tree which struck me a glancing blow on my shoulder. My adversary was in worse case, he could see across the clearing to the tree all right, but failed to spot tree roots on the ground and tripped badly, plus he was suffering from the effect of the blow from the secateurs. He stumbled at a half run and fell into a gorse bush. I heard shouts behind me and the sound of a shot, followed by the scream of a ricochet as the bullet glanced off a nearby tree and streaked off into the ether.

The temptation to panic was almost irresistible but I quelled it with an effort and decided to adopt a slow regular pace through the trees which would give me ample time to see where I was going. I was assisted by the faint glow of light from the sun that still dimly illuminated the sky. It had recently descended over the far away hill and showed up the trees as shadowy shapes. I flitted from tree to tree, then became aware there were sounds of pursuit and further, that the dull glow in front of me could prove deadly as there was a chance it would silhouette me. Another bullet whined past me, I ducked off to the left and started running downhill.

As I hopped and skipped down the slope, I became extremely worried. Whoever was behind me had a torch, or torches, and with the added advantage of vision could not fail to gain on me. There was another shot, but I heard nothing of the bullet's progress, which indicated the shot had been optimistic, could have gone anywhere and probably did.

'Hold your fire' I heard an angry shout and could not help but agree with the sentiment. While logic told me there was little chance of being hit in this light by men on the run with handguns, there was always the chance of a lucky hit.

'Oh God!' I almost whimpered with fright as I tripped over a tree root and fell headlong. I scrambled to my feet, then fell down a slope into the rough track that served as a roadway, the track Bill and I had used only a bare hour before as we changed sites with all our gear.

'What's up?' I heard another voice shout and nearly passed out with sheer fright as a dark shape detached itself from a car parked on the track. This time I was the one with the advantage of surprise, he clearly believed I was one of his henchmen. I didn't waste time in pleasantries, I swung the secateurs again and hit him hard in the gut as I descended on him and he jack knifed onto the track with a loud gasp. I fled over the track and was about to enter the bushes when the car headlights came on and bathed me in brilliant light, which prompted a couple of shots from the trees that hit the track bed and whined in all directions.

I dodged behind a very large tree and plunged into the undergrowth. I heard more shots but none came near me, they clearly had no idea exactly where I was

There was a brief lull while they sorted themselves out, I

took advantage of this to strike off at a tangent away from the blinding lights, they fired another shot but again with no idea of my whereabouts. My eyes were still seeing yellow after images from the headlights; it was like looking through a frosted glass window.

'Come on,' somebody shouted, I shook off the attentions of some of the gorse bush tendrils and kept running. I leapt down the slope, headed off to the left and then struck back up again, the field craft I had learned in the Army coming to the fore. I dodged round a thick tree trunk and dropped on all fours before crawling away from the tree and keeping it between myself and the enemy.

That blasted remaining headlight was still on and there were patches of light shining through gaps in the trees and bushes. I was slightly behind the light by this time, but there was an aura that tended to filter back slightly and cast a slight illumination where I was.

I decided to continue crawling, headed behind the car and made my way slightly upwards. There was a limit to how far I could go, the track at a point four metres ahead went straight to the edge of a sheer drop, so either I would have to shin down a cliff face or clamber up and cross the track again behind the vehicle.

My adversaries were clustered around the car and it was some consolation they were peering indecisively around almost as though expecting to be under fire. Then I had an inspiration. I felt a pebble between my fingers and as they curled around it, I decided to create a diversion. I lobbed it over the car onto the bushes above the car on the other side of the track, it hit something solid and they all jumped back and cowered beside the bonnet.

'For Christ's sake turn that bloody light off!'

We were all plunged into darkness and I sighed with relief. I crawled further behind the car and was confronted by the edge of the sheer drop. I felt my fingers tingle at the thought of it, but as my eyes adjusted to the gloom, I could see that although it fell away steeply it certainly wasn't sheer. I wormed my way over the sill and went down spider fashion, I had no idea how far I would have to go before I hit anything flat but that was the least of my worries. If anyone thought to peer over the edge of the track above me, I would be a sitting duck.

My main concern was to avoid knocking loose stones down the steep slope, they would make sounds like an avalanche in the silence of the night but, luckily, they were making considerable noise themselves while they argued about what to do next.

I found myself on a rocky ledge that made its way along the side of the slope, I wormed my way along it and realised I was heading upwards again. I debated whether I wished to land anywhere near the track again but finally decided to chance it and try to reach the trees on the other side of the track. I cast fearful looks behind and above me but it seemed my pursuers were examining the bushes on each side of the track in front of their car, one using a torch.

I crawled back to a point near the track and rested, it was now or never and if I was going to make the dash it would have to be soon. The quartet was still in front of the car and I decided to make the break. I doubled back across the track, tripped over an undulation in the track and fell hard against the bank on the far side of the track, but had the presence of mind to retain my grip on the secateurs, though what good they would do me right now I had no idea. Had I wished to draw attention to myself it would have been simpler to have banged a drum or used a loud hailer and thus prevented a bruised knee. There was a shout from my adversaries and the torch flashed in my direction. It never reached me, by then I was already in the bushes, having reached them in one bound like a startled gazelle.

'There he is!' a somewhat unnecessary directive with all the noise I was making. I fell over three times in as many metres and cursed angrily. I heard a shot and a bullet hit a tree about a metre away.

I put about 100 metres between me and the torch and sank exhausted against a large tree. I lurched against a fallen log and sat down weakly. I had the urge to fling the secateurs away but saner counsels prevailed. They were still after me and I might need them. There was no point in giving way to finer instincts, these boys had none and they were not playing games. But, had I killed anyone? I had hit somebody very hard with them.

*

'What was that shooting? What the hell was going on?'

In the light of recent events it was not an unreasonable question. I sat down with a bump on a handy log and considered the answer.

'I had a little trouble.' I hazarded, an understatement that perhaps was a little tactless.

'A little troub...!' Bill clapped a hand to his head. 'Bloody Hell! I'd hate to be around when you really run into difficulties. Where's the meat safe?'

The meat safe! I'd forgotten all about that in the excitement. In any case, I certainly wasn't going back for it now!

'What was all that gunfire?' Bill took the secateurs that were still in my hand and examined them. 'What the hell have you been doing with these?'

'I hit one of them across the head with them,' I said soberly.

'My oath you did, there's blood on the end here.'

'They were waiting for me down at the camp,' I explained. On reflection this wasn't strictly true, but it certainly sounded more dramatic. Obviously, what had really happened was they must have previously located our first camp and had intended to creep up on us in the dark, maybe they had just realised the birds had flown when I appeared on the scene.

'Bloody hell!' was Bill's comment.

'Quite so,' I replied. 'I think I shook them off, for the present. But we'll have to do some thinking about whether we stay here or not.'

'Too bloody right we will,' Bill stormed angrily. 'Just tell me again what happened and please don't tell me you think you've killed someone?'

'Yes, I may have done, I think I hit him on the side of the head.'

'Christ, that's all we need,' Bill sank down weakly on a fallen log. 'I don't think the police will go much on *that*!'

The same thought had already occurred to me, as had the possible consequences.

'But I really can't see what else I was supposed to do when they were using me for target practice,' I protested. 'They were shooting at me... not over my head...*at* me! I felt like a clay pigeon.'

'Well there's only one thing to do now. Get the hell out of here and inform the local police.'

'I'm all for that,' I agreed. 'They might be more sympathetic than bloody Ramsey.'

Bill reached into his jacket pocket for his mobile phone, switched it on and listened, then shook it angrily.

'No bloody reception,' he snapped.

'Surprise, surprise,' I replied, this was not unexpected in this area, we had found this in previous years.

'I suggest we get some shut eye, then go down into Halls Gap tomorrow and phone the cops,' snapped Bill

'No. I'll go down on my own. This seems to be my fight, but Christ! I don't even know what it's about,' I rose to my feet. 'We'll never get down there in the dark now and I fancy they'll have the track blocked with their car so we won't be able to use the Land Rover.'

'All right - suits me,' Bill nodded and indicated the secateurs. 'What are we going to do about those?'

'I'll shove them in the back of the Land Rover for now. But for tonight we'll sleep in shifts and we'll do watch and watch about.'

'Amen to that!'

CHAPTER 11

t was 10 o'clock in the morning when I reached the outskirts of the township. I had parked near to, then scouted around, the former camp site but found no sign of my adversaries of the night before. There was a patch of dried blood under a tree near the track, I shuddered and nearly jumped a metre in the air when a bird flew out of a nearby bush.

I was on the alert as I ferreted around but they must have left the area, for the time being at least. Their wounded comrade probably needed medical attention, I fervently hoped he obtained it for I envisaged great difficulty in explaining to an unsympathetic member of the Victorian Police Force why I had bludgeoned someone to death in a Victorian beauty spot, especially when I could provide no convincing proof or reason for any allegations I was being followed, pursued and shot at. My one consolation in following that train of thought was that I'd already reported something on those lines to the Victorian Police. Nevertheless, I still couldn't see how I could justify severely injuring anyone without proving self-defence, but how could I prove that?

I searched around various tree trunks, trying to track my panic stricken run the previous night and searched for bullet scars on the trees. I found one or two gashes that could have been bullet marks, but could equally have been made by birds or teenage vandals.

Descending the hill via the track was a slow and laborious exercise. I imagined I saw sharpshooters behind every tree and rock and more than once nearly drove the Land Rover into bushes when I saw movement, which subsequently turned out to be birds.

On one occasion I was sufficiently alarmed to squeal to a halt and leap out, dodging around the Land Rover, to the astonishment of a car load of pleasure seekers on their way to admire the view from the lookout. I gave an embarrassed grin and a cheery wave, but all I saw as they drove past was the collective question mark over their heads.

On reaching the main road I proceeded cautiously and kept a weather eye cocked for parked vehicles. My progress was a series of stops and starts, so much so I attracted angry horn blowing from a following car after I made a sudden stop in the middle of the road which resulted in him almost ramming me up the back. He roared past me, blew his horn and gestured furiously.

I sat on his tail all the way to the Gap, which caused him considerable discomfort, I could see his face in his mirror as he nervously eyed me, wondering if I was going to accelerate aggressively and cut him out. Had he been aware of the real reason for me sticking to him like glue he could have been even more nervous. My reasoning was, if anyone was lying hidden in the bushes with a loaded rifle, they were less likely to open fire when I was keeping company with another vehicle. Similarly, a vehicle waiting to ambush me by leaping out from a side track would also be hampered if I had a companion vehicle which could supply unwanted witnesses.

There was not much doing in the main street as we passed along it. I left my position on the leading vehicle's rear bumper to draw into the side, presumably to his relief as he continued on through the township and out of sight. I clambered out, had an abortive try on my mobile phone and then looked around for a public phone but it looked as if I'd have to use the one in the milk bar.

My precautions and alertness were justified. That I survived was due to my constant vigilance ever since the incident the night before. As I crossed the road a black Ford Falcon pulled out into the roadway and accelerated in a rush. It had never occurred to me at the time to look for a different car, as the Ford rushed towards me the one thought in my mind was that it wasn't the car I'd seen last night on the track, which had been a Holden.

'K-e-r-r-r-i-st!!'

I propelled myself backwards towards the Land Rover. The Falcon swerved towards me but the turning circle was too tight. It skidded on two wheels, then righted itself as the driver regained control. I caught a glimpse of the short stocky man who had recently peppered me with bullets on my practice fairway. The Falcon screeched to a halt, it had to as a Post Office van was parked by the pillar box. It's rear wheels nearly left the road as it halted abruptly and narrowly avoided climbing up its rear end. It revved up and burned rubber as it reversed. I watched, open mouthed, I stood by the rear of the Land Rover and caught sight of the postman on his hands and knees, he had dodged behind the pillar box for protection.

I was almost paralysed until I saw a hand holding a gun emerge from the rear side window of the Falcon, whereupon

I vaulted into the passenger seat of the Land Rover. As I did so something hit the tailboard, I peered over the top and saw the handgun fire again as the Falcon took off along the street and around the bend. I jumped out onto the roadway, as I did so the .22 rifle that Bill had stashed away next to the passenger seat caught on my foot and catapulted out onto the roadway with a loud clatter.

I leapt down, stooped and picked it up, then looked up and down the street. I was astounded at the lack of reaction, the street was almost empty and the incident seemed to have attracted little or no attention. Maybe erratic driving by Victorian drivers was the norm rather than the exception.

I emerged from the protection of the Land Rover, holding the rifle at the trail, with the idea of returning the rifle to the cab before setting off for the Milk bar again, as I did so another engine started up and I became aware of the Holden from the previous night also bearing down on me, I fell, rolled and scrambled onto the pavement. As I rose to my feet, it stopped and begin to reverse. There were three men in this one, two in the front and one in the rear, again I saw a hand gun come out through one of the windows.

I instinctively raised the rifle and squeezed the trigger; in retrospect I know now it was a stupid thing to do but everything happened so fast. As a tactical move it was fruitless, the gun wasn't loaded, Bill had confirmed that when he locked it away in the cab. As a strategic gesture it did have some effect. It caused the gunman in the car to lose his concentration as he opened fire from their forward turret, the shot was way off and punched a hole in a shop window on the near side of the street. Apart from causing a shattering noise, and scattering broken glass over cakes and buns in the shop window, the effect of the wayward shot was immediate.

Firstly, I had been transformed from a sitting duck into an, apparently, armed man capable of dishing out the same treatment they were doling out. The fact that I hadn't fired a shot and wasn't capable of doing so was totally lost in the general excitement.

Secondly, the local populace realised for the first time that something a little out of the ordinary was going on. Presumably reckless driving, screaming tyres and pedestrians jumping for the safety of pavements were commonplace in Australia whether in cities, towns or crossing the Sydney Harbour Bridge, but when windows began to shatter and gun shots were fired in the main street even the average Australian would sit up, take notice and be aware something was going on that was a little off line.

My adversaries had chosen their moment well, not too many people were about and those that were in the vicinity were not in the immediate area and merely shaking their heads at the woeful driving. Only about four people were near enough to see what was really going on and they dived for cover, except for the owner of the general store and cake shop who had just had bits of his shop window scattered all over his wares.

'What's going on here...what bastard did that?' he shouted in a voice like a bull. He was built like one too, he added more in the same vein, before his eyes focused on me. Since I was clutching a rifle it was a natural reaction for him to put two and two together, I was hardly in a position to deny responsibility. He set off purposefully towards me, clenching his fists, at which point the Holden backed up and opened fire with its rear turret. They were accelerating, with a cloud of dust in their wake so their aim was no better than it had been before. Their first salvo crashed through the windscreen of a stationary car outside the milk bar, there were two more gunshots, followed by a loud clang as the

Holden disappeared around the bend in the main street, leaving me and the general store owner lying in the gutter.

He was momentarily speechless, for which I was grateful as I considered the main force of his invective would be coming in my direction. Further, the reason for the loud clanging noise became apparent, a bullet had struck an item of hardware hanging outside the milk bar and punched a hole in it. I scrambled to my feet still clutching the rifle, an action that galvanised his vocal chords into action.

'Did you do that?' he roared, indicating his shop window. Despite having been precipitated onto the road by the departing Holden he clearly failed to associate it with the previous and more recent gunfire. Since I was the only one bearing any ordnance in sight all his invective was directed at me.

Discretion was the better part of valour, I decided against the idea of using either the general store or milk bar phone to summon the police, I had little doubt that would be done anyway with the various aggrieved citizens in the vicinity who had suffered collateral damage.

I sensed it was going to become more and more difficult to explain my part, passive though it had been in what had just taken place, to a more and more hostile populace now emerging from the woodwork. These included Tom the milk bar owner, whose ornamental copper pot now had a small hole drilled in it, the general store owner with his cake and bun wares spattered with broken glass, and the owner of the car with the shattered windscreen.

As I stood there, brandishing Bill's rifle, all their ire and invective homed in my direction. I began to feel more and more isolated, so I turned on my heel, bringing forth a gasp from the general store owner as my rifle briefly circled in his direction, and headed for the Land Rover. I had scrambled into the drivers' seat and started the engine before they shed their paralysis and advanced over the street towards me.

Tom, the milk bar owner, reached me first.

'What's all this? What the hell's going on?' he asked, looking up at me as I peered out of the drivers' side window.

'I'll explain later, Tom,' I said. 'Just ring the police.'

The general store owner gave a loud roar.

'You bet we're going to call the bloody police and I'll see you in irons, you bloody maniac.' His already red face had assumed a delicate shade of puce, his fists were clenched as he stood by the bonnet. I decided to move out and did so, his fist struck the door of the Land Rover as I drew away.

'Bloody maniac.' I heard him roar again. 'Look what he's done to my window.'

'And my car...' shouted the irate car owner, '...and look what he's done to your copper pot, Tom.'

I had the feeling my position on their popularity list was not high as I drove off. I understood now how bank robbers must feel as they left the scene of the crime. Admittedly the scene was not one any average law-abiding citizen would normally leave in his wake, but I had not been responsible for any of it nor had I started the fracas. I experienced considerable bitterness with members of the human race who jumped to conclusions and condemned innocent people without even listening to their explanations or protestations, merely basing their reactions solely on circumstantial evidence which admittedly, in this case, looked damning. I understood now how soccer players felt on being sent off for retaliation after being on the receiving end of a violent assault from an opponent, while the instigator got off scot free. In my case I hadn't even had the satisfaction of retaliation.

Initially I decided my best bet was to head for Wartook where I would find a land line phone so I could ring the police to try to absolve myself from the trail of destruction behind me, also to ring Jane to tell her she may be seeing me in the near future. The holiday was clearly over, we couldn't spend the rest of the fortnight like the garrison of a beleaguered fort and there would be difficulties if we presented ourselves again in the township in quests for supplies, we were likely to attract a lynch party.

As I accelerated down the road I was once more puzzling over why I, a law-abiding citizen without an enemy in the world, should be hounded and chased all over the countryside and main streets by a private army. What could I have done to merit such treatment? I cruised along deep in thought, twisting the problem this way and that, yet no solution offered itself.

A harsh horn blaring brought me back to the present with a jolt. During my reverie I had drifted over to the wrong side of the road, which was forcibly drawn to my attention by a benevolent passing motorist who gave me a two-finger sign as he swept past hurling abuse. I swung over to the left and parked by the roadside, if I was going to think the matter over, I'd better stand still. I kept the engine running, with the uneasy feeling something could creep up on me out of nowhere and I didn't wish to waste time wrestling with a recalcitrant engine that might refuse to start.

I must have sat for about five minutes wrestling with the problem but got nowhere. All it did accomplish was an alteration to my plans. I scrapped the idea of going to Wartook to find a land line phone. All I could do from there was ring the police, but had no doubt this had already been done by angry shop-keepers and car owners left in my wake. The general store owner would probably have called out the Marines as well. Nor would ringing Jane accomplish any useful purpose, my immediate duty was to travel back, acquaint Bill with what had happened and take steps to move out. I felt my entrails curl when I realised Bill was still in blissful ignorance of the recent catastrophic events. It was hardly fair, if his first intimation of anything being amiss was to be besieged by a posse of angry citizens followed by the Victorian Police Force.

I did a 'U' turn and returned the way I had come. I decided to avoid Halls Gap and to approach the camp from the opposite direction, which would mean parking 100 metres below it and walking the rest of the way. The journey was uneventful, so uneventful I had to quell the tempting idea I had dreamt it all. I was still struggling to believe the events I had experienced had actually happened, when I rounded a bend and came across a petrol station. It was one of those small service stations out in the wilds that cater for the weary traveller's every need ranging from petrol, spare parts, needles and pins, cakes and Coca Cola. I drew in as the petrol gauge needle quivered on the 'E', and spotted a phone-box by the side of the building.

'Fill her up,' I instructed the proprietor as he came out. 'Can I use the phone?'

'Feel free,' he grunted as he thrust the pump nozzle into the Land Rover's tank.

I entered the box, dialled the office number and asked for Jane.

'Hallo!' I said. 'It's me.'

'Hallo me,' she said.

I toyed with the idea of telling her what had happened, but decided against it. I wasn't sure as yet how far the police would be involved; I didn't want them goose-stepping into the office with Jane feeling she had to unload information. We had a few moments of general chit chat, then I saw the service station proprietor had finished filling the tank and was leaning against the side of the Land Rover admiring the view.

'I'd better go, I'll ring you again,' I said.

'Yes, all right,' she said. 'Oh...there's one thing. There have been two phone calls for you. One was from your sister, I spoke to her...she seems nice...I liked her...and she said the same man had been trying to contact you, somebody named Shaw. She said she'd given him this number. She was reticent about giving him your home address and number. Do you know a man named Shaw?'

'Shaw,' I said. 'No, can't say I do.'

'Well he came through on the office phone the next day, yesterday, asking for you. Bob Simmons took the call. Shaw said it was personal so he handed him over to me.'

A personal call and Bob Simmons had automatically handed it to Jane! I felt a warm glow for a second before my mind returned to realities. Shaw? Yes of course, I had heard of Shaw. Mary had mentioned him to me when I had been at the christening.

'Hang on,' I said. 'I do know a man named Shaw, or at least, I've heard *of* him before. Was it Graeme Shaw?'

'Yes, I think it was, I didn't quite catch his first name, but now I think of it, it could have been Graeme. He didn't tell me much, he sounded English. He merely said he had something to tell you that was to your advantage and asked where I could contact you. I explained you were out camping, I didn't say where because of your recent troubles.'

'Good,' I said. 'What else?'

'That was it, except he did say something peculiar. He said something about it being a serious matter and you were to be careful and to watch your back. He was in Melbourne and was travelling to Stawell yesterday. I asked what he meant about being careful, but he clammed up and rang off. He said he'd be in Stawell tomorrow, today that is now, and if I heard from you...would I contact him. He left me the name of the motel where he would be staying.'

'Hmmm!' I said. 'Most peculiar. Well if he rings again, tell him I'll probably be back tomorrow or the next day.'

'Tomorrow, are you coming back so soon?'

'I've had some trouble down here, same as before. We're coming home.'

That was a mistake, I then had to tell her what sort of trouble. I toned it down a little; on reflection the story of a pitched gun battle in the main street of Halls Gap was hardly believable anyway, that is until the newspapers got hold of it. I had another look through the window at the petrol man and realised it was time to go.

'See you soon,' I said and rang off.

'Fifty five dollars forty,' he said. 'Looks like rain.'

I didn't fully agree with his assessment of the weather but didn't feel disposed to argue. I nodded and peeled off some notes. He grunted and went into the office for change.

When I hit the road again, I put my foot down. I realised I'd lost a lot of time and had left Bill in the lurch. I took a side road along the side of the hill which joined the main track up to our camp.

The journey was uneventful, although I started nervously every time a bird flew out of a bush and winced with expectation very time a car appeared coming towards me. I decided I would drive direct to the new camp after all, I didn't feel like undertaking a 100-metre climb on foot. I hit the track and started to climb, roared past our first camp site at a fast rate and scattered stones and gravel over a passing Scout troop. I raced round the bend in the track with the comments of the Scoutmaster ringing in my ears and observed some very un-Scouts like gestures in my mirror from young boys who should have known better.

Bill was brewing himself a cup of tea when I arrived, he didn't look altogether happy, expressing himself somewhat forcibly as I slid out of the driving seat. He enquired as to my recent whereabouts and what the hell took me so long. I ignored it.

'They were there!' I said.

'Who? Shit! Where?' Question succeeded exclamation which in turn was succeeded by a further question as the import struck home. 'In Halls Gap?'

'In the Gap,' I took a mug of tea from him. 'You'll find this hard to believe.'

'After last night's episode I'll believe anything,' he snapped. 'Try me!'

'They tried to run me down in the main street, the same way they did in Stawell a few weeks back, and then...then...' I hesitated, if I told him part of it, I'd have to tell him the lot.

'Go on,' he sensed worse was to come.

'Then they started shooting.'

'They started shooting!' Bill was incredulous. 'In the middle of Halls Gap?'

'In the middle of Halls Gap,' I repeated. 'I think the time has come to go home.'

'Bloody oath it has! What happened next? Bloody hell! You haven't clobbered anyone else have you?'

I assured him I hadn't and gave him a brief synopsis of events, although I omitted my handling of the rifle which had caused people to jump to the wrong conclusions....namely the shattering of the cake shop window, a car windscreen and the punctured copper pot.

'We'd better go back to Halls Gap and inform the police.'

'I'm not going back there, 'I answered bitterly. 'I'll never get out alive. They all seemed to blame me for everything that happened.'

'Why should they do that?'

'Well...er...' I began and tailed off lamely. 'I...er...I was holding the rifle...!'

I had been reticent about mentioning I had been carrying the .22 and apparently joined in the gun battle, gun licences were not easy to obtain. But I realised I couldn't hide much from Bill, he had a right to know, especially as he owned the gun.

'You did *what*?' Bill's voice went up three octaves. 'You walked up and down waving a gun ...my gun! Jesus Christ, this gets worse!'

'No...it wasn't quite like that, but I'm not going back there, that bloody general store-keeper will probably tear me apart.'

'If he thinks you broke his fucking window, I can't say I'm surprised! But we'll have to tell the police.'

'No need, the place is probably already knee deep with constables by this time, if they haven't called out the bloody Army as well. The place will have so many flashing blue lights it will look like a fairground.'

Bill rose and started pulling out tent guy ropes.

'OK!' he grunted. 'Let's get the hell out of here.'

We worked in silence, except Bill nicked his finger and uttered a curse that must have been heard in New South Wales. I stopped work repeatedly and listened, twice I went to the edge of the plateau and listened hard but couldn't hear anything. It took us a mere twenty minutes to dismantle everything and sling it into the back of the Land Rover. Normally we were very meticulous about folding everything up neatly but today we just threw everything into the vehicle in an untidy heap.

'Are we going back through Halls Gap?'

I considered the question, if we did, we'd very likely be apprehended by police and I didn't feel like answering questions at this juncture, especially with the cake shopkeeper hurling abuse. Whatever I had to tell them could wait, whether Ramsey's file detailing my last incident would be in their hands I didn't know. Probably not at this stage unless it had been forwarded onto a police central bureau, with me being the common denominator.

'No,' I said finally, 'Let's go straight home.'

It was quite likely there could be someone from the police waiting for us at Bill's place, it was his Land Rover and somebody may have noted the registration. Tom, the Milk Bar owner, knew our first names, but little else.

We went down the track at a fast rate. I was driving and wanted to be away before the Victorian Police arrived. We would take a fork before we reached our old camping site which would presumably be where the police would arrive first, as Tom knew where we habitually camped and so did some of the other tradesmen in the township.

We bumped and jolted down the track, Bill maintained a stoic silence despite the possible damage I was committing to the springs of his Land Rover. As we rounded a bend, I saw the fork, and veered to the left. As we did so we both caught sight of a blue flashing light coming up the right-hand track from below.

'There they are. Should we stop?'

I kept on going, I'm not sure why I did at that stage, despite my bad odour with some of the citizenry of Halls Gap the police were surely my allies, while my attackers were the worst enemy. Yet I was unsure about my reception. Apart from none of the Halls Gap citizenry being sympathetic towards me, I was beginning to entertain doubts that the roles played by the Holden and the Falcon had been seen at all.

Further, I was intrigued by Jane's mention of this man Shaw

who was anxious to contact me. Anyone who was on my track and gave me polite advance warning, however vague, over the phone could only be friendly. The fact that he sounded English was not unduly significant, in Australia English accents were part of the general scenery.

And yet...I had a feeling this man Shaw may provide the key to the recent occurrences, his warning to Jane for me to be careful certainly seemed relevant as did the expression to 'watch my back!' I wanted to see him as soon as possible without delay and the police could cause an unwelcome delay.

So, I drove on and left the flashing blue lights behind.

CHAPTER 12

It was hardly a triumphal homecoming. For the first time ever in our long relationship, Bill seemed anxious to see the back of me and the sooner the better. It was an emotion I could understand, when after years of solitude you've settled with a young woman, who could be your future wife, you wouldn't want to be too close to a man who seemed to be a magnet for rifle fire.

We had a brief altercation before we entered the house, for the first time he became aware of the bullet hole drilled in the tailgate of the Land Rover. With all the excitement during and after the shooting, I had momentarily forgotten it.

'Good God Phil! How the hell am I going to explain that to the insurers?'

We were still engaged in a heated discussion about it when Marlene appeared. and eyed us quizzically as we unpacked the Land Rover. In view of the difficulties of explaining our premature return, I acceded to his suggestion that I continue on to Stawell as soon as possible and leave him to finish the unpacking. I brusquely agreed, somewhat put out that he felt easier not having me around, but I could hardly argue with his sentiments. I entered the house and changed into the slacks and sweater I'd left there on the day we commenced our ill-fated trip.

'Would you like a cup of coffee?' Marlene asked brightly as I appeared in the kitchen fully changed.

'Er...er...yes. Thank you.'

'Is anything wrong?'

'Plenty!' I said bitterly.

'Oh dear, you haven't had an argument about anything...?'

I shook my head.

'If you think we've fallen out, forget it,' I said. 'But some queer things happened out there directed at me. I'll leave it to Bill to explain...is it sugared?'

'What? Oh yes,' she gave me a long searching look, with her interest aroused and she didn't like being kept in the dark. I hated being mysterious, but I was having qualms of conscience. She had been aware something was wrong before we set out, and now, with the gift of hindsight, I felt guilty I had knowingly exposed her house mate to possible danger, even though Bill too had been fully aware something was going on and had decided to ignore it. I had the feeling Marlene may not see it in quite the same light and decided to get out and leave it for Bill to explain. In any case I'd had enough aggravation one way or another for the last few days.

I drank my coffee faster than I should and burnt the end of my tongue in the process. Bill came in and avoided my eyes as he helped himself to his coffee and likewise burnt his lips. The phone rang and Marlene went to answer it.

'Bugger it!' Bill said for want of anything better to say, then relapsed again into a silence that fast became overpowering.

'I'd best be off then, Bill,' and he nodded. It was my intention to ring Jane from there but on second thoughts I decided it would be politic to get out as quickly as possible. 'I'll give you a ring later in the week.'

'Yes, all right Phil,' our eyes met, he seemed a little embarrassed and almost ashamed. 'It wasn't a good idea, was it?'

I shook my head.

'I thought I'd be safer out there than anywhere. It just shows how wrong you can be.'

'Not necessarily,' he said. 'Maybe you were safer out in the wild. Maybe in a busy main street situation you could have been an easier target...who knows?'

I nodded.

'In view of what happened in Halls Gap, you could be right.' I said and Bill gave a grunt that seemed to signify agreement. Perhaps the trip had been my salvation, certainly the attempt on my life in the undergrowth and bushes when I went back for the meat safe had misfired. I had been on the alert and in an environment with which I was familiar and experienced, which enabled me to remain one step ahead of whoever they were.

'Get onto the police, Phil,' Bill saw me to the door.' Have you told Marlene what's been happening?'

'I left that for you.'

'You bastard, thanks for bloody nothing,' then he grinned and clapped me on the shoulder as I reached the front step. 'I'll be seeing you then.'

'Yes,' I answered feelingly. 'Alive and well, I hope.'

*

My mobile battery was flat, so I stopped not far out of town to make a phone call to the office and asked for Jane.

'I'm back,' I said. 'Or nearly so. I'm at Ararat.'

'I'll see you tonight?' she queried.

'Yes,' I said. 'I'll go home first, then give you a call.'

'All right,' she said. 'Oh, by the way, that man rang again.'

'What man?'

'Shaw, the Englishman.'

'Oh, what did he say?'

'He says he's staying in a motel at Horsham until you give him a call. I've forgotten the name of the motel but I've got the number. Do you want to write it down?'

'Yes, hold on, let me find a pen.'

She reeled off the number and I wrote it down. I wondered if this could be a trap, but on reflection it seemed unlikely a potential assassin would make phone calls and leave a number. I wondered if he had any answers to what was going on.

*

My progress to Stawell was fast but I kept my weather eye well cocked on the road ahead and to the rear. The mirror remained empty throughout apart from vehicles I overtook en route. As I made my way along the main street, I experienced misgivings.

By returning home to roost I was possibly placing myself in the firing line again, further, if the police wanted to interview me my unit would be the first place they would stake out. For all I knew both categories were probably waiting for me, my arrival could well start off another shooting spree reminiscent of the OK Corral.

I turned left into a side street and drove on until I was out of town, turned right and then approached Stawell again from the opposite direction. I parked in an alleyway, donned an old cap I occasionally used on the golf course, then slunk down the street in the direction of my domicile. I put on dark sunglasses as I neared my destination, then had a brainwave.

There was a brush and bucket lying outside the local hotel across the street. It was a feature of the routine of Jim Hewitt, mine host of the hotel. He used these implements to sweep up any broken glass, cigarette ends, bottles or cans that could accumulate out front after a hectic night. The two items more often than not resided in the yard at the rear but it was possible on this occasion Jim had been called in by his wife in the middle of his chores. I picked up the broom and bucket, crossed the street, walked slowly to within 50 metres of the entrance to the units, then commenced sweeping, making slow progress along the gutter and pushing before me large quantities of leaves, plastic cups and cigarette butts.

I remembered reading in my youth a novel by John Buchan, where Richard Hannay, the subject of more than one of his novels, was in straits very similar to mine, being pursued through the Scottish Highlands by German spies. He had reached a road when his pursuers appeared in two dimensions, car and aeroplane. Flight across the countryside and along the road being impossible Hannay assumed the guise of a roadmender, appropriated a hammer left by a workman who had knocked off for lunch and started breaking rocks and patching holes in the road. When accosted by his pursuers he was so immersed in the art of road mending that he lived, breathed and acted the part, thinking of nothing except road mending. He concentrated so hard on it he found it difficult to wrest his mind back to the questions they were asking, to whit - `Have you seen a stranger on this road recently?' So convincing had been Richard Hannay's disguise and demeanour he succeeded in sending them on a wild goose chase. That had been fiction, would it work in real life?

I had made up my third pile of leaves and rubbish outside the entrance to the block of units where I lived. I slowly pushed the heap across the entry and had a good look inside. There was nothing untoward but if people, who seemed to want to kill me as desperately as my pursuers, were waiting for me they wouldn't be standing in the middle of the yard. The entrance to my own unit seemed all right, there were a number of cars parked around the carports which I recognised as belonging to fellow residents.

I left my pile neatly stacked in the gutter just to one side of the entrance and went across it to commence sweeping the roadway. Then I saw them. A car was parked by the kerb, a Falcon which I was sure was the same one I had seen at Halls Gap, with a man in the driver's seat. I hastily looked down at my leaves as he looked up, I could feel prickles along the back of my neck as I busily merged what rubbish I had into another small heap on the ground and scooped it into the bucket.

One man was in the car, which meant there could be another in the near vicinity. I was not sure how they could be so certain Bill and I had left the Grampians, but if one car had gone to check the camp we had used they could easily keep in touch via short wave radio or mobile phone.

I moved back the way I had come, the broom over my shoulder. I was so involved with my role that when I found two little piles near a drain, they offended my eye so much I carefully swept them up and placed them in the bucket. My only fear was that Jim Hewitt would appear and find me wandering around with his broom and bucket. If he saw me and hailed me my disguise would be immediately blown.

I passed the unit entrance and started to cross the street, at which point Jim Hewitt actually did come out. He did a classic double take as he went to pick up his absent bucket and broom and looked around for them both. I decided to grasp the nettle.

'Hi, Jim!'

He peered at me closely as I approached, clearly he didn't recognise me at first but he certainly recognised his equipment. Then he did realise who I was and his face cleared.

'Good Day,' he said. 'Oh, it's you, Phil'.

By this time, I was quite close to him and he didn't have to raise his voice by too many decibels which meant any conversation would not be heard by the watcher in the car.

'I saw some broken glass around the entrance to our units so I thought it best to get rid of it and used your broom. I picked up some leaves as well. Hope you don't mind.'

'No worries.' he said genially as I handed it over. 'That's what's bloody needed around here, someone with a bit of civic conscience to take the initiative. That's probably saved a few punctures or young kids gashing their knees, some bloody fools need shooting...throwing bottles around.'

He was red-faced with a large pot belly, presumably worked on for many years by imbibing large quantities of the wares he sold. He had a rough exterior but a heart of gold, all the down and outs of the neighbourhood knew he was a soft touch for any sob story and he could usually be relied on to leave a drink on the window sill around the side of the building.

He was also one of the heaviest smokers I had ever seen, on the rare occasions I saw him between cigarettes I had to look twice to make sure it was him. He had an appalling cough, I could hear it in the mornings as I lay in my bed across the street, he was better than any alarm clock. He was said to have been a seaman in his younger days, sailing the Seven Seas on a variety of tramp steamers and the hotel was decorated with ship photographs, marine paraphernalia and maps. He was fully aware of the need for atmosphere in a saloon bar and for a particular theme to be pursued. He used the world 'bloody' so frequently that at times it was difficult to follow the thread of a sentence he was uttering. I had actually heard him use the word "forni-bloody-cating" and also to tell someone once he was suffering from "sci-bloody-atica!"

'Bloody nice day' he lit a fresh cigarette from his expiring butt end.

'Er... yes,' I pondered over how to ask my next question without it sounding dramatic. 'Tell me, Jim, have you seen any strangers around here in the last few days?'

'Dunno about bloody strangers,' he replied. 'The bloody police were here this morning.'

'The blood...the police?'

'They were in amongst the bloody units, dunno who they were after, you haven't been sniffing around Mrs Carnegie have you?'

I smiled and shrugged. Mrs Carnegie was one of those well-developed young local wives who roused the sap of every regular drinker at the hotel if she walked past during drinking hours, fully aware of the reaction she was causing. Her firm, pert bust vibrated with every step, while her backside moved rhythmically and jiggled around. If I was her husband, I wouldn't let her out on the street, certainly not in the summer months.

'No,' I answered regretfully. 'I've been away this week. Now if you'd asked me two weeks ago...!'

He chortled, which brought on a severe bout of coughing that nearly brought up his stomach lining. His face went puce and his eyes bulged. I backed to a respectful distance as he slowly recovered, cleared his throat, and spat skilfully into the gutter. I began to feel sick.

'As to strangers, I've had some in the pub the last few nights, they seemed to spend most of their bloody time sitting by the window, but I ain't seen nothing unusual outside.'

'What did they look like?'

'Who?'

'The strangers who sat by the window.'

Hewitt considered at length, had another coughing bout and followed this with an inhalation of smoke he seemed to draw into his boots, so much so I was mildly surprised nothing came out of his lace holes. He disappeared from view for a few seconds as the smoke cloud gathered around him and finally re-appeared through the mist pursing his lips.

'One of them had a bloody moustache, and one of them was bloody tall,' he nodded thoughtfully. 'They sounded English ... bloody Poms I'd say.'

'English,' I scratched my chin. Jane had said Shaw sounded English, which was hardly unusual in Australia, throw a stone in Melbourne and the chances of hitting anyone from England or with an English accent were quite high. Yet it seemed to be additional confirmation of what was going on around me, whatever it was.

We entered the hotel, Jim Hewitt still inhaling and exhaling vigorously. I decided I may as well have a beer while I was at it, I was feeling peckish and a sandwich wouldn't come amiss while I decided what to do and where to go. I could always go to Jane's flat as it was still only 4 o'clock.

I ordered a glass of beer and a sandwich, supplied by Mrs Hewitt, a dried-up woman in her fifties. She too was a heavy smoker; between them they must have polished off about 100 to 120 a day. I often wondered what the ceilings of their living quarters must be like, probably stained yellow or brown by now. Even the sandwiches seemed to taste of stale tobacco, I took a couple of bites then lost my appetite.

'There's one of your mates now,' Jim Hewitt suddenly said. 'Shall I give him a hoy?'

'What? Where?' I swung around as he indicated a man through the window, on the pavement opposite walking towards the stationary vehicle. It was the tall man who had been one of my pursuers over my golf fairway. 'No! Don't do that'

'Why bloody not?' Hewitt asked a question I found difficult to answer, then followed it by a statement that was even worse. "Hallo! He's coming in here.'

Ye Gods! I downed my beer and headed towards the rear of the hotel.

'I need to go for a piss,' I said. 'Look, I'll see you later on... but don't tell him I'm here...OK?'

'Eh?' Hewitt looked puzzled, then shrugged. 'All right. It's your bloody business.'

'Thanks, Jim, I'll see you later, but you haven't seen me, all right?' I ran for the exit door at the rear that led to the toilets and the yard.

'You've left half your sandwich.'

I pretended not to hear that one, the idea of eating anything Mrs Hewitt had breathed all over during preparation did not appeal.

I went out through the back and leapt over the accumulated junk in the yard. I ruminated it was a good job Hewitt was not still at sea, any vessel with all that junk on its decks would have keeled over after leaving harbour.

I hit the pavement and made my way towards where I had left the car. My mobile phone was now charged, I dialled Jane's number.

CHAPTER 13

'It's me!'

'Where are you?' she sounded impatient.

'In Stawell, I'll be with you shortly.'

'I'll put the kettle on,' she said. 'See you.'

While on the road, I looked around carefully most of the way. I had no wish to lead anyone to Jane's flat. Apart from her safety, I needed a safe haven for the night. All was clear as I drove off. I circled the town twice, went around an island three times and kept well away from my own neighbourhood before I zoomed into the driveway of her unit. I tore around the corner of the units and halted in her carport.

She was standing on her balcony as I screamed to a halt. She watched me quizzically as I climbed the steps to her level, but said nothing as we entered her unit. I sat on her couch while she busied herself preparing coffee

'This man Shaw said he'd be there all day.'

'From when? Today?'

'Yesterday,' Jane passed me a cup of coffee. 'I gather he'll be sitting there waiting for you to call.'

'Very strange,' I mused.

'No more so than being run down in the street or being shot at!' she said pointedly.

'No, I suppose not,' I said resignedly.' Very well, here goes.'

I dialled the number but it was engaged. This was such an anti-climax that I actually laughed...thereby is the difference between Hollywood and real life. In a film it would have been snatched up immediately with a blunt 'Yeah?' I dialled again, in case I'd mis-dialled, but it was still engaged. To kill some time I rang Bill Otway, we had a brief chat and he sounded apologetic.

'Any trouble?' he asked.

'I found them parked outside my flat,' I said and became aware of a double take by Jane as she swung around. 'But they didn't see me.'

'Good!' Bill said. 'Well, take care of yourself, old son, and keep in touch.'

Jane was not pleased when I hung up.

'Who was where?'

I had no recourse but to tell her. Her face grew grim as I went through the tale from when we left the Grampians, starting with the shooting affray in Halls Gap, her eyes widened as I embarked on the Wild West part of the story.

'That was on the news at midday,' she said. 'My God! Was that *you*? I didn't take much notice of it at the time as I was in the kitchen but I remember catching some of the detail. That was what I heard, shooting in the main street and people ducking for cover.'

'That'd be right!' I said bitterly, no doubt the cake shop owner had added his two penn'orth for the edification of the Press and the local television stations, casting me as the madman and the villain.

'I'll turn the news on. There should be a news broadcast soon.'

I dialled the motel number again and this time struck gold. The phone was snatched up on the first ring and he gave his name as Shaw. After a brief exchange I agreed with Jane, he certainly sounded English, although as the conversation progressed, I could hear a burr in his accent that indicated a Scots flavour.

'My name is Philip Meredith,' I announced.

'Hallo, Mr Meredith.'

This certainly stamped him as being from Britain. An Australian would have answered: 'Hallo Phil'.

'You want to speak with me, I hear.'

'Yes. But first I must have proof you are the Philip Meredith I'm looking for,' said Shaw. 'In addition, I must meet with you, a phone conversation will not be sufficient.'

'Oh really?' I could not keep suspicion and cynicism from my voice.

'What does that mean?'

Shaw was very discerning. I hadn't been aware I had made my cynicism and suspicion so obvious. I decided to ignore the question.

'Who are you?'

'I am a junior partner in the legal firm of Fell, Pelham and Drysdale of Old Fetter Lane, in London.'

'A lawyer? What does a lawyer want with me?'

'I'll tell you that when we meet.'

'How do I know you are who you say you are?'

'You don't,' said Shaw. 'Any more than I know who you are. But I can try to prove who I am when you arrive here for discussion.'

'Hmmm!' I said. 'What was the name of your firm again?'

He spelt it out slowly and I wrote it down.

'Leave it with me, I'll ring you back,' I said and hung up.

Jane looked quizzical. 'Who is he?'

'I don't know yet, says he's a lawyer. Hang on, I want to check something.'

I reached for the telephone directory and looked in the front. I found what I wanted and dialled it.

'International enquiries...what country?' asked the operator

'London, England,' I gave her the name and address of the firm of lawyers. There was a short delay then I heard a computerised voice saying: 'The number is 01 1261 561 077 . . repeat 01 1261 561 077.' I looked down at the pad where I had written the name and address Shaw had dictated. Everything tallied.

'What was that all about?'

'Well, that much tallies.' I replied.

'What...oh...the law firm!'

'Yes,' I replied. 'It exists, exactly as he said. I gave the operator the name of the firm and the address is right. This is their telephone number. He said he was a junior partner. Now what do I do?'

'Ring them and see if they have a Mr Shaw in the firm and if so, where is he?'

'What...now? There won't be anyone there.'

'It'll be about 9 o'clock in the morning in London.'

'Yes! You're right...well, here goes...but it will cost a bit!'

'Better a few dollars than finding he's a crook or a gunman when you get there.'

That made sense. I thought about it and looked at the clock, which said 5.22.

'Is that clock right?'

'Give or take a few minutes.'

'Are they in front or behind us?'

'I've just told you...now you've got me confused. They are behind us, so it's what I said, about 9 o'clock, or 9.22 to be precise...or is it 8.22?'

I thought for a few seconds. That would be about right, nearly 8.30 am in London. What time would a firm of lawyers start work in London? More than likely about 8.30 am, or they may open their doors early and have flexible office hours.

'It may take some time, I told him I'd ring him back.'

'You're not obligated to ring him back immediately,' Jane said impatiently. 'If you ring him now and fix something up and then ring London and find he's a fraud, you wouldn't go anyway. Why not ring London first and find out?'

'Oh...yes...I suppose so...but I still don't know,' I could see how simple it was and yet I was still trying to find excuses for not ringing London. I still had that feeling of unreality, hovering between the serious and the unbelievable. I had a fear of making a fool of myself talking to a senior partner in a London firm of lawyers.

'Then why don't you have a cup of coffee while you think about it, it did you have anything else in mind?'

I grinned broadly, she certainly looked very desirable.

'There was a thought that crossed my mind.'

'You want to go down to the pub and have a drink with your mates.' she said, drawing attention to her idea of the average Australian male.

'Good idea.' I made as if to go to the door.

'I've got a better idea,' she seized my arm and pulled me into the bedroom.

It was about an hour before I made the call, I was surprised at the speed of the connection. I could recall my father ringing a cousin in England at Christmas years before and he had had to wait what seemed an eternity for the connection to be made as he passed through a plethora of operators, then had to shout to make his cousin hear him.

'Hallo!' I said as a voice answered clearly and distinctly at the other end.

'Fell, Pelham & Drysdale.'

'Hallo,' I said again somewhat foolishly.

'Fell Pelham & Drysdale, how can I help you?'

'My name is Meredith, can I speak to Mr Shaw.'

I could have kicked myself for making such a stupid request, he could hardly speak to me if he was in Victoria.

'Hold on a moment.'

There was a delay and then another voice came on the line.

'Who did you want to speak to?'

'Mr Shaw.'

'Mr Shaw is not available at present. What did you say your name was?'

'Meredith, I'm ringing from Australia.'

'Hold the line a minute,' there was another delay and I heard a muttered conversation in the background, with the word 'Australia' being mentioned. Then there was a clicking noise as another phone was lifted and an authoritative voice came on the line.

'Mr Meredith?'

'Hallo, Mr Shaw?'

'No. My name is Matthew Pelham, I am the senior partner. Mr Shaw is away on business at present. Can I assist you?'

'You definitely have a Mr Shaw?'

'We do. He is a junior partner in this firm,' I digested that one in silence and Pelham spoke up again. 'Are you there?'

'Yes,' I answered absently, trying to think what to say next.

Then I decided there was only one thing to do, stop horsing around and get to the point.

'Listen, my name is Meredith, Philip Meredith. I am ringing from Stawell, in Victoria, Australia that is. There's been some damned odd things going on and I've had a call from a Mr Shaw who says he's from your firm...!'

'That is correct, he is and he is also in Victoria...wait a minute. What did you say your name was?'

'Meredith...Philip Meredith.'

'Philip Bromyard Meredith?'

There it was again, that damned name Bromyard cropping up. What the blazes was going on?

'Look...what is all this?' my irritation was increased, I was conscious with the time the call was taking my money, or Jane's, was ticking away.

Mr Pelham ignored my question and asked me one. 'You have had a communication from Mr Shaw recently?'

'Yes.'

'How long ago?'

'About half an hour ago, no...nearer an hour.'

'Well, he is very near to you, he is in a motel in Stawell, the Horseshoe Inn to be precise. I would suggest you call and see him as soon as you can'

'What is all this about?'

'I can't discuss it over the telephone. Mr Shaw is empowered to tell you all about it,' said Pelham. 'If you have been in contact and he is near to you, I suggest you contact him again as soon as you can. All I can say is, you will hear something to your advantage - if you are who you say you are'.

'What? Can't you be more explicit than that?'

'Not over a phone line, Mr Brom...Meredith,' there it was again, what was it with this name Bromyard? 'Just get in touch with Graeme Shaw as soon as you can, it is very important. Make it soon. Goodbye Mr Meredith.'

'Well,' I said in exasperation after I had put down the phone and turned to Jane.

'What did he say?'

'Well, bugger all, except he confirmed that Shaw is who he says he is, it certainly doesn't look as if he's anything to do with these people who've been chasing and shooting at me. He really is a lawyer.'

'Well there are lawyers and lawyers.'

'Maybe, but this one seemed genuine,' I said. 'Pelham sounded like the sort of upper class pompous ass you would expect a London lawyer to sound like.'

'I hope you don't tell your clientele and agents that,' she said primly.

'I meant *London* lawyers,' I said. 'I'd better ring Shaw.'

The number was engaged.

'Hell!' I said.

I tried again about ten minutes later and got through. I had Shaw on the line very quickly.

'Meredith,' I said. 'I'm coming to see you. I just had to check you out, that's all.'

'I know,' Shaw answered. 'Mr Pelham has just rung me. Come round as soon as you can. I'll be here.'

CHAPTER 14

The motel was on the road to Horsham, I passed and repassed it three times before I was satisfied I wasn't being followed. Darkness was setting in when I finally nerved myself to drive through the motel entrance; as the sun disappeared behind the distant hills.

'Which is Mr Shaw's room, please?' I said brusquely to the receptionist as I peered at her through the glass. I also examined my reflection to check over my shoulder without turning around. I had thought I'd heard someone come in behind me and my nerves were screaming but there was nobody there! She looked at the chart and gave me a smile that in happier circumstances would have sent prickles up my spine.

'Seven,' she said. 'That's around the corner to the left, third unit past the rockery.'

'Thank you,' I climbed back into the car and cautiously circumvented the quadrangle bounded by the units. I had been round once and was starting on a second circuit when I realised by going in ever decreasing circles, I would only draw attention to myself.

I parked at a point distant from No: 7 and switched off the lights. I climbed out and peered around. There were lights on in five of the units, not all were occupied, but there was a light in No: 7. I approached the unit with exaggerated caution; it had reached the stage where I felt a complete damned fool. Since my arrival I had been creeping around the undergrowth and peering around corners.

I decided to grasp the nettle, advanced to the door and knocked. I placed my back against the wall and carefully cast my eyes all around the units and quadrangle. The door opened and I turned towards the light.

'Mr Shaw?'

'Mr Meredith, I presume.'

I resisted the temptation to make some crack about Livingstone and Stanley as I thought neither of us would be in the mood for jokes. I merely nodded and after a cursory look into the room and a glance through the crack between door and doorpost, I sidled in.

There was nothing unusual about the room. It duplicated virtually every motel room I had occupied over the last few years. It had the usual double bed, single bed, television and kettle on the bench alongside the wall together with a wash hand basin, toilet and shower at the far end. I strode to the toilet and peered in, there was nobody there. I opened the wardrobe and peered in that as well, it was empty.

Shaw cynically eyed my erratic progress around the room.

'Satisfied?' he remarked laconically as he watched.

'Just checking, that's all,' I was in a boorish mood, but also felt a little foolish which didn't improve my temper. He nodded, from his demeanour he didn't seem to consider my actions untoward.

'Very wise,' he said. 'I've been doing that myself for several weeks.'

'So what's all this about?' I asked.

'Take a seat,' he ignored the question. 'Can I get you anything?'

'What have you got?'

'Scotch, beer!' He indicated a bottle of Scotch and a beer bottle on the refrigerator. 'There's even a drop of gin in the fridge.'

'Whisky,' I suddenly had the suspicion he could be attempting to drug me. God Almighty! I was becoming paranoid.

Shaw poured two drinks out of the same bottle. Maybe he too thought I needed reassuring. I took the opportunity to observe him. He was about my own age, somewhere between 24 and 30 at a guess. He was tall and lean, black hair flecked with grey, and a thin black beard running around his cheeks and under his chin. His hair cut could best be described as a long back and sides, while his beard was a merely a light covering of his visage and certainly not bushy. He came over with two small glasses of whisky clasped in his fingers. His eyes were a peculiar shade of green, they were not still as they flickered over me; he was clearly observing me in the same way I was observing him. He placed the whiskies on the table before me and invited me to take either one.

'Cheers!' I selected one of them and he tossed back half of the other glass while I sipped cautiously at mine. It tasted normal, as far as I could see, with no sleep-inducing additives.

'Cheers,' he responded and put down his glass.

'Now what the hell is all this about?' I repeated.

Shaw sat down and stretched his legs. He reached for his wallet and produced a business card which he handed to me. It indicated he was a partner in the London legal firm of Fell,

Pelham & Drysdale, Old Fetter Lane, London. I checked the telephone number. At least that tallied. It was the number I had rung about an hour or so before.

'This proves nothing,' I said, determined to be bloody minded.

'On its own, perhaps, I would tend to agree with you,' Shaw nodded in agreement. 'But you've already checked, haven't you?'

'Why do you say that?' I answered testily, although I already knew.

'Telephones work both ways,' he remarked.' I had a call from Matt Pelham less than an hour ago.'

'Hmmm!' I took another sip of Scotch.

'I'm glad you are taking precautions, phoning the office in London was wise and I commend you for it,' he stood and went to the shelf on the side, returning with the whisky bottle. 'More?'

'Er...yes...thank you,' I tossed back the remainder and proffered the empty glass. I deduced that if he had drugged it, highly unlikely since he had poured his own from the same bottle in front of me and drunk his first, I would probably be feeling sleepy by now.

Shaw refilled both glasses and sat down again.

'All right, we've established who I am,' he said. 'Have you any objection if I establish who you are.'

'I am Philip Meredith, I live in Stawell and work for the Jupiter Insurance Company as an outside sales rep, you can check all that out if you wish.'

'I already have,' he commented dryly. 'But that isn't the information I am after. Can you answer a few questions?'

'I suppose so.'

'Where were you born and when?'

135

'In Queensland, I'm aged 28.'

'Can you be more specific, where were you born, what town?'

'Townsville.'

'Birthdate?'

'Look, what is all this?'

'Just tell me then I'll tell you.'

'2nd April.'

'Who was your father?'

'Roland Benjamin Meredith...he had the name Bromyard too, but he never used it.'

'Do you know when he was born, and where?'

'1965. He was born in Goulburn, New South Wales.'

'Birthdate?'

'22nd September.'

'Good. When did he die, and what of?'

'About nine years ago, he picked up some disease in Asia. He used to work in the overseas department of one of the banks, spent some years in Singapore and later in Papua New Guinea. He picked up something in PNG and he apparently just wasted away. I didn't know him all that well, he was away much of the time.'

'Did your father have any siblings?'

'Yes, there was Nancy and...er...Janet, Keith and Ralph, all younger than him.'

'What are the married names of your aunts, your father's sisters?'

'Hells bells, I'll have to think about that. Hmmm! Yes... Chadwick and...let me think a minute...Sherwood.'

'Good. Where are Ralph and Keith?'

'Now you've asked me, I know very little about them. I have a feeling Ralph went to Canada, I believe he married and has four children including a couple of sons. Keith joined the Australian Army and was killed in Vietnam; I don't think he was married.'

'Who was your grandfather?'

'Donald James Bromyard Meredith, he was born in Wagga Wagga in 1918...and, if I remember rightly he was married in Wagga Wagga about 1950. He died sometime in the 1990's in Queensland.'

'Who was his wife?'

'His wife...? Good God!' I scratched my head. 'I think it was another Nancy, probably my aunt was named after her. I think her maiden name was Thorpe.'

'Do you know of anyone further back, his father, for instance?'

'Not a great deal, I think his father came from England, I believe his name was Samuel,' I looked at Shaw somewhat defiantly. 'I think Samuel had some other sons in addition to my grandfather but I don't know where they or any descendants are. Anything else?'

'No, that will just about do, I think.'

'Oh, hang on. I do remember something about Samuel, there was a family story about him. I think he was born aboard ship as they came over here. But don't ask me who his parents were or where they came from, I haven't a clue.'

'His mother came from Bicester, the male line emanated from somewhere in Gloucestershire, so I believe.'

'How the hell did you know that?'

'Because I have been living, breathing and sleeping the Bromyard family details for the last several months,' Shaw rubbed his chin. 'I think I know the family tree off by heart.'

'Bromyard?'

'Samuel's mother was Virginia Bromyard, he was born

in 1885 on the Sea Prince. She arrived here as a widow and shortly after arriving, set up house with her sister and her sister's husband, who came here on the same ship. Within three months she parted from them and went to live on her own, I can well imagine why, and three months after that she married Thomas Meredith, another immigrant from the same ship.'

'So that's where the Bromyard name came in,' I said in wonderment.' 'I've never found out before this why that name kept cropping up from generation to generation.'

'Probably from force of habit,' said Shaw. 'Family names often do that without any thought as to the reason why. Your name is Philip Samuel Bromyard Meredith?'

'Yes, that's correct.'

'The name used to be hyphenated, Virginia Bromyard and Thomas Meredith had several children of their own, their name was Meredith, but they don't really concern me. The hyphenated version only applied to your great grandfather and eventually his offspring, of which there are several. Apparently, the name was officially registered when he was 17. Thomas Meredith insisted on it, he did it so that his stepson would never lose his real father's name.'

'Nice of him.'

'Yes, and very useful too. It enabled us to trace you.'

'The hyphen disappeared sometime in the nineteen twenties; I think. My father didn't bother with it, while my grandfather was a real old Aussie and thought it was snobbish, so he dropped it. My father never bothered to resurrect it.'

'Again, that was very useful.'

'Why, what do you mean?'

'The original hyphenating of the name enabled us to trace you, and we weren't the only ones looking for you. Its discontinuance had the effect of masking the name to a degree.'

'I don't follow you.'

'Take a look at this family tree, you'll see your ancestry going back several generations.'

He reached into his brief case and handed me a large folder. It was very thick paper and the chart was obviously computer produced. I looked at the top of the chart and observed the date alongside it was pre-dating European settlement in the country in which I lived.

'Nathaniel Bromyard, born 1735 in Ludlow, Shropshire,' I read out loud. 'My God! How did you find out about all this?'

'I didn't, somebody else did,' said Shaw. 'But it's authentic I can assure you of that. Take a look at the rest of the tree, it goes to the present day in several lines.'

He pointed out several places on the chart, I glanced over it. It digressed onto several computer produced sheets. Then, as the ramifications of it sank in, and I saw the beginning date on the first sheet at the top of the tree, my interest was aroused as it showed the presence of the name 'Bromyard' over several generations.

'This is fantastic,' I burst out. 'How long did it take to find out all of this?'

'Less than six months and it cost a considerable amount of money, over £6,000,' Shaw replied. 'Normally a task like this could take years, but we were in a hurry.'

'You must have been,' I commented. 'It's more than I'd ever spend, although it's very interesting. Can I have a copy of this?'

'Yes, but not yet, this is the only one, in Australia anyway. It isn't complete, space being what it is we couldn't fit in all the descendants of your Great Grandfather Samuel, including your grandfather's siblings, although there are quite a few. We only discovered them recently when we found out about the widowed Virginia,' said Shaw. 'Can you see yourself on the chart?'

'Yes, descended from Isaac Bromyard, I see he only lived to age 25.'

'Yes. That was a tragic happening, he and his wife Virginia were emigrating to Australia, and he was killed in a street accident in Liverpool a matter of days before they were due to board the ship. She decided to continue with the journey as they were planning to emigrate with her sister and her sister's husband and they were all the family she had. She seems to have been a strong-minded woman, since she and Isaac had burned their boats she would have had nowhere else to go when she was widowed. She gave birth to your ancestor, Samuel, on board ship. Virginia later married Thomas Meredith after arrival in Australia, which is where your present surname comes in.'

'What was the object of this exercise?'

'It all started from John Brodie-Matthews,' said Shaw. 'You can see him down the left-hand side of the tree. When he was a very young boy his father, Jonathan Bromyard, was killed at the Front in the Great War in 1916, Jonathan's widow Ann Bromyard, formerly Matthews, Brodie-Matthews' mother, married a second time to Gordon Brodie when John Brodie-Matthews, then still named John Bromyard, was a small child. He had a name change similar to your forbear, but in his case he took, or was given as a child, the maiden name of his mother and the surname of his step-father, thus becoming John Brodie-Matthews. We know the marriage between Gordon Brodie and Ann Matthews lasted, he survived the Great War and inherited the family business, which dealt with electrical goods. He died in 1948.'

'So his wife was widowed a second time.'

'No, she had pre-deceased him,' commented Shaw. 'However, when the son, or step-son, John Brodie-Matthews reached adulthood, he did much work tracing his family back, as many of us do. He knew from his birth certificate who his real father was, and that he originally had a different original name. He researched the Bromyard family and traced his ancestry back to Nathaniel Bromyard in Ludlow in 1735. We had the more difficult task of tracing forward from the past to find male descendants of Nathaniel.'

'Why?'

'As you can see there were very few male descendants who survived,' Shaw ignored my question, 'Your male relatives in past generations seemed to be very unlucky every time there was a major war, if they missed one war another one got them. If you look through, you'll see not even young children were immune, young Anthony Bromyard and his sister were killed in the Blitz with their mother and father.'

'What happened to Brodie-Matthews' own sons?'

'One was killed in Korea, the other died of a drug overdose.'

'What happened to him?' I pointed to another John Bromyard who had died recently.

'He was murdered,' said Shaw shortly. 'He was poisoned in a Melbourne bar.'

'Murdered? In Melbourne?' I sat up straight. 'Wait a minute, I read something about that in the newspapers. It caught my eye because of the name. That was some weeks back, or was it months? The Waverley Bar or something wasn't it? Initially they thought it was a heart attack, then found he'd been poisoned. Who killed him?'

'The same people who are trying to kill you!'

CHAPTER 15

t took a few seconds for this to sink in, then I nearly choked over my whisky.

'What?'

'I said...the same people who are trying to kill you.'

'How did you know someone is trying to kill me?'

'Not everyone takes the precautions you did, checking I was who I said I was.'

'Maybe I'm just naturally over cautious.'

'Perhaps, but not everyone goes to the exaggerated lengths you did when you arrived here. I was wondering how many times you'd go around the car park. After that you came creeping up to the unit like a professional burglar.'

'All right,' I grinned with embarrassment. 'So I've had a few problems.'

'Like that business at Halls Gap?'

'You heard about that?'

'Every man and his dog has heard about that' said Shaw. 'It's been on all the news channels. A Wild West shoot out in the town and your name prominently mentioned.'

'Oh God! When was this?'

'There was a news flash about two hours ago, didn't you see it?'

'Er...no,' I felt myself blush. That could have been while Jane and I had been in her bedroom.

'Well, there'll be another news broadcast shortly. Maybe you can tell me what's been happening to you before it comes on.'

I started on the saga of the past few weeks, beginning with the shooting episode on the golf course with Frank Gilmore. He listened without interruption as I proceeded, made a few notes as I reached Halls Gap, and exhibited some amusement at my comments regarding Mrs Hewitt's sandwiches. I finished the story with the night's happenings, my call to him and the conversation with Mr Pelham.

'Well, the news is on again at 7 o'clock,' Shaw collected the glasses and placed them in the wash-hand basin. 'You'll be interested in the Halls Gap shootout; it had some similarities with the Wild West.'

'It was not a shootout,' I protested. 'I never fired a shot, that damned rifle wasn't even loaded.'

'That's not what the news broadcast said.'

'Don't I know it,' I said bitterly. 'Everyone seemed to be under the impression I started it!'

'You'll say more than that if they describe it the same way they did last time,' said Shaw. 'From what was said I assumed you went on a shooting rampage and shot up every shop in the town.'

'Why doesn't that bloody surprise me?' I said bitterly. 'That owner of that blasted general store really made a meal of it. But why should anyone kill John Bromyard, and be trying to kill me?'

'I'll try and fit it in before the news broadcast, I'll just switch it on with the sound off so we don't miss it when it *does* come on. If you promise not to interrupt, I'll give you the bare facts and why I'm here.'

'All right, fire away!' I replied and winced, hardly a tactful choice of words in view of recent events. 'After the last few weeks nothing will surprise me.'

But I was wrong.

'It's a long story, Shaw began.

'I don't care how long it is,' I replied. 'As long as it explains what the hell's been going on.'

'I'll give you a brief synopsis which will give you some idea of what it's about.' said Shaw. 'Firstly, there is in England a large industrial complex known as Brodie Industries and the man heading it was John Brodie-Matthews, the man on the family chart. He inherited the business from his step-father Gordon Brodie. It was a thriving large-sized business when he took it over, but John Brodie-Matthews transformed it into a national and international industrial complex.'

'I know the name, aren't they in Australia?'

'They are, they're well represented in Commonwealth countries, the US and Canada. Brodie-Matthews swallowed up many other electrical firms and made the company into a huge conglomerate, approaching the lines of ICI or Courtaulds, or to give you a rough Australian equivalent, BHP. He also did well on the Stock Market, surprising how well you can do when you have a lot of money and assets, in addition he made vast profits on the property market. He was a multi-billionaire when he died late last year.'

Shaw went to the washbasin to replenish the jug of water.

'No more whisky,' I shook my head. 'Just water.'

He poured water into my glass and placed the jug on the table.

'He was worth billions, I'm not sure of the precise figure as much of it was tied up in the business, but he had considerable wealth outside it and amongst other things he took over an unfashionable soccer club in one of the lower echelons that subsequently reached one of the upper divisions. The management of the business, and the bulk of his shareholdings, went to Philip Goodman, who was Managing Director before Brodie-Matthews died. He's a good bloke, also a distant relative, but a different family so he doesn't appear on that tree. Anyway, we're not concerned with him at this stage, suffice to say there was a legacy of about $100 million to be divided amongst many relatives. Brodie Matthews was very family conscious, especially when he discovered his real name should have been Bromyard and originally was.'

'Was there anything special about the name Bromyard?'

'It wasn't aristocratic if that's what you mean, but it was his own name, that was important and special enough to him. It is also very rare as you don't often come across it. Bromyard itself is a small town in Herefordshire, I've been there a few times, and John Brodie-Matthews bought a house there when he was well into his family history research.'

'All right, so what happens now?'

'Let me finish, then I'll tell you,' said Shaw. 'His family life was marred by tragedy, his elder son was killed in Korea in the early 1950's, his younger son Michael got into bad company and died of a drug overdose, while his wife and daughter were killed in a road smash. Brodie-Matthews re-married soon afterwards...too quickly and disastrously so Matt Pelham, my senior partner reckons...to a widow, Eileen Fisher. He met her whilst on holiday in Paris.'

'Romanic setting,' I remarked.

'That's about all it was,' Shaw replied. 'Matt reckons she

caught him on the rebound and the marriage wasn't a happy one. We've discovered that her first husband. Marcus Fisher, had been a very unwholesome character, involved in criminal activities from facts we've dug out recently. We now know he had Underworld connections and was involved in drug dealings, illegal immigration, prostitution, gambling and God knows what else.'

'How would an astute man like you say Brodie-Matthews was, not carry out...?'

'...character checking...a good question, why indeed?' Shaw grimaced. 'If only Brodie-Matthews had been as thorough checking on his future wife as when he checked new business connections. He normally went through their financial histories and personnel with a fine-tooth comb! But he slipped up where she was concerned. Matt Pelham said it was a sad case of love being blind!'

'And he knew little or nothing of this before he married her?'

'Seemingly not but he certainly found out later. I believe his new wife was not altogether forthcoming about past histories and the like when she persuaded him to marry her, but it was hardly in her interests to do that. But even worse, Laurie, her son, was not and is not a savoury character either. He was about 25 when Brodie-Matthews married his mother and he's been regularly in and out of trouble with the law. He has criminal and underworld connections and is also running businesses and protection rackets, mainly in the gambling and night club fields. He's Brodie-Matthews only living close relative of the next generation, albeit it by marriage, although Brodie-Matthews does have a sister. But Brodie-Matthews in his later years fell very much under the domination of his second wife, plus his health was not good.'

Shaw paused to take a sip of his whisky and carried on.

'He was in bad health and dying for about two years; he had always been a heavy smoker and contracted lung cancer. He was prevailed upon to change his will so that Laurie Fisher, his stepson, would inherit a sizeable slice of his personal estate, somewhere in the order of £80 million plus. And so it stayed until this time last year, when he sent for Fell, our then senior partner, and changed it by codicil with a somewhat odd clause.'

'What's a codicil?' I asked.

'An addition' replied Shaw. 'It's similar to an endorsement on an insurance policy.'

'Oh...OK.'

'He stated that this money, all £80 million, would go to the nearest male relative who bore the name of Bromyard as a surname, who was the direct, senior male descendant of Nathaniel Bromyard, the first man on his family tree. The preferred person concerned was to be a descendant of the most senior male line emanating from Nathaniel Bromyard born in 1735. If such a claimant didn't turn up within 6 months of his death, then it would revert to Laurie Fisher and Fisher would receive the legacy.'

'Sounds simple enough,' I hazarded.

'Simple my foot, it might sound so but believe me it was a hell of a task. I've learned a lot about genealogy and ancestor tracing over the last few months. Tracing is usually done backwards, that is starting with your father, then his parents, then his grandparents and so on and the same with your mother's lines. What is not so easy is tracing forward from a point in the past, say 150 or 200 years ago, and finding all the descendants of people living at a particular time. It's a monumental task, especially as people can leave town and go virtually anywhere, and you've no means of tracking them and finding where they are.'

'Why not?' I asked.

'I'm not going into that now, we haven't time,' Shaw gave a dismissive gesture. 'All we knew was the make-up of John Brodie-Matthews' segment of the Family Tree. He was descended from Charles Edward Bromyard born in 1846, who was the direct descendant of Nathaniel in the senior male line. We explored all Charles Edward Bromyard's descendants from his eldest son, another Charles, and drew a blank. There were no other surviving male descendants. The Great War killed off Brodie-Matthews' father, uncles and cousins, two were in the RFC, the other was killed in the trenches, while another went down with the Repulse in 1941 off Malaya. We went back and investigated Edward Bromyard, second son of Charles Edward Bromyard and found the same story of repetitive tragedy. Two sons killed in the trenches and another killed 28 years later in the Blitz in London together with *his* only son. So we went back to an earlier generation and started on a brother of Charles Edward Bromyard named Samuel, again the Wars intervened. Ian was killed in 1918, while Frank went down in the Dorsetshire off Colombo in 1942. Frank's son Ernest immigrated to Australia, he died in 1972, while his only son John was the one murdered a few weeks back in Melbourne.'

'Poor bastard.'

'I don't like to speak ill of the dead, but bastard is what he was, if he'd inherited the only ones to have benefited would have been the local bookmakers and the brewery. He'd left his wife, refused to pay her any maintenance or their mortgage and was living with some tart in St Kilda. Can't think what she saw in him, he was overweight through excesses of the barroom and the table.'

'I gather you didn't like him!'

'Too damned right I didn't,' Shaw said savagely. 'Although initially I was relieved to find him as it could have finished this damned job I've been doing almost full-time for the last five months.'

'So what you're saying is, I am now the senior Bromyard?'

'From what we have uncovered of your own family...yes that seems to be the case. We then investigated Samuel's brother Isaac, but initially we gave up when we found he died aged 25. Then we recently made a chance discovery that he'd had a son, another Samuel, who was born after his death aboard an immigrant ship travelling to Australia.'

'So I am due to inherit something?'

'Could be, but it isn't that simple,' said Shaw. 'As mentioned, I've been on this investigation for nearly six months, all I've told you in the last fifteen minutes or so took endless time to research, check and then counter check. We became involved with a professional researcher who strung us along and cost us valuable weeks and we had worse than that. Somebody, and it's obvious who, is trying to stop us finding an heir. Since Brodie-Matthews died our senior partner Fell was killed in a house fire, he was an expert genealogist as well and was working on the research. A professional genealogist who took it over was assaulted in the street and finished in hospital, while records vanished from a genealogical society in London...happily they were only copies but it took time to track down and view the originals. I was attacked near my lodgings one night, I was lucky, but I got this scar.'

He indicated a scar under his hair-line.

'I share digs in London, my cousin plays for one of the London Premier League Football clubs and he and some of the other players occupy rooms in the same block. I was set on in an alleyway late one night near the flats on my way back home from the Underground station. My cousin and his team mates had been to a celebration after winning an FA Cup tie and came up from the opposite direction, if they hadn't arrived when they did I'd have been another hospital case.'

'Good God!'

'We found John Bromyard in Melbourne, but found him too late. Our opposition, Laurie Fisher, found him as well. We'd been in touch with him for a couple of weeks before they got to him, someone laced his drink in a Melbourne bar. I shouldn't have mentioned Fisher's name I guess, but we all know he's the one behind it. He's been employing another genealogical researcher to find out facts, and people, and then trying to destroy or misfile records to put anyone else off the scent. But we scored first with you, we were thrown initially when we assumed, like Laurie Fisher's researcher, that Isaac, the other brother of Charles Edward Bromyard, had been childless. I didn't know you existed until I came here looking for John Bromyard, then a researcher in England uncovered an old newspaper cutting of Isaac Bromyard's death just prior to emigration and the report mentioned his wife Virginia was pregnant, yet she still emigrated on her own. Well, she wasn't quite on her own, she and Isaac had been intending to emigrate with her sister's family as well.'

He paused, considered topping up his glass, but then pushed the bottle away.

'I had the date they left Southampton, and traced their arrival in Australia through the Latrobe Library in Melbourne. There is...was, mention of Virginia Bromyard and her infant son Samuel, born in 1885 on voyage in the Sea Prince.'

'How did you find that out?'

'I'll go into that some other time, no time now, suffice to say I isolated the shipping records. I tried to find a trace of any marriage involving Samuel Bromyard about 1900 onwards, but no joy. Then it occurred to me his mother may have married again and changed her name and possibly his as well. She had, she married Thomas Meredith. I found the marriage of Samuel Bromyard Meredith and from then on it was relatively easy, the name Bromyard appeared to be carried on as a second name by succeeding generations. But your troubles over the last few weeks indicate that somebody else has now locked onto you, either our genealogical researcher was followed or he was careless. We know for a fact his house was burgled some weeks ago and the information may have been compromised.'

'They seem to be well organised.'

'They are, and ruthless with it. I found where you were about a week or ten days ago, I think they were either level or ahead of me. They want you out of the way so Laurie Fisher, who's in severe financial trouble, can inherit.'

'Which will now come to me.'

'Not so fast, we have to get you to London first to formally claim it.'

'Well what's the problem?'

'We had six months after John Brodie-Matthews died. We've only about 3 weeks to go, if they either kill or detain you for that length of time, Fisher wins, we'd hardly have time to do any more digging into other family lines. He won't be fussy about killing you either, you've heard of Al Capone? Well, he's cast in the same mould.'

'What's to stop him killing me after I've claimed the money?'

'There will be no point in doing that. It will be too late after your identity is proved and the inheritance is yours, if you die it will go to *your* next of kin, who I assume is your sister Mary. Nothing can stop that, certainly the will can't as it will have done its job and will have no traction on your estate. Certainly, Laurie Fisher will then have no claim on it.'

'It seems an odd addition to make to a will,' I mused. 'Is it legal?'

'It is, and I've come across stranger clauses in wills than that,' Shaw looked at the clock.' Hello...we have about five minutes to go to the news...we were dealing with a will last year where a woman shunned her relatives and left her house and money to her cat.'

'Her cat!'

'Her cat, 'Shaw grimaced. 'It was a bugger of a cat as well, fat, bad tempered and vicious. The relatives contested the will and it was modified eventually, but you can see Brodie-Matthews' will was not as odd as some.'

'Has this man Laurie Fisher tried to contest it?'

'He had thoughts about it, he had a very stormy interview with Mr. Pelham after the reading of the will, but Brodie-Matthews had inserted another clause to the effect that if anyone did contest it, all the money would go to charity.'

Shaw looked at the clock again. The TV was still running with the sound turned off.

'Brodie-Matthews wanted the name Bromyard, a rare enough surname as it turns out, to benefit from his efforts over the years as he was very family conscious, yet he appreciated that any court proceedings could put the money in limbo for years if he didn't put a sunset clause on it...shades of Jarndyce v Jarndyce if you know your Charles Dickens.'

'Yes, I'm with you...Bleak House.'

'Ah, you're with me. Good,' Shaw smiled. 'Matt is also of the opinion that Brodie-Matthews was aware who and what he had married, and where the money would go if he did nothing. He made the original will before he was aware of the true nature of his wife and son's origins. He made this codicil without his wife's knowledge, he probably lacked the courage to defy her and strike him out altogether, but put in this clause to be bloody minded. His wife wasn't present when the codicil was made, she didn't like it when she discovered it and tried to get it reversed. It was because of her, she's a greedy, grasping bitch, by the way, that Brodie-Matthews brought it down to 6 months, originally, he wanted 18. He was very much under her thumb, but his keenness for genealogy and his biological family gave him some resistance. Plus, he was a sick man at the time as well. No man will completely alienate his immediate family when he knows he's sick and will become worse.'

'So Fisher knows he can lose the lot if a claimant turns up?'

'He got off the mark quicker than we did, he employed a genealogist to find out who the next in line would be, he had a few months start because his mother tipped him off whereas we didn't start until John Brodie-Matthews died. Our task was made difficult too, more so as Fisher's man in some cases had deliberately misfiled records after he'd looked at them, fortunately those were copies and the originals were still in existence. But it all took time, and so many of the lines fizzled out in the various wars that I began to wonder if we'd ever find a claimant. But Matt Pelham was determined to pursue it to the end, he was an old friend of Brodie-Matthews, he knew the Fishers and was...is...determined to stop Laurie Fisher inheriting.'

'How much did the research cost?'

'Thousands, but it all came from the Estate,' Shaw moved over to the television. 'Let's see what's on here.'

There was a brief preview of a program scheduled later that evening, then the news announcer appeared on screen. He read off the preamble, then leapt into the headlines:

'The Prime Minister's air liner has made a forced landing at Florida, a bomb exploded outside the Croatian Legation in Sydney, windows shattered by a gun battle in Halls Gap and the AFL announces admission prices are to increase next year.'

'My God! I even came in front of the Footy!'

The Prime Ministerial headline was hardly worth the air time, the plane's pilot heard a noise he didn't like shortly after take-off and very sensibly returned to the airport for a check. The Croatian bomb explosion was alleged to have been placed by dissident Albanians, it had caused no casualties but had broken some windows and pushed in the wall of a nearby shop. I was glad I wasn't the loss adjuster who had to sort that one out, would it constitute an Act of War? I hoped it wasn't one of ours.

'Police are investigating a shooting affray in Halls Gap that took place this morning when a considerable number of shots were fired...!'

As he commenced reading the item a camera shot of the Halls Gap main street appeared on the screen, which then homed in on the frontage of the cake shop which had a broken window and stock scattered over the pavement. I had a healthy suspicion that much of that was to impress his insurers, I couldn't remember any stock being scattered around. I could see the cake shop owner gesticulating to bystanders and police in the background behind the reporter.

'And here - to report on the incident - we have our news reporter, Gary Needham.

Gary Needham duly fronted up, with the shattered window in the background and a furious shop owner in the background mouthing off to a police officer.

'Early this morning a man with a rifle rampaged up and down the main street, fired several shots and smashed a number of windows in the main street of Halls Gap...'

'What the hell...?' I burst out. 'That's bullshit!'

At this point the camera homed in again on the shattered window, then zoomed onto the cake shop owner.

'...and then he threatened Dan Blain, the local store owner, who bravely held him off with a large stick.'

'You bloody liar!' I commented bitterly as Dan Blain appeared on the screen.

'Tell us what happened, Mr Blain.'

Blain needed very little prompting. He took about three or four minutes to tell the biggest pack of lies and exaggerations I have ever heard in my life. The .22 rifle or popgun grew in size until it was in the same category as a Kalashnikov AK 47, while my visage had become not only sinister and cruel, but also of Middle European origin, clearly influenced by the bomb blast at the Croatian Legation. He started to tell the story a second time, despite the attempts of Gary Needham to cut him off, which enabled my description to become tall and heavy, bearded, armed to the teeth with a semi-military outfit...I think he hastily added the prefix 'semi' in case his insurers invalidated his claim for his broken window as War Damage... while I had been uttering expletives in a foreign language.

As a general description it was not only well wide of the mark but very welcome, this should put the police off the scent for years. I had then apparently peppered the street with an incredible number of shots, hitting an indeterminate number of vehicles and frightening the townsfolk out of their wits, before firing directly at Blain himself who had nobly fended me off with a long stick, which he had fortuitously found on the footpath.

The interviewer finally managed to cut him off, Needham must have had the same reservations as I did, wondering where all the bullets had come from. From the number of shots that were allegedly fired in such a short space of time, I must have had a Bren Gun. The interviewer then interviewed an Inspector Parrett from Ararat, and I could see Sergeant

Ramsey in the background taking down notes from our friend Tom, the shop owner.

The police inspector's statement when interviewed was guarded and much more restrained, which caused me some concern. The Inspector was non-committal, watered down the Middle European aspect and toned down the hysterical description given by Blain. He said they were following various leads and expected an arrest very soon. He also cast doubts on the use of the word 'peppered' as applied to shots in the main street and tried to modify that as well.

The interviewer tried to hint at a Mafia slant, there had been some shootings in the greengrocery trade some months back, but the Inspector wasn't buying into that and commented dryly that there were plenty more likely areas for a fruit and vegetable war than Halls Gap.

The Inspector was also reticent about the beard, but commented they were anxious to interview a tall man and his companion who was shorter and with a moustache, both of whom were dressed in camping gear and driving a four-wheel drive vehicle. I didn't like that. The description wasn't comprehensive, but it certainly applied to Bill and myself and proved the police were no fools and not misled by Blain's wild exaggerations. I presume his insurers wouldn't be either, although I hoped they would be, if they interpreted it as War Damage his insurance claim would finish up in the bin.

The news then drifted off onto the AFL price increases for the next season, Shaw rose to his feet and switched the television off.

'So you're in the news. I gather that was you?'

'It was.'

'What really happened?'

I gave him a brief description of the Halls Gap shooting

spree that was more accurate than Blain's had been, he listened intently and pursed his lips.

'My God!' he said. 'You were lucky. There's no doubt they're now becoming utterly desperate, the time limit is nearing its end and they know I'm in the vicinity. I'm afraid I'm the reason why attempts on your life have intensified. Before this they merely had a watching brief, no point in arousing attention by killing you or John Bromyard...or trying to...unless there was a danger of either of you making moves to claim the estate. Bromyard was near to it. When I locked onto him, I didn't know you existed and I don't think they did either. We already had his flight booked when they got to him, I've no idea how they found out about him or how they managed to commit the murder. I'm sorry, but I may have enabled them to take action against you when I was tracking you down.'

I felt myself go cold all over. I could have been a sitting duck for weeks once they knew of my ancestry and whereabouts.

'What do we do now?'

'We get you back to London, damned quick.'

I could feel the sweat of fear beginning to permeate my whole being.

'I'm not so sure I want the money,' I said unhappily.

CHAPTER 16

'Not want it?' Shaw looked at me with surprise and some hostility. 'Why not?'

'Too much bloody trouble and I may get killed.'

'Ye Gods! I've been working on this case for six long months and when I finally find who I'm looking for, he decides not to bother. Bloody Hell!'

I thought about it. I could do all the things I wanted to do, travel the world and buy the house I wanted with enough land to build my own putting green and fairway. Then I thought of John Bromyard, and the shootings over the last few weeks.

'It's all right for you,' I said with some bitterness.

'All right my arse!' snapped Shaw. 'I've been a target like you have over the last month, I've had to change my location repeatedly, and I'll be as much in the firing line as you until we reach London.'

'I've no wish to be in any firing line,' I said angrily.

'You're already in it, and you'll remain in it regardless until the deadline expires, whatever you decide,' Shaw retorted. 'They're not the types to take unnecessary risks and they won't leave anything to chance now. They've already proved that, they're getting desperate now and aren't too fussy where or how they try to get you, they even tried the main street in Halls Gap, and didn't they try to run you down in Stawell?'

'All right, so I waive my rights under the Will and tell them so, I'll advertise it.'

'Pigs arse you will, you can't do that. You can't vary the terms of somebody else's Will, although you can certainly do whatever you like with the cash when you've got it.'

'All right, I'll tell Fisher he can have it, all of it, when I inherit.'

'You'll do what?'

I repeated it.

'Don't be bloody ridiculous,' Shaw snorted. 'Even if he believed you, you're not dealing with gentlemen of honour here, he wants the money, you're in his way and he couldn't risk you changing your mind. He takes no risks and no prisoners. Have you ever seen a drug addict, Mr Brom...Meredith?'

'What? No, I can't say I have. I don't quite follow.'

'Well I have, some of our senior staff saw Brodie-Matthews' son occasionally and they watched him go downhill when the habit got a hold on him. Apparently from a pleasant young man with excellent prospects he turned into an emaciated, quivering wreck who was only capable of looking forward to his next fix. There are hundreds like him in London, Melbourne and Sydney, who've had their lives wrecked by unscrupulous pushers who are now making profits by peddling the stuff to 10year old kids outside primary schools.'

'Look, I still don't know...!'

But Shaw was in full flight and ignored me.

'What's more, I saw the effect it had on Brodie-Matthews, it broke his heart. I had many dealings with him after that, he had many of his son's photographs in his office, and he mentioned him during almost every business conversation I had with him. If that money goes to Fisher it will go to a man who is a social pariah, a bastard of the first degree. He is into drug rackets, prostitution and immigration rackets that virtually amount to white slaving, and various other criminal activities. His sort is a blight on society, I hate him and all he stands for.'

'Why does he need money so desperately?'

'He's had troubles, the narcotics investigation people are breathing down his neck, and there are also gang rivalries. He lost a large night club due to fire, and the insurers are quibbling about the payout. He has to lie low on the drug rackets, and he needs a large influx of cash to build everything up again, which he will do if he gets hold of Brodie-Matthews' fortune. Do you want to help him?'

'How do you know he's into drugs?'

'You find out a lot when you're in the legal business, much that can't be proved but you know it's right. We become involved in police circles and with many private detectives who are ex-police. Take it from me, many young drug addicts here and in London are in that state due to bastards like Laurie Fisher, and he's one of the people at the centre of the web.'

I lapsed into silence, his arguments and statements were convincing. I agreed with him, with the circumstances as presented by him, it was quite unlikely the aggravation I had been suffering would stop now, they couldn't take the risk. In the immediate future it wouldn't make much difference whether I wanted the inheritance or not, I was a barrier to Laurie Fisher inheriting.

'So what do we do now?'

'Our best bet is to make for Melbourne and take an international flight to London, the quicker the better. They wouldn't be able to do anything on an air liner and we'll take precautions at the other end when we reach London.'

'Why do we have to go to London?'

'Because that is one of the provisions of the Will, it states that the claimant has to present himself to our offices by a particular date. That date is now very close, roughly three weeks away.'

'What happens when we reach the other end?' I asked. If I was going to play the part of a clay pigeon, I preferred to know something of the arrangements.

'We move in with our own heavy squad,' said Shaw. 'We have regular contact with three firms of private investigators in the normal course of business. We shall hire all three to carry out a bodyguard job. They are pretty tough types too, most are either ex-police, SAS or Marines and they've been around. Some have acted as mercenaries in trouble spots throughout the world.'

'And they will guarantee my safety?'

'We can never guarantee anything, but make no mistake, to get past that lot they'll need a tank. Once we are in the offices of Fell, Pelham & Drysdale we're safe.'

'All right, I'm on,' I said, and suddenly thought of Jane. For the first time in my life I had something to live for and I didn't like the thought of risking the relationship. At that point the phone rang and Shaw snatched it up.

'Hallo!' he said. 'Yes, he's here.'

'Who is it?' I asked.

'It's a woman.'

'Hallo!'

It was Jane. I listened to what she had to say and I saw Shaw was watching me closely. I put the phone down and turned to Shaw.

161

"That was my girl-friend,' I said.

'Yes...yes,' he said impatiently. 'She told me that.'

'She has just received a phone call from Marlene...Bill's live-in partner,' I explained as clearly the name meant nothing to him. 'The police have just been and Bill has been taken away for questioning. Marlene is in a panic, and not in a good temper, so Jane says.'

'Damnation!' Shaw ejaculated. 'So now they'll be onto you as well, we can hardly expect your friend to withhold information.'

'No,' I agreed. 'He'll spill the beans, or what beans he knows. He was very keen for the police to know what was going on anyway.'

'I can understand that,' said Shaw. 'But it does present a problem. If they run you to earth, we'll never reach London in time.'

'I'd say we've no chance at all then.'

'We have some jokers in our pack,' said Shaw. 'We have a private security firm in Melbourne working for us. We must reach them and the sooner the better.'

*

I insisted on calling on Jane on the way out, she was clearly upset when we finally left, and I felt equally upset, which nearly resulted in me deciding not to bother to claim the inheritance. Then I thought of all the money being used by a criminal gambling and drug syndicate and my resolve hardened.

I tried to explain to Jane what it was all about, but she began to ask so many questions that we could have been there for a week. Shaw quickly supplied the solution, he had brought with him all the genealogical records, and realised he could resolve two problems if we left the lot with Jane. She could discover what it was all about, and secondly, we wouldn't be carrying his large folder around with us that would be an encumbrance. It wasn't as if it was the only copy anyway, the original was in London.

After a tearful departure, we made a quick visit to my flat to pick up my passport. These two journeys could have enabled the enemy to lock onto us but I doubt whether they would have made any difference in the long run, Fisher's men would have had all the exit roads watched anyway. Where it could have been deadly was that I could have led them to Jane, from their track record to this point they would not be above using a hostage, but in hindsight I'm sure now they didn't lock onto us until we appeared at my own apartment, which they must have staked out.

There was a party going on at one of the neighbouring apartments when we arrived to collect my passport, my next-door neighbours were Italians who had an extremely large and noisy extended family, and they seemed to hold parties and reunions every other week The stereo had been dragged out onto the balcony, as was usual on these occasions, loud, music was blaring out and probably keeping everyone awake for miles around. I entered my apartment for my passport, accompanied by Mario, my neighbour, his friend Dino, plus three of their mates who had all had too much to drink, all of whom locked onto me with enthusiastic invitations to join their celebration, whatever it was, and they considered it their bounden duty to thrust glasses of wine at me.

In hindsight, it's likely Mario, Dino and their friends, over-enthusiastic company though they were, did us a favour. There was a musty aroma in the apartment, something like stale cigarette smoke that assailed my nostrils as I foraged around and I thought I heard a noise in the kitchen as I passed by the

door after exiting the lounge room clutching my passport. I felt
adrenalin run through my veins and stuck close to Mario Dino
& Co, who had all entered the apartment with us and entreating
us to stay. They were all built like genial gorillas. I headed for the
front door, flinching as their stereo hit my eardrums at full blast.

Shaw was involved with three more revellers on the threshold
and now I know what I do now, the presence of so many others
was our luckiest factor that night. To have waylaid me in my
apartment would have been their best bet, but with Shaw
outside and the balcony resembling Flinders Street Station on
Melbourne Cup Day, they had to pass up the opportunity.

We clattered helter-skelter down the steps to ground level.
I raised my glass to Mario up above and made the pretence of
swallowing the remainder of the glass before I surreptitiously
tossed the contents onto the flower bed as I set it down. I
regretted having to do that, what I had tasted so far of the wine
had been excellent, Mario and his family knew their wines
well, but I needed all my wits about me. Mario beamed at me
from his vantage point on the balcony and shouted something
I didn't quite catch which was probably in Italian anyway,
then we headed for the car, flung ourselves aboard and took
off like a drag racer.

'Some party,' commented Shaw. 'Pity we had to leave it.'

'Don't worry about that; they hold one nearly every week,' I
said tersely. 'The last one ended with a fight in the courtyard
and the police had to be called in.'

'What? Then we *should* have stayed.' commented Shaw
which amused both of us. Maybe he wasn't a cold, humourless
lawyer type after all.

We hit the road for Melbourne and I put my foot down. It
occurred to me we would have to stop for petrol sometime but
the tank was nearly full and I thought it would be enough.

They must have picked us up by a not so shrewd calculation, it was a fair bet Melbourne would be our destination and as there was only one main road in that direction it was only a matter of time. I became aware of their lights in the mirror after roughly 30 minutes on the road. They stayed there so I put my foot down and kept it there.

We were in the country miles from anywhere when they made their first attempt. They reached a point close behind then attempted to draw abreast of us after they had been creeping up slowly for some time. As we approached Beaufort, they tried to swerve us off the road. They nearly succeeded, but as they cut across us, I swung the wheel to the left and traversed a service station forecourt.

'Hold on!' I gasped to Shaw as I swung the steering wheel violently to the left, knocked over a rubbish bin, raced over the forecourt and headed for the other exit on a side road. The tyres squealed in protest as we described a turning circle about the size of a 50cent piece and scorched up the road to Raglan. I heard a squeal of brakes and tyres as they tried to emulate my manoeuvre and a 'bonging' sound as the long-suffering rubbish bin was propelled violently into the service station frontage. In the mirror I saw them swing violently across the road and into a fence on the other side, they backed out and took off after us again but we had gained ground.

'How long have they been onto us?' shouted Shaw.

'Too bloody long,' I was angry with myself for being so easily followed. 'They've been following for some time.'

'Bloody hell!' Shaw was furious. 'What a lousy place to be caught, miles from anywhere.'

'Everywhere on this stretch of road is miles from anywhere, but they haven't caught us yet,' I said grimly. 'Hold onto your balls.'

From frequent travelling in the area I had the advantage of knowing the road and where the bends were, but they possessed an equal advantage in that all they had to do was keep our tail lights and headlights in sight. I maintained a good pace and managed to keep them at a distance, thanking my lucky stars it was a dark night. If a driver is breaking speed records, ample warning of approaching vehicles is given by their headlights. On the other hand, we obviously stood out like a beacon to our pursuers, our headlights cleaving the darkness must have been visible for miles.

After travelling for a considerable length of time I glanced at the fuel gauge and wasn't happy, after soaking up a significant mileage at high speeds it was just over half full and at a rough guess this would give us about 140 kilometres. Melbourne was roughly that distance, but we wouldn't get that far if we tore around the countryside like this. Fuel consumption rose alarmingly the faster you travelled.

'They're catching up again!' Shaw looked over his shoulder.

'Shut up!' I retorted, the last thing I needed was negative input. But he was right, I looked desperately ahead for solace but there was none. My only recourse was to put my foot down, thereby decreasing the overall distance we could travel. The needle crept around the dial, at one stage I was touching 140 kph on a road that was hardly suitable for half that speed. The wire fences on each side of the road flashed past, and I ruminated on the possible consequences if we hit a cow or kangaroo at this speed. I had seen the results of collisions with kangaroos, cars off the road with severe damage and injured occupants, while the kangaroos were history.

I was aware of headlights approaching ahead and slackened speed, but as the lights in the mirror grew larger, I slammed my foot down again. The lights ahead grew brighter and I cursed the oncoming driver who was one of those thoughtless morons who always drove on main beam with an absolute disregard for anyone else.

'Dip, you bastard!' I ground out, but the other still came on and I angrily flicked my lights to main beam in retaliation. We passed him on a slight right-hand bend, he hooted furiously as we passed and I heard a shout, presumably his code of ethics dictated he was the only one allowed to be unmannerly.

We screamed around the right-hand bend on two wheels, I nearly panicked as I felt the wheels begin to drift on the gravel and my adrenalin ran as a tree loomed closer and closer and finally flashed past us, there was a knock as we gave a nearby bush a slight nudge.

'Christ...be careful!' gasped Shaw.

'What do you prefer, a scratch on the bodywork or a bullet up your arse?'

He appreciated the logic because he held his peace, I heard him suck in air as we nearly straightened out the next bend. I looked in the mirror and found we had gained about 400 metres, the oncoming thoughtless driver had his uses as he must have dazzled our pursuers as well, but it was no great margin. The distance could be made up in in less than a minute.

I had been toying with the idea of turning abruptly off the road onto a farm track and dousing the lights, hoping they would streak past without seeing us, but had to dismiss that plan as impracticable. To do this I'd have to switch off the lights before making the turn, otherwise they would see us deviate. We also needed a good lead, which we didn't have, and to try and negotiate a right-angled turn at this speed would save them the expense of a bullet. Further, the brake lights would give us away.

We roared through a small township, I caught sight of the

name 'Chute' and then we were through it. Our speed was such we must have woken the entire population of three men and a dog and set every bird on the wing within a radius of five kilometres. A glance at the mirror showed they were still with us, we had gained even more but the lead was quite meaningless, except it did away with the possibility of anyone taking pot shots at us. That was the good news; the rest seemed to be all bad.

The fuel position wasn't good either, we weren't desperate but there was still a long way to go and the chances of us reaching a large town in the near future was remote. What we needed was scores of people thronging a main street, with possibly a few policemen in attendance as well. Secondly, I wasn't too sure where I was going as my directory was in the pocket behind my seat, where it normally reposed, but I was hardly placed to consult it, nor was Shaw who wasn't cognisant of local roads anyway. I didn't know the road we were on; I thought it came out somewhere on the Castlemaine-Ararat Road but wasn't sure where.

Maybe if I turned right at the end of this road, we could reach Castlemaine, then head for Melbourne, assuming we had enough fuel. Could we stop in Castlemaine and yell for help? But if we did the police would become involved and then my part in the Halls Gap 'affray' would have to come out and my chances of reaching London in time to deprive Laurie Fisher of the cash he coveted would be nil.

We roared through Mount Lonarch, with the others still well behind us and continued northwards. The sky became lighter to our right as we cleared some trees that ran for a long stretch along the eastward side of the road.

'What time is it?' I asked Shaw.

'Half past three.' he announced.

Half past three! My heart sank into my boots. It would be another two hours at least before we could expect to roll into a township and see any people about, Castlemaine would be a ghost town before 6.00 am. I looked in the mirror again; they were still hanging modestly some distance behind. I didn't like that. They knew all they had to do was bide their time. On the other hand, how much fuel did *they* have?

We reached the intersection and swung right to head for Maryborough, the signpost said it was 34 kilometres. Then I realised why the enemy had been biding their time, the Pyrenees Highway was much wider than the road on which we had formerly been travelling, there wasn't much more traffic and it was more conducive to speed. I realised they had increased speed and were drawing closer, I grimly accelerated and we bounded forward. This kept them at a distance but I could see this was going to be a war of nerves.

The speedometer reached 120kph and stayed there, but so did they. This was worrying, if we continued at this pace we'd burn up all our fuel in double quick time. No doubt the enemy, blast them, would have had the foresight to fill up to the brim before we left Stawell.

'How far to Melbourne?'

Shaw clearly believed all we had to do was race to Melbourne and cruise up to the airport lounge.

'Too bloody far,' I answered savagely. 'And we have a problem.'

'What's that?'

'We'll run out of fuel at this rate.'

'Have we enough to reach Melbourne?'

'More like Castlemaine…if they don't catch us first.'

'What do we do then?'

'I don't know.'

As we flashed through Maryborough I did have the mad idea of searching around the town for the police station and crashing the car through the frontage, but the enemy were so close by this time I couldn't entertain the plan, and even in our straitened circumstances I wasn't sure I could deliberately ram a building. Naturally being a law-abiding citizen, I had automatically slackened pace when reaching the town, but not being so civic minded they just kept on coming...fast. I pondered on the irony that when speeding to keep an appointment with a client there were police traps everywhere, raising revenue from hapless motorists, but when it was a matter of life or death and you really needed the police there wasn't a constable in sight.

As we passed through the other end of Maryborough and sped on down the highway, I heard popping sounds, a look in the mirror indicated flashes emanating from their side windows. I realised to my horror they were shooting at us. It didn't last for long as they must have realised the chances of hitting us at that speed were remote. Further consideration dictated that had a lucky shot hit us and we'd gone out of control they could have been close enough to be involved in the subsequent smash if we somersaulted all over the road.

The sky was getting brighter as we headed for Castlemaine. It was now four o'clock. I pressed my foot down and we kept going.

There was no point in awaiting the inevitable, we could cut out any time and could well be exposed in the middle of a long, straight stretch of road with no cover. I put it to Shaw and although I had some initial opposition we finally reached agreement. The needle had been approaching and then quivering near to the 'E' for too long and we were still short of Castlemaine, the high speeds had caused abnormally high fuel consumption. I also felt incredibly bitter about the Victorian

Police Force in general and Sergeant Ramsey in particular. Where the hell was he when I needed him?

From Ararat to Beaufort to Maryborough via Amphitheatre I had broken every road rule and speed limit in the book, yet there had been no sign of any police. My recent driving had been highly erratic and dangerous for country roads, some of which were unsuitable for anything faster than a tractor or farm cart, yet Ramsey was presumably sleeping peacefully in his bed whereas three weeks prior he had waylaid me for travelling at a much lower speed on a wide, two-lane freeway for which he had fined me $150. There was something wrong somewhere.

'That lot will do.' said Shaw and I tightened my lips. There was little wrong with his choice, there was a large tree covered area where the road curved round it in a right-hand bend. I pressed my foot on the throttle and we bounded forward. I saw our pursuers recede in the mirror as I made our last desperate fling, they were roughly three quarters of a kilometre behind as we swung round the bend and temporarily lost them from view.

'There's a lay-by,' cried Shaw, I swung the wheel hard over, wrenched at the handbrake to avoid giving the game away with flashing brake lights and we fish tailed in a cloud of dust. We bumped and swirled to the end of the lay-by as I changed down and tried to use the engine as a brake, we forged into the trees at the far end, scraped the bodywork against bushes and there was a harsh bump and jerk as we hit and circumnavigated a ditch. We ground to a halt in the trees about twenty metres in.

'Quick, let's go,' I shouted. We left the car and ran or staggered into the trees. I became aware of our pursuers' headlights as they roared past us on the way to Castlemaine. We didn't kid ourselves they would be fooled for long so we kept on running, we heard the sound of brakes being applied and I hoped they did a somersault. It wouldn't take them long to find our car. When chasing a vehicle 500 metres ahead which suddenly disappeared, it wouldn't take too much intelligence to work out where to start looking.

CHAPTER 17

There was a cold nip in the air as we ploughed through the undergrowth, I was wearing a sweater but Shaw was wearing just trousers and shirt. I had had great difficulty in persuading him to don casual clothes before we started out, my suggestion that he wear a sweater had been treated with scorn, it had been a warm day and like many Englishmen he tended to assume Australia was subject to high temperatures through every hour of every day, even though he'd been in Australia for some weeks.

I called for a halt and listened, we could hear their car engine, it sounded as if they were at the lay-by. I could vaguely make out voices. I looked at Shaw and jerked my thumb in the direction from which we had come.

'I'd say they are back at the lay-by. We'd better head this way.'

The sky was becoming lighter in the east, it was approaching 5 am and there were streaks forming across the sky, the wings of a flock of high-flying birds lit up with a reddish hue from the sun's rays, although the ground below was still swathed in darkness.

'Where the hell are we going?' grumbled Shaw. his voice sounded petulant; I could hear the quiver in his voice as he shivered with cold. A sudden transition from a warm car to a cold, nippy Australian morning must have been traumatic, it was bad enough for me and I had a sweater on. It should be warmer when the sun rose, assuming we lived that long, although daylight would be a curse as we could be spotted more easily.

'Damn!' I said as the trees came to an abrupt end. Beyond was a paddock roughly a kilometre wide, with more trees in the distance, or so it seemed. In the dim light we could see little more than a smudge.

'What now?'

'Run,' I said laconically. 'But not too fast, maintain a steady jog trot; and watch your step. We don't want to run ourselves into the ground or twist an ankle.'

In any case we didn't require speed at this stage, the opposition would be unsure of our movements or direction in the semi-darkness. An added advantage of a steady jogtrot was that it would warm Shaw up and stop him shivering.

We first found out about the sheep when we ran into them, it was surprising they allowed us to get in amongst them as far as we did without becoming aware of our approach. Shaw fell over one, nearly doing a handstand over its back, while I took such a violent evasive action that I nearly did twist an ankle. They scattered with a loud chorus of 'baaaa's' which unfortunately gave us away. I heard a shout from behind, happily a fair way off, but not far enough.

'Bugger it!' I held my hands to my head. 'Those bloody sheep have given us away - are you all right?'

'I'll live,' he replied, an unfortunate turn of phrase, I shuddered at the possibility we may not! He was all right, but his natty shirt was mud stained and I could just see the pained expression on his face. I suppressed a grin and also the almost irresistible urge to utter some joking comment, something on the lines of being a true Aussie now...riding on the sheep's back...but decided now was hardly the time.

'Come on, head for those trees.'

We jogged along and reached the next clump of trees without further mishap. I stumbled over a tree root but soon recovered myself. I looked back and way back in our wake could see dim movements in the murk, I could just make out a man's shape.

'Come on, we'll head this way.'

I wasn't too sure where we were heading but the sun and therefore Castlemaine were to our right, so we were still heading north, presumably in the rough direction of Bendigo. I thought of a prolonged trek to Bendigo and then realised I was ravenous.

'We'll have to try and head for Castlemaine,' I gasped between gulps of air as we jogged in and out of the trees into another paddock. 'Hallo! There's a railway.'

We reached the railway track; a typical country branch line and all the sleepers looked as if they were the originals laid way back in the 1880's. The tops of the rails had a thin reflective sliver of silver on their tops, indicating there was traffic on it but not too frequently.

'This track leads into Castlemaine,' I said to Shaw. 'We'll have to stay away from it, it's too exposed, but if we keep it in sight, we should be all right.'

Shaw nodded. He was beginning to shiver again as the cold air fanned his perspiration. We crossed the track and continued heading north, then veered over in an easterly direction. There were more trees over there and I felt safer with foliage in the vicinity. I looked back and could make out more movement in the murk but they were still some distance behind. Our latest direction change might throw them off, but visibility was marginally improving as the sun's rays began to take effect.

'Come on,' I said. 'Make for those trees over there.'

We headed in that direction, passed through the tree belt and tried to keep it between us and where we had last seen our pursuers. So far, they hadn't appeared, but if they did, they couldn't fail to spot us as the sun was now over the horizon and bright rays were hitting the tops of the trees, making them appear as if they were on fire. The railway track we had crossed over had vanished, it must have curved away to due south, although I still reckoned it was heading for Castlemaine.

Another railway track appeared ahead with a road behind it. I could see vehicles moving on it and they still had lights on. I thought hard and tried to picture the map of the local area. I had rarely ventured this far on my rounds as Castlemaine and Ballarat were covered by a colleague, Peter Glavich, who I occasionally met for lunch at Maryborough or Beaufort. I made occasional business forays in the vicinity when Peter was on leave, but not often. After some thought I deduced it must be the Ballarat-Castlemaine Road, and was congratulating myself on my sense of direction when I saw something that turned my heart to stone.

I spotted two figures ahead in the middle of a paddock and beyond them was the roadway and the railway track. I also saw a stationary car which was little more than a blob.

'Shit!'

'What's up?'

'The bastards are ahead of us as well...look!'

'Bloody Hell!' Shaw looked ready to collapse. 'How did they get there?'

I didn't bother to respond; it was clear how they had. They had dropped two men to follow us on foot, and two others had gone ahead in the car and approached from the opposite direction. Yet how could they have known exactly where we would appear? Had we gone west they would have missed us completely. Perhaps we were just unlucky.

'Quick! Over here.'

There was another collection of trees in the southerly direction, the two ahead had just dropped into a slight depression in the terrain and we could possibly reach tree cover before being seen. I bent double as I went into a jog trot and headed for those trees.

I risked a glance behind, a hazardous undertaking as I kept running, and my heart sank. Two men had emerged from the tree clump over to the west and were running in our direction, and the two men ahead had appeared from the dip in the ground and were also heading for us. They were all well behind us so there was no chance of being shot at by either party as they must both have been nearly a kilometre away.

We grimly ran for the foliage. This was the largest plantation so far and could almost be dignified by the name of forest. As we neared it, I changed my view about it. Plantation it was not, it seemed to be a motley collection of wattle trees of all shapes and sizes, mature trees growing haphazardly alongside saplings with heavy undergrowth and blackberry bushes. This had an advantage; they wouldn't be planted in regimental lines, which would have enabled our pursuers to see us for long distances between the rows.

We plunged in, Shaw fell headlong into a blackberry bush and tore his shirt, I pulled him out and decided not to tell him of the possibility of snakes as we were in enough trouble as it was. We skirted a rusty old car body, jumped over its wheels lying some distance away and threaded our way through more thorn bushes. Progress was not easy, low branches tore at our hair and twigs tried to thrust themselves into our eyes. The wood was thick, it was difficult to see far ahead and I tried to think what our pursuers would do. Previously it had been small clumps of trees, but now we had reached what was metaphorically a large island of trees and shrubs in a grassy plain and were lost inside it.

I tried to put myself in their position. I would be inclined to send a search party of two in and despatch the other two around it to wait for their quarry to break cover and flee. They would probably assume we would flee in the same direction in which we and they were currently travelling.

'Stop and listen,' I commanded.

I strained my ears while Shaw looked at me and scratched his beard.

'They're coming,' he said.

'I know they're fucking coming...!' I broke off, no point in becoming exasperated. 'Yes...all right they're coming but how many and where from? Listen again.'

We listened hard and Shaw shook his head.

'Can't say,' he said. 'I think we'd better keep going.'

'Wait,' I said. 'They'll probably expect us to burst out in the same direction we've been going. I reckon we should head off this way.'

'The hell with that, I'm keeping on going.'

'But that's what they'd likely expect us to do, they're making so much noise they're almost acting like beaters in the grouse season.'

He ignored me, turned and ran ahead, I followed. We jogged for another ten minutes but then I seized him by the back of the shirt, extending his tear by another two inches.

'Blast you! This is my best...!'

'Shut up! Fuck your shirt! Look!' I pointed ahead, there was movement between the saplings about fifty metres ahead. There were two men there, both carrying guns.

CHAPTER 18

We flung ourselves flat on the ground and Shaw looked at me.

'What now?'

'You're asking me?' I snapped irritably. 'You were the one who decided to go this way. I thought you might have some ideas.'

He briefly digested that in silence, looked back the way we had come, then said:

'They'll be on us from back there soon,' a comment that wasn't much bloody use at all. He also seemed to consider it was my fault.

'I was aware of that!' I answered irritably. I gritted my teeth, raised my head and peered over the long grass and undergrowth. The two men ahead were still some distance away, it took me a few seconds to spot them again and I noted with satisfaction one of them had caught himself on a prickly bush. We did have one advantage, we knew where they were and, right now, they didn't know where we were. They seemed to be heading to our left, so I wormed my way to our right.

We covered about twenty metres on our bellies before we hit some gorse. This made my hair prickle, I had heard, rightly or wrongly, snakes tended to gather near gorse bushes and felt my adrenalin begin to run. I skirted the bushes with Shaw on my tail, threaded my way through another dump of old motor car tyres and reached a second car body.

'Charming,' commented Shaw. 'What time is it now?'

I looked at my watch, it was approaching 6 o'clock. We had covered a considerable amount of ground in the last hour, not much as the crow flies, but the activity had done enough to cause a ravenous stomach to conjure up visions of food displays in my mind and aromas I was sure were not actually in the air.

I peered back the way we had come. Through a small gap in the undergrowth I could see our two pursuer groups had now merged into a single unit of four. It wouldn't be long before they abandoned their northward progress and started on an east-west approach.

'Come on!' I commanded and struck off again to the left.

We ran at the crouch; I risked a look back and realised we could become too exposed. We needed more trees and bushes before we abandoned the crawl. So I dropped onto my belly again and Shaw followed suit.

We reached thicker undergrowth and I burrowed underneath it, trying to avoid as many of the prickles as possible. I heard Shaw curse and saw him back off and try again, cursing again as the same snags caught him. Then he was through and we lay panting on the far side of the bush. I could hear sounds behind us, they had clearly decided on a course of action. They had one advantage, they could advance at a jog trot without it mattering whether we saw them or not, we didn't have that luxury and had to progress warily.

'We'd better keep crawling,' I advised and Shaw muttered under his breath. We cautiously inched our way forward then Shaw uttered an exclamation.

'Shut up,' I hissed angrily. 'Do you want to rouse the entire bloody neighbourhood?'

Shaw muttered something that obviously wasn't polite, scrabbled with his fingers at the earth and flicked a white object at me. It hit me on the right ear and I nearly blew our cover there and then.

'What the hell was that for?' I hissed furiously and regarded the object balefully. It was a golf ball, mud covered and stained, but clearly a fairly new one. I rubbed it on my jumper sleeve, it began to come up pristine white and I could read the identifying mark 'Hot Dot 7'. It was quite a good ball; I pursed my lips and dropped it into my trouser pocket. Why I did that I still can't fathom, the chances of living long enough to tee it off seemed remote at the time.

Shaw didn't answer my question; I knew the answer anyway. I suppose as leader of our little safari I had become dictatorial and intolerant of shortcomings. I rubbed my ear, which hurt and commenced crawling forward again. I can only assume that with all the excitement of the past few days my brain was not functioning properly, it wasn't until I came across another ball lying in my path, and then a third, that the full import struck me, then only after Shaw put the idea in my head.

'How the hell are we going to dodge the bastards?' he was asking after I picked up the third ball and was cleaning it. 'We must be miles from anywhere, I doubt if there's a living soul within miles.'

'Well somebody dropped these and...! Good God!'

'What?'

'These bloody golf balls. We must be just off a golf course, there must be fairway close by.'

'I don't follow you.'

I didn't bother to explain, obviously Shaw was no golfer, but it was clear enough to me. Many golf architects thread their fairways through clumps of trees, up hills and around water courses. They actively encourage plant growth just to make things more difficult. They are an unsympathetic breed of men who possess extreme instincts of cruelty and sadism, who exploit their hate of their fellow men by the construction of bunkers, untrue greens and dog leg fairways with the addition of thick undergrowth liberally laced with stinging nettles if they can find any. Sometimes the bushes are already there, so they design the course around them. I calculated this small forest bordered a fairway, but judging by the maturity of the trees they had been here long before any golf course was constructed.

I tried to gauge where the fairway could be, it must be near. Maybe it could be within twenty metres or so. I experienced a flush of excitement. This could be our salvation.

The first ball must have been struck by a lousy golfer; it would have been the king of all sliced or hooked shots. We inched our way forward for another ten minutes before we finally reached a line of bushes and a cyclone wire fence. We also encountered three more balls on the way, which indicated to me we were not only getting warmer but the tee must be to our left. most golfers are righthanded and lesser golfers tend to slice more than hook.

I parted the bushes and peered through. True enough I was looking at a fairway and away to the right I could see a green with a yellow flag in the hole. Further away to the right, in the distance, I could make out a brick club-house, surrounded by conifers. There were a few ant-like people around it, the usual run of early morning starters. Away to the left was a small tractor and two men in a bunker.

'What now, do we head for that building?'

I considered the problem. Our pursuers were not far behind, we'd gained a little ground initially as we had gone in a straight line whereas they had had to wander around erratically to cover all possible options. Nevertheless, they were able to walk or run about upright, whereas we had to crawl or proceed doubled up, consequently they could travel faster. I could hear them not too far away so we hadn't much time to spare.

There was another clump of bushes on the other side of the fairway, I indicated it to Shaw and suggested we should make a run for it. He thought it a good idea.

We emerged, wriggled under the cyclone fence and began to run. I risked a quick glance behind us but saw nobody. My heart was pounding, more from fear than exertion. We reached the bush and dived headlong into it without being seen.

'Now what?'

'Good Grief! Haven't you got anything better to do than ask what we're going to do next,' I hissed angrily. 'You're the one who landed me in this mess.'

'I thought you were the one who lived in this God Forsaken country and knew his way around.'

His reply was just as heated and unjust as my original comment. I realised squabbling amongst ourselves would get us nowhere, quite apart from the risk of our ripostes being overheard by Fisher's men. I contented myself by muttering something on the lines of telling him to go and stuff himself, then cast my eye around the neighbourhood. Apart from a slight change of scenery I could see little to encourage us. The club-house was still in view and a few early morning golfers were in sight on various fairways.

'Is there anyone behind us?'

Shaw raised his head and had a long look.

'Not yet. Oh sod it! There they are.'

I peered over a dead branch and received a sharp jab in the chin for my pains which brought tears to my eyes. I blinked to clear them and followed his pointed finger. A couple of heads were peering through the cyclone fencing but luckily, they were glancing from side to side as well as in our general direction which indicated they had no idea where we were. They were standing roughly where we had been before we crossed over the fairway, I wondered if they had followed our progress or whether it was coincidence.

'What n...?' Shaw began, then stopped himself. I smiled to myself for a brief moment.

'Stay put!' I said shortly. 'So far they're not sure where we are and there are two other clumps of bushes we could be in. What's going on in the other direction?'

Shaw wriggled over and had a look.

'Nothing, I can't see anyone.'

'Hmmm!' I lapsed momentarily into a reverie. I found my thoughts drifting in the direction of Jane and wondered if I would ever see her again. In fact, I wondered if I would see any of my colleagues again. I was suddenly brought back to reality with a bump.

'There's someone heading this way,' hissed Shaw.

I had a look and was startled to see somebody was taking a practice swing on the tee over to the right.

'Hell!' I muttered. 'Where did he spring from?' It concerned me a little that we hadn't seen him before, if he could suddenly materialise without being spotted, then so could Laurie Fisher's men. Then another man appeared on the tee, followed by another. A fourth man arrived as suddenly as the others, his head appeared from over a small rise representing one of the bunkers.

'I've got it. That must be the 10th hole,' I said. 'They've just decided to do the back nine holes. That makes sense.'

I had often done that myself if I fancied a round in the early morning, it made a change from always doing the first nine if you were pressed for time and had a full day's work in front of you. While most players who decided to have a round at the same time of day usually congregated around the 1st tee and joined a queue to tee off, starting at the 10th often avoided this, unless several others had the same idea.

'How come they're playing at this early hour?' asked Shaw. 'It's only just before half past six.'

'People do,' I said. 'I've done it myself. Some courses get so crowded you can be queuing up for hours to tee off and then when you do finally tee off you're liable to fall over the group in front of you. Golf courses get very congested during peak hours, so some players start this early and then go to work.'

Shaw digested this in silence as we watched the golfers tee up and drive off one after the other, the first one landed on the fairway, two others plonked down in the rough near us, one of them landed in some surface water and skidded. The fourth announced its arrival by thrashing through the leaves and dropping to earth between us with a motley collection of broken twigs.

'Damn! We'll have to get rid of that, if they come looking for it, they'll find us and it might alert those other bastards. Where did he hit it from?'

'They're all over there,' Shaw indicated to the right. I gauged the direction and then lobbed the ball out so it lay in line with the tee and just before the bushes, about where the striker would expect, and hope, it would be. I ruminated I was at least doing someone a good turn, he would be well placed to land it on the green from there with a short putt to follow if he was lucky. Maybe that one good deed could cause the gods to look in our direction, give an approving nod and stack a few odds in our favour.

'After they've taken their next shot, we'll start walking over to the green up there,' I said to Shaw. 'We might make it without being too obvious, using these four golfers as camouflage. Once we've passed the green we'll have to think again.'

Shaw nodded, wearing only a shirt, now torn in a couple of places, he was beginning to shake again with the cold. He had my sympathy. I was at least wearing a sweater. A brisk run over to the neighbouring parallel green wouldn't do him any harm.

The quartet continued homing in our direction, they provided a useful service in that they tied down our pursuers as well. Rampaging over a golf course brandishing firearms was a little difficult when confronted with the respectability and normality of a golfing foursome. Further, not carrying golf clubs was another factor that would cause raised eyebrows.

Those members of the quartet who landed on the fairway took their second shots, the first landed on the green, the second player's shot I lost completely, the third landed in the rough near to the green. The last player continued moving towards us and to our horror he walked straight past his ball, which could hardly have been more prominently placed and was clearly heading for our bush. He must have kept his eye on the ball and estimated where it had landed. I felt myself go cold, I was feverishly turning over convincing reasons to justify lurking in the bushes as he came within 10 metres of us and began swishing at the undergrowth.

'Can't you find it, Tom?'

'No. It landed in here somewhere.'

'Hang on. I'll give you a hand.'

The third player, whose original shot had skidded on the surface water, had already taken his second shot. He wheeled his buggy over and nearly trod on the ball, where I had lobbed it. He stopped short and picked it up.

'What was yours?'

'Top Flite 3'

'Well it's here! This is it.'

'It can't be.'

'Well, it's a Top Flite 3.'

'What! Let's have a look.' Tom abandoned his undergrowth swishing and went over for a look. 'Good God!'

'Is it yours?'

'Too right it is!' He turned it over and over. 'Well, that's bloody unbelievable, I thought I saw it go in those bushes.'

'Well, it must have hit something and bounced out, unless you misjudged the flight.'

'But I swear I saw it go in,' he scratched his head in perplexity and for one awful moment I thought he was going to disbelieve the evidence of his own eyes and start searching in our haven again. Then he shrugged.

'Yes, it's mine for sure, there's that small cut over the maker's name, the Top Flite `3'. Well I'll be damned!'

'Your lucky day,' commented his companion and called out to the other two players. 'OK lads, we've found it.'

If there is an Almighty God, I felt that he owed us something for the immense pleasure we had given to one of his creatures. Tom, the player we had assisted, took his shot and it was a screamer, it almost appeared to curve upwards as he despatched it and it must have landed about ten feet in front of the green. Such was the way on it, it bounced forward, careered up the lip of an undulation, leap frogged a bunker, popped over the top and landed within a short distance of the flag. I reckoned he would probably have a 20centimetre putt.

'My bloody oath!' I commented; it was the kind of shot every golfer dreamed of. I watched them go off towards the green. 'Well, we've made somebody happy today. Come on! Let's go!'

We emerged and commenced trotting across the parallel fairway, heading for another green in the distance. The four players had their backs to us as we trotted, while behind us our pursuers, hopefully, had their view blocked by the bush from which we had just emerged. I glanced behind us as we progressed and checked that the bushes lay in line with where we had last seen Laurie Fisher's men. We were still short of our goal, a green on a round plateau with steep banks, when I perceived movement to the one side of our late haven.

'Walk!' I snapped to Shaw. 'Grab that rake.'

Shaw obediently slowed down and looked quizzical.

'Do what?'

'Get hold of that bloody rake and start raking, look as if you're enjoying it and know what you're doing. Just look busy.'

We busied ourselves, Shaw raking over the sand in the bunker, while I started clearing away the odd flotsam and jetsam that seemed to accumulate round every bunker, old twigs and branches and a few paper handkerchiefs. I harvested them into a heap, then carried them over to the waste bin standing adjacent to the next tee. I had already used this occupational camouflage technique successfully with Jim Hewitt's bucket and broom outside my apartment a few days ago.

I noted it was the 8th tee, I had not been far out in my estimation. Our recent acquaintances, the foursome, were on the 10th and were now walking towards the 11th. They walked across the summit of a rise and disappeared over the ridge.

I looked again at our pursuers, they seemed undecided what

to do and our activities and alibi/disguise appeared to have worked, for the time being. We did have the advantage that when they had seen us the light had been dim, so they wouldn't be too sure what we were wearing. We had been merely a speeding car and then two shadowy shapes flitting through the half-light, previously easily identifiable by the fact we had been running away from them. Three of them gathered in a huddle in the middle of the 9th fairway and had a conference, joined later by the fourth when he emerged from the bushes adjusting his flies, clearly, he had been relieving a call of nature.

There was a danger they could approach us either to converse or ask if we had seen two suspicious characters, in which case they could recognise us facially. I assumed they would know Shaw, having followed him from London. Possibly they must know me as well if they had been stalking me for weeks and trying to run me down or fire shots at me. We were presently in their middle distance and looked like part of the golfing landscape, but that wouldn't last indefinitely.

Shaw carried on raking the bunker, I couldn't guess whether any of our pursuers were golfers, but from their behaviour during our short acquaintance I tended to doubt it. Yet even a layman would begin to think it odd if we stayed there much longer, a bunker wouldn't need that much raking.

'Where are they now?' asked Shaw, who was raking so conscientiously he didn't raise his head. He said later he was scared to look up in case it attracted their attention.

'They're still standing on that fairway, over by those trees,' I replied as I watched them from under lowered lids and out of the corner or my eye. 'I think we'll have to move from here. Don't turn around, stay facing that way.'

Shaw obeyed, not quite knowing why. I had just caught sight of his shirt, spattered with mud on the one side from his encounter with the sheep. The Ungodly would certainly think that was strange, a man with a mud-spattered shirt at this early hour. That would give us away for sure.

'I suggest we go that way,' I pointed down the 7th fairway. 'Otherwise they'll see the mud stains on your shirt.'

'Oh!' Shaw looked down. 'Will they think this odd?'

'Very!' my answer was short. His query came under the heading of a 'damn silly question'. I was still considering our problem when there was a dull thud and a ball plonked down bang in the middle of the fairway, bounced a few times and came to rest. A second ball pitched a few moments later, slightly to one side of the fairway, then bounced and rolled into the trees on the right.

As the inevitable third ball arrived, I had a glimmer of an idea. I started walking down the fairway towards the balls, signalling to Shaw to follow.

'Bring the rake' I ordered.

The rake, of course, belonged to the bunker and should have stayed there, but I doubted whether that fine point of golfing etiquette would have registered with members of the London Underworld. Shaw hoisted the rake onto his shoulder, which bestowed the aura of a professional groundsman, and we advanced towards the first ball. I had a careful look around and picked it up.

The four approaching golfers were still out of sight over the crest of the ridge, in fact it was likely there was still a fourth ball to come and it would be just my luck to be standing underneath it when it came down. I felt a tingle of apprehension, while Shaw, the non-golfer, stood in blissful ignorance of the fact that Nemesis, in the form of a golf ball, could suddenly appear out of the blue and possibly land on his head.

'It's a long time coming, where the blazes is it?' I was

muttering when I heard it. It scattered some twigs and a few birds as it came down in the trees.

'Pick that other one up, that one over there,' I said. 'Be quick about it, while those bastards over there aren't looking.'

Shaw did so, and stood with it in his hand.

'Now lob it into that clump of bushes,' I ordered and did so with the ball I had retrieved. 'Quickly now.'

Four heads appeared over the ridge and four golfers slowly approached. They strode purposefully forward, two headed for the fairway and two others in the direction of the trees. The two fairway men slowed up and looked perplexed; there was not a ball in sight.

They looked around with some surprise and then eyed us with some suspicion. I had some sympathy with that. If you were on a course you knew well, when a ball disappeared over a ridge you would have some idea where it would have pitched. I assumed an innocent look and picked up a cigarette packet from the turf.

'G'day,' I said, having decided to open the proceedings.

'G'day,' came the answer, followed by another puzzled look around. 'Have you seen any golf balls around here?'

'Heard 'em all go,' I said and indicated the trees. 'They all landed in there.'

'What? All of them? Are you saying they all landed in there?'

'One of them hit that divot and pitched almost at right angles,' I remarked. 'Another pitched and rolled. Did you see the other one, John?'

Shaw stood gazing into the middle distance; sublimely unaware I was addressing him. Maybe I was being overcautious by using a non-applicable name, the thought crossed my mind of a possible interview the police may conduct later with a equally possible witness who had seen us.

'Did you see the other one...*John?*' I said again, through gritted teeth. He caught on this time.

'No. I heard it though, it went in there. A couple of birds flew out'

I breathed freely, and shrugged.

'Bad luck,' I said sympathetically.

They stood there, disbelieving, for a couple of seconds, then shrugged and reluctantly headed for the trees where their colleagues were already beating about. I heard them discussing the matter as they went.

I had a wild plan in my mind, which depended on all four golfers going into the bushes and abandoning their buggies. Two of the buggies had sweaters wrapped around the buggy handles. These could come in useful with Shaw still dithering with cold.

'Right in the middle,' I called out helpfully and received three waves of acknowledgment, but they still looked puzzled. I could understand that, as an experienced golfer I would have had a fair idea where my ball would have landed, unless it developed a late swing in direction or hit something. I hoped that explanation would have occurred to them too, as they relinquished their buggies and, armed with a club apiece, advanced grimly into the undergrowth and then plunged into the bushes. I watched them go with some trepidation, hoping the first two wouldn't find their balls too quickly.

'What are Fisher's men doing?' I asked Shaw.

He raked around in a circle, looking in all directions.

'Over to the left, in the other bushes.'

'The ones we were in?'

'Yes'

'Good,' I had a quick look around in all directions and then peered into the immediate undergrowth. The four golfers were still searching. I couldn't guarantee they'd be doing that for too long, they would be anxious to get on with it, give up the search and start off with dropped balls. The area they were in was in a slight depression, so their buggies were out of sight because of the rise in the terrain, plus the thick foliage of the trees.

'Come on,' I said. 'Grab a buggy.'

'What?'

'One of these two, down in the dip where they can't see what we're doing.'

'But we can't do that.'

'Oh yes we can. We're not stealing them, we're only borrowing them.'

The average insurance policy's definition of theft occurred to me as I grasped the handle of one of the buggies. `*With the intention of depriving the owner permanently thereof...*' Well, we weren't. We only needed them to get over the next rise away from the view of our pursuers.

Shaw seized another buggy with a jumper attached and started pushing. We hastily scuttled around the side of the bushes down into a dip, and then struck straight across an adjoining fairway.

I risked a hasty look back. Both sets of bushes were waving around as our pursuers and the golfers were investigating undergrowth. We trundled our buggies as fast as we could and crossed the fairway without mishap. Then we set off across the next and passed through a belt of trees clearly planted by the sadistic course architect. They acted as a useful screen and would give Laurie Fisher's men another decision to make, while the golfers would similarly have problems when looking around for their missing buggies.

'Put that sweater on.' I commanded. Shaw stopped and pulled it on, he had been shivering again and his teeth were chattering. The cold this morning was quite intense, although the temperature was increasing slowly as the sun rose higher.

'Now head this way,' I said, after a careful look both ways. I could just make out a flag fluttering in the distance and headed for it. I had no idea now whether we were on the first or the back nine holes now, having been completely disorientated by crossing fairways at right angles.

Like most golfers, I judged my progress and the geography of any golf course by following the fairways in an orderly fashion although occasionally one could lose one's sense of direction if a bad hook or slice meant crossing or hitting up parallel fairways in the wrong direction. We had crossed more than one fairway at right angles, so now I had no idea where we were. What we had to watch was that we didn't progress too far along the back nine in the opposite direction, this would make us conspicuous and could result in the professional or any golfing staff asking us where the hell we thought we were going...what we were doing...or worse, who the hell were we?

We were approaching a green and I decided we would have to merge in with the general landscape. I produced a ball from the bag and indicated to Shaw to do the same. I addressed it with an 8 iron and swung. It wasn't a good shot as I was out of practice and had other matters on my mind. I topped it and it ran along the ground, bouncing its way along the fairway until it stopped about 20 feet short of a bunker. It was strange, after I saw where the ball had landed, I remembered the advice of the young golf professional Stringer when he had gone round with myself and Gilmore, 'don't look up too soon to see where the ball has gone!' I shook my head in disbelief, that had been in a normal world, how much abnormality had occurred since then?

'Now you.'

Shaw took a club out of the bag, I shook my head.

'Not that!' I said impatiently, and took the wood from his fingers. This was hardly the club to use for a shot at a green less than 40 metres away. 'Use that one.'

He addressed the ball with a stance that would not have disgraced a No. 11 batsman in a village cricket match. He dug out a divot as big as a soup plate. I winced, picked it up and stamped it back into the fairway. The ball had been struck by the divot and rolled about five feet.

'Have another go.'

He over compensated and missed it completely, I ground my teeth and looked around nervously. This performance could probably draw more attention than crossing fairways at right angles. He tried again and connected. The ball kept a low trajectory and skidded well over the green, lobbed over the bunker, hit a tree about 7 metres beyond, reared up into the air, came back and landed on the green.

'Good God!' I couldn't believe it! Even a poor putter could drop it in from there. I thought back to the painstaking care I usually took when just short of any green, never had I landed a ball that close even with an orthodox shot using a 9 iron.

'Is that good?' asked Shaw.

'You could say that!' I remarked coldly as we walked towards the green. I cast my eyes all around us but nobody was in view. The golfers could still be hunting for their balls, while our pursuers could have exhausted one clump of bushes and be probing the next. With our bags and buggies, we were technically invisible but for how long, I had little doubt the golfers would soon emerge and could recognise their own property at a range of half a kilometre.

I took my next shot, it was a beauty, if other matters had not been so serious, I could have had a flush of pleasure, I actually remembered Stringer's advice. When I finally looked up, the ball was describing a graceful parabola over the bunker and finally pitched within a metre of the pin, rolled slowly beyond it and pulled up with about 10 centimetres to spare. We walked onto the green and Shaw somehow managed to miss his short putt and trickle it over the lip into the bunker, a feat I would have thought impossible, even for a novice. I had a hasty look around, picked up his ball while he was still replacing his club in the bag, and lobbed it onto the green, I didn't want to waste too much time in one location while he shot sand all over the place.

'That's the best way,' a voice said from the bushes and I nearly fainted on the spot.

CHAPTER 19

swung round, I was being addressed by a small man in a highly coloured shirt wielding a scythe. He was smoking a large pipe from which he emitted clouds of not unpleasant smelling tobacco smoke. He emerged from the bushes and swung his scythe with careless abandon, skilfully applying an even cut to the long grass.

'G' Day,' I said, still trying to quell my beating heart and with a degree of shame. I felt like a hunt member caught shooting the fox. 'We've...er...my friend has been caught in every bunker so far and I think he's had enough. I thought I'd give him a helping hand on this one.'

'Good on' yer!' he responded. 'You're a real gent! I don't think he saw you do it.'

'Er...no. I don't think he did.'

Thank God for an understanding man, he'd probably been caught in many a bunker himself. He eyed me for a moment before he re-applied himself to swishing his scythe.

'Nice mornin'' he observed.

'Yes, indeed,' I indicated to Shaw to take his putt, praying he wouldn't select a wood or a no. 3 iron to do the job. The scythe man temporarily ceased his operations to lean on his implement and observe Shaw's efforts. Shaw was eyeing the clubs in his bag with some perplexity and finally pulled out a no. 4 iron. I promptly guffawed with laughter, which I hastily cut short as it began to border on the hysterical. Shaw looked up questioningly.

'What the hell is the matter with...?' he began irritably, but I laughed even louder and managed to give a brief shake of the head followed by a sideway jerk and a flick of the hand, both of which, I thought, evaded the attention of the scythe man. Initially he looked equally puzzled at Shaw's club selection and then began to laugh as well.

'Good idea, the way you played the last shot,' I said pointedly and could have bitten my tongue as I recalled Shaw hadn't seen the actual destination of his previous effort into the bunker. Luckily the scythe man saw the funny side of that as well and politely turned his back for another chuckle. Then I had an inspiration.

'Try using mine,' I rummaged in my golf bag. 'That bent shaft on your putter could be causing trouble.'

I thrust my putter into his hand with a muttered instruction to tap it gently as it was only about a metre to the hole. Shaw took up his tail end batsman stance again but our spectator didn't appear to see much unusual in that. I reflected that many experienced golfers, even top professionals, adopted eccentric or unorthodox stances when putting. He finally putted, after a wild jab that missed the ball altogether, which could have been interpreted as a practice swish...and holed out! I blinked with surprise but recovered myself and uttered 'Shot!' The scythe man likewise muttered an approving grunt. He grasped his scythe while Shaw had the sense to look nonchalant.

I was shaking as I squared up for my own putt, the state I was in I could easily miss a short one. I nearly did as it went off to one side, wandered thoughtfully around the lip of the cup before it decided to drop. I dropped the flag back in and nodded to the greenkeeper.

'See you later,' I said as we walked off.

He nodded and carried on scything. As we moved off, he called to us and I felt a surge of adrenalin.

'The fourteenth is over there,' he indicated with a wave of his arm.

'The fourteenth?'

'Over there.'

'Oh...the fourteenth, thanks,' I said. We had to pass close to the scythe man and I could almost hear the wheels and cogs turning over in his mind, how could two such early risers have reached this far and how come they didn't know the way to the next tee. I could feel his eyes boring into me as we passed. He took a vicious swipe at an offending hummock of grass and cleared his throat.

'You had an early start.'

It was a statement, not a question. I had two alternatives, feign offhanded nonchalance, or else agree. I had the third possibility of ignoring the question altogether but decided to keep the relationship on a friendly basis.

'Not that early, we started at the tenth.'

'Oh!' he digested that one as we passed him and began moving away. Another 20 seconds and we'd be almost beyond his sphere of operations and conversation.

'New here, ain't yer?' he swished at another hummock.

'Like hell!' I determined the best form of defence was attack. 'We usually play on Thursdays.'

'Oh! All right mate,' he answered almost apologetically. 'No offence. It's just that we've had a bit of trouble recently, people hopping over the fence and playing a few holes.'

'Without paying a green fee?'

'That's right, mainly young lads, Fred Fairley's been off his tree about it.'

'Oh yes, Fred would take it badly, he's a stickler for things to be done properly, isn't he?' I hoped my character assessment of the absent and unknown 'Fred' was accurate.

'Aye, he does that.' For the first time I placed the accent, it was English North Country, probably Yorkshire. The accent was nearly lost, but it was still there in the background. He had probably been in Australia for years.

'Come on,' I muttered to Shaw out of the side of my mouth. 'Don't look back for Christ's Sake!'

'You convinced him all right.'

'Don't kid yourself, he had to show us where the next tee was and I told him we were members who played here every Thursday. That may have escaped him for now, but don't bank on it.'

I didn't breathe freely until we had placed a convenient bush between us and him.

'What now?' asked Shaw.

'Play golf, if you can,' I said cuttingly. 'We tee off from the 14th.'

Shaw played the 14th like a cricketer, and a bad one at that. We were still in view of our scything friend and I squirmed as Shaw took guard, I half expected him to ask for 'middle and leg!' I couldn't take his shots for him, nor was it possible to pick up or kick the ball onwards, though I did succeed once when the scythe man disappeared temporarily behind the hump guarding a bunker.

'Damn and blast the man!' I muttered angrily. We were well out of earshot, but still within his view. The problem was, at this hour he hadn't got much else to occupy his attention, apart from keeping the grass down. Shaw's performance was not in the vein of a man who played every Thursday, every Christmas Day was more like it.

'Swing the club more slowly!' I cursed him angrily as another divot circled gracefully through the air. 'Pick up that bloody divot and stamp it back or we'll have Farmer Giles storming up here slagging off, especially if you leave it lying in the middle of the fairway.'

'Who?'

'Our scything friend. Oh God! Look who's over there.'

It was, of course, inevitable we should be in view eventually of either the four golfers or Laurie Fisher's men. On the parallel fairway there were four men, clearly the latter. They were still a good distance away. I looked back and saw the scythe man was nearly out of sight. I squared up to Shaw's ball and hit it. I could not believe it as the ball described a high arc and dropped on the green, well ahead of us.

'Where are they now?' I asked Shaw as I still maintained my act and watched the ball.

'Still there, looking the other way right now. Oh Hell! Look who's over there!'

'Bugger it!' Another four men were bearing down on us, two with buggies and two without. They gesticulated angrily at us so it was clearly time to make a hasty departure. Without their intervention our disguise may have lasted a little longer and fooled our other pursuers, but an angry punch up would certainly attract attention now. The thought crossed my mind that four angry golfers who had had their early morning round interrupted and their buggies stolen could be a more dangerous proposition than four London gangsters.

The golfers were running in our direction now, and fast. They were less than 100 metres away. I relinquished the buggy and turned tail.

'Come on!' I snapped. 'Run like buggery.'

They still gained initially as they had steam up. We headed towards the 13th and surprised our friend with the scythe.

'What's up?' he asked, pausing in mid swing.

'Four blokes coming in this direction, I think they may be some of the blokes Fred Fairley was on about, I don't reckon they're members.'

'What?'

I repeated it, and he downed his scythe.

'We'll see about that,' he said.

'We'll go and look for Fred,' I said, whereupon we scampered in the direction of the distant club-house.

The groundsman waited grimly by the 13th for the arrival of the four golfers. He'd hold them up for a few minutes until the misunderstanding was sorted out and they proved they were the members and we weren't. I gesticulated angrily to Shaw, who looked back and paused to watch the proceedings. He followed me and we scuttled over the rise by a bunker and headed round to the east towards the now risen sun.

'Come on, quickly!' I hissed and we set off at a canter. There was no need to elucidate, although the club members had been temporarily held up by our scything friend, the disturbance had attracted the attention of Laurie Fisher's cohorts. I heard a shout in the distance and they started to run in our direction, three of them heading for us and the fourth heading off in another direction, presumably in the direction of their vehicle.

CHAPTER 20

The railway was first drawn to our attention by the stationary goods train. It was quite a long train and consisted of mostly box wagons, but there were some open trucks. We jogged towards it; Shaw gasping as I ran ahead of him. He was thinner than I, but clearly out of condition, although even Shaw seemed fitter than those behind us as we drew well ahead of them. It was the car that bothered me, it was liable to appear anywhere, and anytime we crossed a road could cut off our escape, but thankfully the one road we did cross merely had a man and small boy thrashing around in the bushes, looking for errant golf balls. We leapt a fence, continued towards the railway and crossed the track about forty metres ahead of the train which was stationary at a signal.

'Hold it!' I shouted to Shaw who was still running like a scalded cat. 'Run round in a circle and head for one of those open trucks, we'll cadge a lift.'

The locomotive gave a disapproving toot as though it had

heard my plan, we continued running away from the line while our chasers could still see us, then when the train blocked their view we turned around, threaded through the undergrowth and ran alongside one of the open wagons. The train was beginning to move.

'What about the guard?'

'They don't have guards now, just drivers,' I shouted. 'Come on!'

I ran alongside one of the slowly moving wagons, seized a handhold on the end, swung myself off the ground and clambered aboard while Shaw followed suit.

'Just hang on here.' I shouted as I hung onto the side of the wagon. 'If we climb over the edge of the wagon, they'll see us.'

We waited until the train had covered some distance, I risked a glance behind and saw they had crossed the line behind the train and were heading off in our original direction.

'Now!' I shouted, we climbed up the last few rungs and rolled over into the wagon. We were not visible from the locomotive, there were some box cars in front of us and the track was curving slightly to the right. The clicketty-clack of the wheels gathered in intensity as the train sped up and we began to breathe more freely. I looked up at the blue sky and saw the faint roundel of the moon which appeared and disappeared spasmodically as we passed by the occasional tree.

'Where are we heading now?'

'Castlemaine at a guess,' I said. 'But don't bank on it being safe, those bastards have a car and can get there before we do.'

*

I stood and cautiously peered over the top of the wagon. I could see Castlemaine station just ahead, there was another train at the platform, one of the diesel passenger rail cars prevalent on these country lines. We slowly coasted into the station, ground to a halt and the rail car took off in the opposite direction. I looked around, we could just see part of a nearby street from where we were and I was struck by the number of flashing lights.

'What can you see?'

'Police!' I hastily ducked down again. 'Three of them in the station car park.'

'Any sign of those other bastards?'

I shook my head, whether they had any idea of our being on the goods train was problematical, it may take them some time to realise we had vanished into thin air, especially as we had been more fleet of foot and steadily gaining on them. With luck they could spend valuable time culling the immediate countryside before they thought of other possibilities.

'Would the police be after us?'

I pondered the question, frankly I wasn't sure. The incident at Halls Gap would still be fresh in their minds and under investigation, they would know by now it was me who had been involved. Bill wouldn't have kept mum or committed perjury on my behalf and I wouldn't expect him to. Marlene certainly wouldn't allow him to do either; it would be quite pointless and could land him in serious trouble. The police would wish to ask questions about the alleged fusillade of gunfire in Halls Gap, but the one patch of bright light was that if the police had recovered any bullets none of them would be a .22.

They must have locked onto Jane by now, they would know my car number, and it was quite possible that by now the police could have found it where we had abandoned it. With the disturbances we had caused at the golf club and the theft of the buggies, a report of the buggy theft could have been made to the local police and it wouldn't be long before they associated the two events and were interviewing green-keeping staff.

To search Castlemaine would be a logical step for the police, and possibly for Fisher's men, but luckily the latter had less manpower or vehicles with which to saturate the countryside, as far as they were concerned, we could have fled in any direction from the golf course. The police could also be armed to the teeth, they may possibly assume I was still carrying a shooting iron after my last public appearance in Halls Gap, if they hadn't already unearthed it from the back end of Bill's Land Rover where I'd left it. If they had they could have established that it hadn't been recently fired, if at all. I wondered if Bill had been able to explain the bullet hole in the tailboard.

'Can we get off without being seen?'

I considered this question at length. I was not so sure I wanted to get off the train, it was heading in the Melbourne direction and it seemed a good idea to stay put. All we had to look out for was Laurie Fisher's men, they could have put two and two together and assumed the train was a possibility; they could have seen it moving off when they reached the boundaries of the golf club.

I peered over the top of the open wagon. There was a long slow rumbling as another train passed us coming in the opposite direction. The oncoming locomotive hooted when it was level with our wagon, nearly deafening us, followed by the clickety-clack of the trucks as they passed. I watched it go, then was jolted backwards as our train jerked into motion.

We lumbered slowly out of Castlemaine Station, I peered through a crack between two of the wooden slats on the side of the wagon and saw the platform slowly pass us by. Below us I could see an open space with a cricket pitch in the centre and some practice nets, with the inevitable four Australian Rules football goalposts at each end of the oval. A car was parked by the side of the road, with two men looking at a map while a third was walking over the oval towards the toilet block. At the wheel was a fourth man. My blood ran cold as we moved over a bridge and then I lost sight of them Undoubtedly these were Fisher's men, on the credit side they hadn't seemed too interested in our train but that state of affairs could change anytime. They had done well to have moved in the same direction.

Our motion slowly increased and the truck began swaying from side to side with the faster speed. I glanced at Shaw and grinned.

'Not a bad ride considering it's free.'

'Not bad at all. What time would we reach Melbourne?'

I shook my head, this was a question I couldn't answer. A passenger train could make it in about what...an hour? An hour and a half? Would a goods train be quicker, having no stops, or slower, having a long line of heavy trucks? Further, there was no guarantee this goods train would be heading for Melbourne, it may be heading for Ballarat or Geelong. It also occurred to me I was ravenously hungry, my mind turned towards obtaining food.

'Hell! I'm hungry.' said Shaw, it was as if he'd been reading my thoughts.

'My oath!' I shrugged.' No idea what we can do about it, I didn't feel disposed to hang around in Castlemaine.'

'We could have done worse.'

'Hmmm!' I disagreed with that but said nothing more. I was struggling to think about railway routes, where they went in Victoria, roads I knew very well, but railways? Would it be Daylesford next, or was that too far west? This train may or may not be heading for Melbourne, most railway systems in Australia headed for the capital cities, the systems were like a spider's web with the state capital at the centre, but with goods trains there was no guarantee. I dismissed the problem, we'd see soon enough when we arrived in the next town, could be Kyneton, maybe Woodend.

'No chance of food then?'

'No!' I answered shortly and told him what I had seen as we had moved out from Castlemaine. He looked grave.

'We'll just have to starve then.'

'Too right,' I said.

CHAPTER 21

must have fallen asleep. I awoke with a start and noted the sun was high in the sky, the wagon was swaying from side to side and I had a mouth like the floor of a parrot's cage. My stomach was uttering noises of protest.

'Where are we?' I asked Shaw.

'We passed through a place called Elphinstone about ten minutes ago,' he answered. I peered at him to try and analyse his mood. Had I lost status as the action man who always knew what to do and where we were?

'Good!' I said, more for effect than anything else. It was in one sense, I had worked out where we were heading, definitely southwards towards Melbourne, Kyneton would be next then Woodend.

'Any signs of our friends?'

'Difficult to say,' Shaw shook his head. 'I've been looking at the cars on the road, it runs parallel for long stretches, but I haven't seen anyone keeping pace with us.'

'Hmmm!'

It looked as if we might have a clear run into Melbourne, all we had to do was try and alight at a point somewhere near the city, although I was a little hazy what to do once we got off the train. We also had to consider the possibility the train could stop to load or unload freight somewhere, ours was not the only empty wagon. We'd have to stay alert as I didn't want to be submerged under tonnes of wheat.

I considered another point that had struck me. With all the excitement I had been airily thinking of reaching Tullamarine Airport, boarding an aircraft and enjoying a comfortable flight to London. I knew Shaw had a return ticket and his passport, I had my passport all ready for a possible flight but no money, or not enough to purchase a ticket. I mentioned this to Shaw.

'No worries' his reply indicated he'd been in Australia long enough to pick up some of the phraseology. 'If I can get near a telephone, I can ring Jack Lester. He's an ex-copper; and runs a private security company in South Melbourne. He has a connection with a security firm we use in London, he's on our payroll for this case. He'll supply the cash and any transport we need. It's just a case of getting hold of him.'

'How did you involve him?'

'I didn't.' Shaw explained patiently. 'We employ many firms of private detectives, there are many in London. When we realised what was likely to happen in this case, we asked Rod Fillery, a private security investigator in London, for any recommendations. Fillery has connections with Jack Lester and recommended him, and Lester located John Bromyard before I reached here. Both Lester and Fillery used to be in the Metropolitan Police in London and after migration Lester was in the Victorian Police Force for years.'

'You'd better tell him to bring some food as well.' I said. The lack of sustenance was becoming a problem, the sun was now high in the sky and my watch indicated it was nearly 11.00 am. We'd had no breakfast and had been involved in strenuous activity since the early hours.

'Good idea! I feel like an empty drum.'

'So do I. But if we hop off the train at its next stop, we may not get back on it again. How much cash have you got?'

We sorted out our pockets and solemnly counted what we had. It came to $160, plus a few cents.

'How were you going to pay your motel bill?' I asked with a touch of sarcasm.

'Diners Card' he answered snappily, clearly my irritation had aroused a similar antipathy in him. 'Plus, things are so damned expensive in this country I ran through my cash quicker than expected.'

I forbore to make any comment. We had enough on our plates as it was without arguing with each other. The worst problem was not so much the lack of food, that was bad enough, but thirst. I was dry as a chip and no doubt he was too. Natural functions were another issue, up to now we had managed to balance on the step rungs at the end of the wagon and urinate over the wagon behind. So far neither of us had had more pressing needs, but it was only a matter of time.

The clickety-clack of the wheels gathered in intensity, we seemed to be speeding up. I peered over the edge of the wagon, we were fairly flying along. I could see signs of a town ahead, it must be Malmsbury, we had passed through Taradale not long ago. I groaned as the pangs of hunger gained in intensity and settled myself back onto some empty sacks.

At Malmsbury we could wait no longer, as the train rumbled into the station and halted, we scrambled over the side and headed for what looked like a nearby hotel. We both felt weak kneed and had trouble in keeping to our feet initially. When we reached the hotel, the landlord eyed us suspiciously as we entered, after catching sight of myself in a mirror, I had to admit he had good reason. I had stubble that didn't look too pleasant which ran from one ear to the other, while Shaw's previous wispy beard had grown and was unkempt. The stolen sweater from the golf course hid his muddied shirt.

'Sandwiches?' I asked and received a brusque nod in response. I ordered a couple of beers and two lots of sandwiches each, which caused the landlord to raise his eyebrows but he made no comment. The pub was nearly empty apart from two old men playing dominoes in one corner, they surveyed us at length, then decided the dominoes were more worthy of their attention.

'What do we do now?' asked Shaw as we munched away.

'Drink up quickly and then head back for the train. If I was a passing motorist, I wouldn't pick us up!' I said, 'I feel naked with the road so close, if they're going to be anywhere, they'll be covering this road somehow or other.'

Shaw nodded in agreement, then went to the Gents toilet while I kept an eye cocked on the road. He was away for some time and I kept an anxious eye on the train. It was being loaded with some merchandise and looked as if it may take some time, but I didn't want it to go and leave us.

We returned to the station and nonchalantly strolled around it. There was next to no cover, on the other hand there weren't many people around. We had negotiated the road with some difficulty, there had been a fair amount of traffic on it and we waited until there was little or nothing in sight. I didn't want our gangster friends to arrive, make enquiries of the local populace and someone to remember two dishevelled characters standing by the road in the vicinity of the railway station.

The train was still standing silently and I could see the driver on the platform deep in conversation with someone standing on the side of the track. As I watched, the light on the signal down the track changed to green. I indicated to Shaw to circle around the rear end of the train and walk up the blind side, blind that is, from the view of anyone on the station platform.

'We'll have to hurry. It'll be off in a minute. The signal light has changed,' I said shortly. 'Get hold of that sledgehammer.'

Shaw seized hold of a sledgehammer by the side of the track and put it over his shoulder. I picked up a crowbar and shouldered that, then we ambled slowly up to the train, I hoped, looking like track maintenance workers. We crossed over two heaps of sleepers and reached the train, our former home seemed to be in the same state of emptiness as before. We looked hastily in all directions before we stepped in between the trucks and the rails. I had my heart in my mouth as I thought of the possibility of the train starting off with us in between truck and track. We tossed aside our camouflage, the sledgehammer and the crowbar, shinned up the rungs and fell into the wagon.

After about a minute there was a jolt, we began to move and the speed slowly increased.

'Things are looking up' Shaw said brightly but I forbore to answer. I felt a cold sensation on the back of my hand. It had started to rain.

CHAPTER 22

Maybe it was my time in the Army that caused me to sleep with one eye open, whenever matters went smoothly, I often became suspicious and wondered when the crunch would come. I can remember my cousin, who had a wild troupe of children, saying the time to start hunting for mischievous children was not when there was a babble of noise, but when complete silence reigned. Silence meant trouble. In this case it was complacency that was nearly our undoing.

We were lying on and under the tarpaulin in relaxed mode when we passed through Wood End Station, that is, I was lying on top with my hands propped under my head while Shaw was lying asleep with only his head showing, in deference to rain which had been falling but had now stopped.

Some distance after Wood End Station the line passed under the main Calder Highway, as we passed under the dual highway bridge, I opened one eye and coldly regarded the structure. There were two heads peering over the top, heads which turned and engaged each other in animated conversation followed by fingers that pointed at us. One of them placed a mobile phone to his ear. I had closed my eyes and drifted off into dream thoughts again, before the import of what I had seen hit me. They disappeared and seconds later a car moved off the bridge.

'Bloody Hell!' I sat up with a jolt and Shaw cursed me irritably.

'What?'

'They're onto us!'

'What? Who? The Police?'

'Who the hell do you think?' I snapped.' No! Not the police. Bloody Fisher's mob.'

I peered over the top of the wagon, the road was heading away from us on our right, but the car was not now visible. It would not be long before the road and the railway were in close proximity again which would be dangerous. I looked to the left of the track, Mount Macedon dominated the skyline, I looked long and hard at it.

'Where are they?'

'Over there.'

Shaw cautiously poked his head over the side of the wagon as I pointed and shaded his eyes.

'I don't know which car you mean but I can see the highway,' he said and added.' Is there anything we can do?'

'Yes. Get off the train damned quick. It's served us well but it's no haven for us now.'

'Where do we head if we get off it?'

'Head in that direction and up the hill.'

'How do we get off?'

That was a good question, the wheels were fairly clacking along now and I didn't fancy leaping off onto railway ballast and gravel. I had a wild idea of wrapping ourselves in the tarpaulin and jumping off, but quickly discarded it as impracticable.

I cursed myself soundly for underestimating our pursuers but on reflection our best bet must always have been to have stayed on the train as long as we could. Their leader must have used his head and been prepared to take a punt on which direction we had taken, but it was clear they hadn't all headed in the same direction if we had to contend, so far, with only two of them. They must have another vehicle or vehicles somewhere, I wondered how they had managed that and the answer soon occurred to me, Fisher's men were criminals and obviously very adept ones, procuring another car, by fair means or foul, would be child's play to them.

'Bastards!' I muttered, while admiring our main enemy's leadership I put it on record that I hated him. But I had to concede logic was on their side. Heading to Melbourne was our likely choice, in fact our only choice if in the long run our destination was London. We needed an airport, Tullamarine, and there was only one main road that led there. So, they would calculate we had either hitched lifts from obliging motorists from town to town or else we had found an alternative means of transport. Having observed a train pass the golf course, travelling at a slow speed, at which juncture we had disappeared, two and two made an easy four and was worth checking.

'That signal up ahead is red.' Shaw called out.

'Is it?' I peered ahead and strained my eyes. Sure enough, there was a red light ahead. I willed it to stay as it was and there was a perceptible slackening in the intensity of the noise from the wheels.

'We're slowing.'

We were anxious as the locomotive approached the signal, the wheels beat out their tattoo more and more slowly, I prayed it would stay red long enough for us to jump. The train slowed even more, before a green light showed through the mist.

'Damn and blast!' I shouted. 'We've got to get off, *now!*'

I clambered over the front of the wagon and climbed down the rungs, swung by one hand and then dropped. We were on an embankment; I jumped and rolled down it. Shaw followed me and fell to earth about thirty metres ahead of me. The train rumbled on, the wheels still beating out their regular tattoo as the long line of wagons went past.

'Come on,' I shouted. Shaw scrambled to his feet and moved towards me. I headed away from the direction of the road, I had no wish to be exposed to view from their car. There was a clump of trees on the north side of the line, we headed for those.

*

It was beginning to drizzle as we headed across a paddock, the trees before us were clinging to the side of Mount Macedon. We were wet and miserable as we ran on and on. I risked the occasional glance behind us but saw nothing to excite comment. The train was ambling along in the distance and would soon disappear behind a rocky outcrop, but I couldn't see the road beyond.

We reached the hillside and landed amongst undergrowth, we crossed a road heading for the top of the mountain, a favoured tourist lookout. There were a few cars heading in both directions, but it wouldn't be a popular day for admiring the view with low cloud and drizzle.

The ground was slippery underfoot as the drizzle hardened into rain, we kept going and soon saw the main road ahead. We enjoyed a good view of it and I peered long and hard at it to try to pick out any stationary vehicles, but couldn't see any.

'Come on,' I commanded. Shaw nodded and fell into line behind me. We must have looked a villainous couple, which was a worry if we were to try and hitch a lift. Our best bet would be a truck, most drivers were capable of looking after themselves, but would even a truckie pick up two hitchhikers who looked like prison escapees?

It took us some time to reach the main road, traffic was frequent, but I was wary. I felt anyone who was cute enough to follow the train would also deduce where we'd be likely to pop up.

We headed off to the right, following the road in the Melbourne direction

'What do we do now?'

'Bloody well pray.'

The small truck was standing in a layby on the same side of the road as we were walking. The layby was typical of many constructed by various councils alongside main country roads, it had a table and seats of solid timber construction with a latrine at the far end. One man was adjusting ropes that secured tarpaulin around the load while the other was checking the other side of the cab. The load was stacked up behind the cab, occupying half the tray, which had low sides. The latter half was empty except for neatly roped, folded tarpaulins. Either they had delivered half their load or only had half a load to start with. They had clearly stopped either for a toilet break or a sandwich or both and were carrying out routine checks around the vehicle. The rope man eyed us warily as we approached and said something to the other who joined him and also gave us the once over.

'G' Day' I hazarded, trying not to sound too hearty or ingratiating.

The rope man inclined his head and answered in like vein. They examined us closely and stood with arms hanging loosely by their sides, giving the impression that if any trouble presented itself, they knew how to handle it.

'My name's Phil,' I hoped the use of first names could be a relaxer. 'We were heading south, towards Melbourne that is...' I faltered because I wasn't too sure where Melbourne lay at that stage after slugging through undergrowth and jumping off trains. 'I was hoping you could give us a lift, to Melbourne.'

If they were travelling to Melbourne, or a western suburb near it, it would suit us, and give us access to public transport in the form of buses, trams and trains. The truck owner's name on the tailboard included Melbourne which was encouraging.

'Maybe,' said one, he didn't sound ecstatic.

I had reached a point near the cab, there was nothing to excite comment...or wasn't there? I caught sight of a little red and black doll fastened to the driving mirror.

'You're another Essendon supporter...go Bombers!'

He raised his eyebrows and regarded me with a mite more acceptance.

'I am, as for Melbourne, we might be going that way,' he said cautiously.

'There's no room in the cab.' the other said emphatically.

'We can ride on the back, if that's OK,' Shaw felt it was time he contributed to the conversation. 'We won't be any trouble.'

'Oh yes?' was the reply but I wasn't too sure how to interpret that as they both wandered to the back of the truck and had a muttered confabulation. Then they returned, clambered aboard and slammed both doors. My heart sank but the driver looked down through his open window.

'Better get up there, then,' he said. 'But get under the tarp, if the cops see you, we'll all be in the shit. Right?'

'Great!' I shouted joyously as we clambered over the sides. 'Good 'on yer, mate!'

To shelter under the tarpaulin suited us fine, quite apart from the hazards of the police and Fisher's men it had started to rain again. We inserted ourselves under the tarpaulin as the truck swung out onto the road. I found a small bale of something I could use as a pillow.

After a few minutes Shaw said 'What was all that about Bombers?'

'It's Essendon...an Australian Rules football club in Melbourne...no...more than that! They are one of the tribes!'

'What do you mean? A tribe? Are we talking about aborigines?'

I explained the intricacies of Australian Rules Football, the 12way split that had existed in Melbourne for generations, dividing the populace amongst 12 local football clubs. Things had slightly changed in recent years with the introduction of interstate club franchises from Perth, Adelaide, Sydney and Brisbane, but basically the same premise applied. I explained the Melbourne tribal divisions were now ten, not twelve, one had relocated in Sydney and another had merged with a Brisbane franchise, but the tribal loyalties still existed. For immigrants into Melbourne or Victoria generally to feel accepted, their first priority was to adopt one of the football 'tribes'. For all sales representatives it was also a useful talking point when conversation flagged.

'Ah! I see,' said Shaw eventually. 'But how did you know which one he supported?'

'There was a photo clipped to the dashboard behind the steering wheel, and a small black doll with a red diagonal stripe hanging under the mirror. That told me one of them, probably the driver, supported Essendon, so I knew what to say. I assume it's the same in England with Soccer clubs.'

'To a degree,' Shaw agreed. 'But it's national. You're dealing with nearly a hundred possibilities in England and Wales, not just 12, or 10, which means several clubs use the same colours. But in London there's a similar situation, you'd recognise which team anyone supported, out of about 10 possibles.'

'Well, a bit of football knowledge got us a lift.'

We lay flat on the tray as the truck passed through Gisborne, swung left around the bend and passed the Post Office. We left the town behind and after some distance, I rose and sat near the tailboard admiring the scenery.

But then we passed a car parked by the side of the road with two men standing by it, they looked like the two I had seen on the bridge when we passed under it on the train. They were smoking cigarettes and checking the road as we passed by. As we passed, one of them was speaking into his mobile phone.

'Christ! Get down!'

At this point the truck swung around a right-hand bend and mounted an upward slope. We lay flat on the tray as we left them behind, I peered through a crack in the tailboard and felt a thrill of fear as they were both looking in our direction as we drew well away, this damned slope could enable the floor of the truck to become more visible to their line of sight. Our truck rounded the bend and they vanished from sight. I hoped and prayed we had not been seen.

We kept a weather eye open after that, if any vehicles approached from behind, we cowered under the tarpaulin. I created a small fold so I could peer through it and still remain covered, keeping a lookout for any vehicles that could have contained Fisher's men, but I saw nothing. We lay prone, it was not comfortable, but we were heading in the right direction, and the rain had stopped.

Our progress became more rapid and smooth as the truck entered the Calder Freeway, to a degree I felt more secure as

Gisborne was left further and further behind, and our last sighting of the ungodly became more distant. But I wasn't complacent. I knew when one relaxed that was the time to watch for danger.

As the truck's progress became more constant, I actually dropped off to sleep, despite the hard and unyielding surface on which we lay. A loud horn blaring woke me, I poked my head over the right side of the truck, but the altercation was nothing to do with us, it seemed a car had changed lanes in front of another coming up fast and the latter was stating his opinion about the attempted manoeuvre.

The situation resolved itself with an exchange of gestures, I cast my eye around the carriageway generally behind us, then a black car caught my eye. It was keeping pace 70 metres or so behind, there appeared to be three men in it. Almost alongside it but slightly behind it was another car, both were keeping their distance from us. I dropped down behind the rear tailboard and gave it some thought.

Could it be? I tried to peer through the crack in the tailboard, observed that although many vehicles came up fast behind us and overtook, these two remained in position.

I could feel the hair prickling at the back of my neck. Could we have been seen and recognised outside Gisborne when we ascended that slope? If so, then we were not out of trouble. Yet situated as we were on a freeway, the idea of them attempting to run us off the road was unlikely. Danger would arise when we left it, if indeed this was them.

There was nothing Shaw and I could do about it. It would be difficult to attract the attention of our two trucker hosts, and if we did that what could we do? Get off and run? As long as we stayed put and were travelling at a fast pace on a busy freeway, we were reasonably secure.

I communicated my fears to Shaw and he looked grave.

'What can we do?' he asked.

'Nothing,' I replied. 'We couldn't do anything even if we wanted to. We can't ask the driver to stop in the middle of a freeway, and it wouldn't do us any good if he did, the buggers would just stop as well and pick us off easily.'

'So what can we do?'

'Stay put, we're travelling to Melbourne at a fast pace, which suits us anyway. If we're put down in a city street there'll be plenty of bolt holes. Just hope and pray it's not them...!'

But it clearly was, another peep through the tailboard cracks when one following vehicle was slightly closer confirmed our worst fears.

The Calder Freeway merged with the Tullamarine Freeway, which in turn became the City Link. The evening shadows began to close in, which suited us, when we did finally alight, the darker it was it would improve our chances. As we progressed, I realised we didn't know the exact point where our two hosts were heading, were they by-passing Melbourne or heading through it? The answer came when we struck off the freeway at a point I recognised as Footscray Road, we turned into Dudley Street and crossed over the railway tracks. We turned into Spencer Street, and paused at traffic lights outside Southern Cross Station. City traffic being what it is, our pursuers were marooned several vehicles behind us, I tapped Shaw on the shoulder.

'This'll do, we'll get off here. Over the side, quick!'

He followed without demur, my feet hit the road, the lights were still red. I went quickly up to the passenger door, hammered on it and gave a thumbs up sign as the passenger's face turned towards me. He reciprocated, gave a wave and we made for the pavement, the lights changed and the truck and other traffic moved off.

'Good!' I commented as we watched their tail lights disappear. 'Now, our next move is...?' I paused, for once I was stumped.

'Find a telephone,' said Shaw. 'My battery's flat.'

'So's mine.'

'Have you got any loose change?'

I had, we dodged into an adjoining street looking for a phone kiosk but there were none to be seen. I knew there were a few shops just around the corner after the next set of lights.

We found a phone box, but it had been vandalised and was out of order, it accepted money and refused to give it back. I found a milk bar and purchased a bun, which we divided into two, which replenished our supply of small change. Then we had to wander around to find another phone. I espied a wall phone in another milk bar which we entered to make a call. Shaw utilised it and spoke at length, pausing to ask me where we were. I could see the street number of the milk bar on the facia above the door, backwards but readable.

'What road?'

'Church Street off Little Bourke,' I replied.

Shaw replaced the phone and re-joined me.

'They should be here soon,' he said. 'They'll be driving a white Ford Falcon Station wagon.'

'Good enough,' I answered. 'In the meantime, we get out of here and stay in the dark outside to keep out of sight. I don't trust those bastards. They put two and two together too easily.'

It was just as well we did as two cars, a black one and a grey one, both drew up by the same milk bar and two men entered it, one from each vehicle. I watched them for about 5 seconds before I froze with fright.

'It's them! Get down!'

CHAPTER 23

t hadn't taken them long to discover the rear end of the truck was bereft of personnel, they had quickly tracked back to a point where they assumed we'd disembarked, had I not hated them so much I would have admired their ability to put two and two together. We ducked behind a stationary car to the discomfort of the woman in the passenger seat. We peered nervously around the rear of the vehicle; they were still there. A car door slammed, then our shield abruptly drew away leaving us exposed. We hastily scrambled to our feet and dived into the nearest shop, a newsagency.

'Er...Herald Sun please,' I said as we cowered behind the central stand in the shop. I accepted the newspaper and retreated again behind the central stand. Then we wandered to the back end of the shop and started to admire the greetings cards and wrapping paper. The newsagent raised an enquiring eyebrow as we did so. He obviously thought we were behaving suspiciously and worth watching. I could hardly blame him.

'Have they seen us?'

'Not yet,' I answered grimly. 'I'd say they're following the route they assumed we would take. It looks as if they've just stopped to ask questions and maybe grab a bite.'

I regarded the car across the street from our vantage point at the back end of the newsagents. I could still see the men in each car and two in the milk bar. They seemed to be buying refreshments, but would obviously be asking questions as to whether the proprietor had seen anyone like us. My heart sank as I observed the milk bar proprietor jerk his thumb at the phone Shaw had been using. I looked around for a back entrance, or exit, from the newsagent. There wasn't one.

'We'd better stay here then.'

'Not a good idea, they can see us in here as easily as we can see them over there. It's getting dark and we may have more chance outside. In any case, our friend behind the counter here is getting nervous.'

The newsagent was indeed eyeing us warily; there was a limit how long two unprepossessing individuals like ourselves could loiter at the back of his shop. We could cause trouble for ourselves of a different nature if we hung around too long where we were, the newsagent could reach the point where he became ultra-nervous and called police. I knew there had been hold ups of shop-keepers in this area in recent months. If we got ourselves arrested, we'd be safe from Fisher & Co but it would scupper any chances of reaching London in time.

'Come on, let's get out of here,' I began moving towards the door.

'Where shall we go? I told Jack Lester we'd be around here.'

'I'm not meaning to go far, just out of here and off the main street.' I answered.

'Why can't we stay here?'

'Because mine host is looking uneasy, also this place is well lit and from where our friends are outside, we stand out like dog's balls,' I said with a trace of sarcasm. 'It's only a matter of time before one of them looks in this direction.'

Shaw had little option but to follow, he certainly didn't want to stay there on his own. If the newsagent was entertaining suspicions about our *bona fides,* these must have been enhanced by our mode of exit. We crept up to the doorway peering furtively from side to side, then slunk into the darkness like a couple of old lags, dodging from pillar to post and pressing our backs against walls of buildings. I could understand how the police identify suspects after commission of a crime, they merely look for anyone trying to look inconspicuous. We finally ducked down an alleyway, miraculously we made it without being seen.

'Where did you say your colleague, Lester, was going to pick us up?'

'Outside that milk bar.'

'Shit! That's all we need.'

Shaw said nothing as we leant against the wall and I peered round the corner into the street. One car was still parked outside the milk bar less than 50 metres down the road. The second one had taken off and moved slowly down the street, they appeared to be checking a truck, a likely candidate for carrying hitch hikers. One of them emerged from the milk bar, looked around, then gave a discernible double take as he looked in our direction. I jerked my head back but knew I'd committed a faux pas. When chasing somebody, it was logical to assume a head poked around the corner of a building that suddenly withdrew was worth investigating. That damned street light almost above me would have made my head stand out like a beacon.

'Damn! Get back,' Shaw obeyed, I peeped around the corner

again and nearly had a fit. Two men were hurrying in our direction while the car abruptly moved away from the kerb with its right indicator flickering.

I gazed at the oncoming duo with horror. The first man was tall and thin, wearing a dark suit, white shirt and tie. His features were thin and hawk-like.

He had seen me peering around the corner. We were still 40-50 metres apart, he and his companion were still on the other side of the street. Then my temporary paralysis snapped.

'Run...this way!'

Shaw and I ran from the intersection. We reached another intersection, turned right into it and then right again, thus heading back towards the main road. I calculated another right turn would bring us back to near the newsagents and milk bar where Shaw's friend Lester was due to pick us up.

'How long ago was it you rang?' I panted.

'Dunno! About 15 minutes, maybe longer.'

'Where was he coming from?'

'South Yarra.'

'How long would it take him to start out?'

'No time at all. He's used to emergencies and I told him they weren't far behind us.'

'Good!' I tried to work it out. South Yarra was just south of the main city business district, which was where we were, how would he get here? I became so wrapped in the calculation I nearly ran into a lamppost.

'Bugger it!'

We turned the corner and found ourselves back in Spencer Street with the Southern Cross Station nearly opposite. We turned left and hurried down the pavement, keeping a watch over our shoulders, we were not being followed...yet. I turned into a doorway.

'How long will Lester be?'

'I'm trying to work it out,' I snapped irritably. 'Say about 20 minutes give or take a minute and assuming he comes like a bat out of hell!'

'Oh God! That long?'

I could only agree with his sentiment. It seemed an eternity, with Fisher's men not far away.

I willed myself to remain calm and stay where we were. A few times I thought I saw someone who looked like one of Fisher's men, but each time was a false alarm. It looked as though we'd temporarily given them the slip, but that wouldn't last. Yet surely Lester should be near us soon. There was a fair amount of traffic about, could he be in one of those passing vehicles?

'They should be here soon, what did you say their car was?'

'A white Ford Falcon station wagon, registration OCP...!'

'OK, as long as you know it. We'll stay another few minutes then we'll have to move.'

We eventually crept out of the doorway and cautiously emerged onto Spencer Street again. As we peered around in the direction from which we had come, I caught sight of two of our adversaries on the other side of the street, then I spotted the others on the near side.

The two men opposite caught sight of us first and after looking to left and right, started to cross towards us, one placing his mobile phone to his ear.

'Quick, up here.'

I turned left into Little Collins Street and took off like a rocket with Shaw trailing behind me. I spotted a hotel on the corner and caught Shaw by the arm.

'Into the pub, quick!' I hissed. 'They can't start shooting in there.'

'What about Lester?' Shaw protested.' He'll never find us. He can't search every building in the city.'

'There's bound to be a phone inside the pub, ring his office or mobile from there and tell him where we are, tell him...' I looked up at the facia as we went in through the door. '...it's called the Saint and Rogue!'

We plunged into the bar room, thrust our way in and collided heavily with a group of four men standing near the bar. Drinks spattered in all directions as we ploughed into them.

'You silly bastard! Look what you've done.'

'I'm sorry...sorry,' I spread out my hands in a placatory gesture. 'I'll buy you all another.'

The bar room was full of drinkers, many standing but quite a few occupying tables. It was round about 5.30, and was the type of bar to which many office workers would gravitate after a day's work. In years gone by bars used to close at six, which precipitated what was known as 'the 6 o'clock swill' when office workers would line up drinks prior to the early closing. Although those days were long gone, in places the tradition still persisted. The four drinkers we had collided with didn't look like office workers, they were dressed in jeans, chequered shirts and/or overalls and looked like construction workers. They must have been workers from a neighbouring building site, I'd noticed scaffolding nearby as we entered the hotel. They looked as if they were well-established, and could be unpredictable.

This aspect suited me, if our gangster friends caught up with us here, a well-oiled quartet, or more, could be useful allies.

'Come to the bar,' I said, unnecessary since they were already steering me in that general direction. As I hit the bar with my midriff, the door burst open and the tall thin, hawk faced and suited man entered, while two other men simultaneously entered from the rear of the premises. As an outflanking manoeuvre I had to admit it was well executed, but by virtue of our own unorthodox entry we now had a crowd of people around us with whom we had a tenuous relationship and who were temporarily beholden to us as we were buying them drinks. Starting to rough us up or commencing a gun battle in here could cause severe complications. I jerked my head at Shaw as we approached the bar, a wall telephone was visible through the hatch in the next bar room. He got the message and headed in that direction.

'Five beers,' I called to the barman and placed a large proportion of our meagre monetary resources onto the bar counter. I spoke loudly for the benefit of the tall thin man in the suit who was trying to get close to me, for him and his companions to see we were in company was vital. The nap hand of drinks temporarily disassociated Shaw from the attention of both pursuers and drinking partners.

I contrived to retain a central position within the quartet, there was no harm in allowing Laurie Fisher's men to see I had friends, however tenuous or unpredictable the relationship was. Through the hatch I caught a glimpse of Shaw, he had reached the other bar-room, had a phone to his ear and was dialling.

I stood at the bar with my new found 'friends' and even managed to eye the tall thin suited man with an element of defiance. My four present companions were still in an aggrieved mode and seemed undecided whether or not to soften their mood, perhaps they may become more malleable after another round. I was now on the outer fringe of their group, which concerned me as I wanted to remain well within their circle as much as possible. I eased myself back within their fold, looked around and calculated the brawl possibilities.

The bar-room was full and many present were in working clothes, tattoos were prevalent. The majority were presumably from the nearby building site and stoking up before heading for home. The general tone and physique of some of the drinkers made even Fisher's men, hovering on the periphery and trying to merge in, look average. They were trying to get as close as they could to me so I sought to inveigle myself within the drink school foursome who were disposed to be more friendly now their spilled drinks had been re-imbursed. It occurred to me, if Fisher's men attempted to seize us in here, with the current clientele a brawl could easily erupt without too many questions being asked about who started it or what it was about. I resolved if they did try to seize me, I'd ensure I landed a blow on one of my new drinking partners. Another of their drinks being spilt could act as the catalyst to start fists flying.

My four 'friends' were still a little unpredictable although the temperature was definitely cooling. They could now be classified as friendly after the supply of replacement drinks.

Fisher's men were still orbiting the outside of our fivesome, the tall man in the suit was prominent and when close to looked to be a vicious bastard. I caught his eye and a shudder went through me, he looked cold and calculating, as if he was already working out how to dispose of my body.

Four glasses landed one after the other on the bar, I hastily swallowed mine and followed suit. If ever I needed friends, it was now, I needed to continue to curry favour and invest money in protection. There was a pause, they seemed much more friendly now, but I decided another round was essential to cement our 'relationship'. I looked around and saw two of our stalkers had placed themselves strategically by the exits while the tall thin man was still hovering on the periphery of our drinking school. Two more men had entered the main door of the bar, Fisher 'reinforcements', probably summoned by mobile phone.

Shaw, for the present, appeared to have been forgotten by everyone, he was still on the phone on the other side of the hatch in the other bar-room, which was reassuring. He put the instrument down and made his way into our bar-room, uttered an 'Excuse me!' as he brushed past the tall thin man and joined us. Shaw's facial expression when he saw who it was would have been comic if the situation had not been so serious. I raised a questioning eyebrow and Shaw nodded.

'Five more please,' I said to the barman. His eyes thoughtfully flickered over my companions, he hesitated, then shrugged and obliged. It was obvious he'd seen them before, was considering the aspect of trouble and weighing up whether trouble was more likely to eventuate if more went down the hatch, or if drinks were refused. He clearly decided the latter course involved the most risk.

Four of the drinks were despatched quickly, too damned quickly for my liking as I was considered to be a part of their circle as long as drinks were current. I was still sipping mine as the glasses plonked down again. I eyed my new 'friends' uneasily, I seemed to be between the devil and the deep blue sea, I wasn't sure if funds would extend to another round.

'No worries, mate,' said one of them. 'What you reckon, Sam?'

He deferred to the beefy and tattooed individual who looked to be the unofficial standard-bearer of the quartet. Sam seized my arm and steered me to the bar.

'All right,' he said not unkindly. 'Have this next one on me. You've paid your debt, eh?'

'I'll buy the next round.' said Shaw.

'No, you won't, I will!' Sam jerked his thumb at the barman and my adrenalin began to surge as the tall thin man came closer. It seemed I was still in trouble and would have to fight him off if he tried forcibly to pluck me from the group. If I could maintain my presence with this quartet, I still stood a chance. Shaw now had most of the cash we had between us and I may have to get him to buy the next round, if I was still alive to drink it. If we could keep on buying drinks, we were also buying time, Lester and his men must be near at hand by now and after Shaw's call knew where we were.

Sam ordered another round, but when the drinks arrived, they disposed of them more quickly than I liked, not being used to imbibing too much beer at one sitting all I could do was sip mine. There was more than a trickle of perspiration making its way down my back and neck as Fisher's men crowded closer, the nearest one breathed over me and I nearly threw up, not only from fear...he smelt as if he had been eating cow dung. But I also detected a minor change in their demeanour, they were clearly puzzled and uneasy about our four companions who were still in close proximity. These four, having extracted their pound of flesh, had mellowed considerably and Sam had actually bought the last round. Their drinks had been spilt, which had cost me heaps, but by acting as a defensive barrier they had repaid us with interest.

But two other drinkers, obviously acquainted with Sam & Co, had arrived and they began to regroup, break up and move away which enabled the thin man to insinuate himself closer to Shaw and myself.

The suited man and one of his companions inserted themselves into our space and isolated us from the now separated members of our former drinking group. My ribs were thrust against the hard edge of the counter. I tried to push myself away from the bar back towards the fragmented Sam & Co. where I considered I may still have some credit. Shaw was outside the circle and seemed momentarily forgotten.

A red face planted itself less than a foot away, I debated whether to land the first blow, I had nothing to lose and might be lucky but something hard jammed into my ribs and I nearly fainted from sheer fright.

'Say nothing, just do as you're told. Make your way to the door, now move!' said this new adversary. 'Grab his other arm, Bert.'

A hand seized my neck in a vice-like grip, my eyes nearly popped out of my head and everything started to go hazy. The suited man had decided it was time for action and to cease horsing around. They began dragging me from the bar, made easier as my drinking school seemed to have partly dispersed and lost interest in me. Another of his companions, named Bert, presumably the one I had slugged on the mountain, seized my arm and began to shepherd me towards the street door.

'No… no!' I gasped, but received a blow in the ribs. In itself it wasn't too drastic, but it pushed me backwards, the back of my rib cage hit the hard corner of the bar and it hurt like blazes. The next short armed punch was only a glancing blow because I saw it coming and managed to twist, but couldn't avoid colliding with the woodwork of the bar again. It was a sample of just how nasty Fisher's men could be once they really got started.

'Take it easy over there' I heard the barman say, then I managed to twist to one side and a knee intended for my groin hit the outside of my left thigh. I hit out instinctively with a left-handed back hand blow and by a lucky chance the hard edge of my hand landed on the end of the tall thin man's nose.

All the bitterness that had accumulated over the last 48 hours was in that vicious chop, a blow that could have done credit for any contender for the World Wrestling Championship. The thin man's head jerked back and his nose seemed to explode. He staggered into the arms of one of his companions who pushed him back in my direction.

'You want to rough it, do you, Bromyard?' he hissed, a statement that must rank as one of the most unjust and ironic of the century after all that had been dished out to me over the last few weeks. Despite the damage to his nasal organ, he managed to grin most unpleasantly, presumably savouring what he had in store for me when he got me to a secluded place. He moved forward again menacingly but didn't seem his usual confident self, with watering eyes and a stream of blood emanating from his nose. His hand reached for my throat, he was breathing heavily over me and gave me an aroma of stale beer and the frankfurters he must have purchased from the milk bar.

I was conscious of a draught of colder air as the bar-room door into the street opened and closed, but could not see who had entered

I felt myself go numb as I anticipated the beating I was about to receive, even if I landed another lucky punch, I had no doubt his four companions would soon sort me out. His grinning face squared up to mine, but this was the point when I dimly became aware of a change of circumstances.

The grin abruptly disappeared from his features and was replaced by a grimace of sheer astonishment. I was dimly aware of a rush of feet, shouted commands and dark blue uniforms, I was released and fell back against the bar. Two uniformed police materialised, the tall thin man was bundled up to the bar and his hands secured behind his back. One constable frisked him and produced a pistol which was laid on the bar.

'What's the hell's going on...?' I asked Shaw as another of Fisher's men was similarly treated, he resisted and tried make a dive for the street door but was seized and manhandled by two more police before landing across a table about a metre away, which scattered its alarmed occupants.

Shaw jerked his thumb at a newcomer who had joined the

fray accompanied by three other men, these were not police but appeared to have entered with them. He was a very large man well over 6 feet and built like a tank

'This is Jack Lester!'

CHAPTER 24

'Hi, Phil', Lester shook my hand in a crushing handshake that inflicted more damage than anything Fisher's men had done. 'I see you've managed to keep yourselves entertained.'

'I wouldn't put it quite like that,' I answered shakily as the tall, suited man was being ushered out. Lester seized my arm and steered me and Shaw in the same direction. There were three other men with him, plus more police.

Two more of Fisher's men were standing on the pavement as we left, they must have seen the influx of police and as yet had not formulated a Plan "B". For a few seconds there was a Mexican stand-off, as they stared at Lester their eyes flickered over him and his companions. Lester paused and eyed them levelly while his colleagues formed a phalanx around me and Shaw. Then the realities of the changed situation percolated through, and they hastily vanished in a northerly direction as police uniforms began to emerge from the doorway.

'Good riddance,' Lester said as he watched them go, and added as police members started off in pursuit. 'I don't think they'll get far. Well, we'd better get out of here. We have a schedule to keep.'

We were bundled into the back seat of a car outside which took off with a very large man at the wheel and Lester in the passenger seat.

'How...?' my voice began to tremble and I started again. 'How was it the police arrived...how were they involved...?'

'I alerted them to what was going on,' Lester turned round to face me. 'I said there was trouble, who they were and they were likely armed ...how right I was. But that wasn't all, as Graeme pursued this case it was quite clear an unsolved murder was in the equation, John Bromyard in the Waverley Pub. I'd already tipped off Victoria Police to look in the direction of Laurie Fisher's mob. They contacted London, so they knew who they were looking for, but they didn't know where they were. Graeme's call about an hour ago indicated not only where you were but where they were, so I rang Detective Sergeant Alan Tyson, an old buddy of mine in the Homicide Squad, he was handling the Bromyard case. He asked the Special Ops Group for assistance and they gave it priority.'

'Did they get them all?'

'Don't know yet, but they caught the boss man in the pub. This could solve that Bromyard murder for them, up to now they'd made little progress. I'd say you're safe from them now.'

*

Jack Lester was more than bulk and muscle, he was also a good organiser and leader, with a view of how other people or adversaries would think, how they would think what you would think and then what he had to do to combat any subsequent conclusions.

Within moments of arriving at his offices in South Yarra we were ensconced in his operations room, a window in the room looked out into the internal corridor but otherwise the room was completely enclosed. I felt thankful for that, I had visions of someone taking a pot shot from an adjoining building, not an unreasonable thought in view of recent events.

'You have to reach London, right?'

'Right!' agreed Shaw.

'How long do we have?'

'About 15 days, I'm not sure exactly, I've lost track of dates over the last week or so.'

'I guess they'll be expecting you to fly straight to London from Tullamarine, or may consider the possibility you'd travel via South Africa. So what we'll do is fly you via the United States and back to England that way. You...' he indicated Shaw '... will have to stay here. We want you to be seen around here for a few days and then at Tullamarine as well. In the meantime, Phil will fly to San Francisco or LA with Tiny.'

The plan seemed a good one, not infallible but it made sense. The man referred to as Tiny, who had been the driver from the city, nodded in agreement. He was about 6'2' tall and must have weighed about 16 stone.

'What about the costs?'

'Bugger the costs, no doubt the Estate will provide for that, I'll charge Matt Pelham for the privilege and I've no doubt Pelham in turn will debit the Estate. Money is no object just now as everything will collapse if Phil fails to make it.'

I felt my adrenalin run and prickles run up and down my guts at that. Despite his offhand manner I realised I wasn't out of the wood yet.

'That's OK by me,' said Shaw.

Lester planned the route with care. He eliminated any semblance of directness, the first flight was to Auckland, then Hawaii then to the States. A flight would take us to the Eastern Seaboard and we would then be booked on a transatlantic flight.

They brought in a make-up man, from conversation I discovered he also worked for one of the TV studios in Melbourne and whilst he was working on me he told me of some of the television actors on whom he had carried out make-up jobs. As he listed some of his subjects, I recalled some of the numerous police and detective series he mentioned. I looked at myself in the mirror afterwards and marvelled, my appearance had certainly changed.

'What about my passport photo?' I asked. 'I look different.'

'This is to get you to the airport and inside it unrecognised. When the time comes to present yourself to Customs you can muss yourself up a bit and look more like your photo.'

'But what about my passport? I may be stopped at Tullamarine airport. I'm probably wanted for that shoot out at Halls Gap,' I protested. 'There could be a flag on my passport.'

'There won't be,' grunted Lester. 'I've been in touch with an old buddy in the police, they know all about that shoot out, the gun you were holding never fired a shot.'

'How would they know that?'

'Trust me, they know. Plus, they've been viewing the incident through CCTV in Halls Gap and it confirms your story.'

'But aren't they after me?'

'No, they want to interview you but you're not in the wanted category. You can handle that part of it when you get back.'

I lapsed into silence. I deemed it better to ask no more questions, Lester appeared to have everything under control.

Shaw and I had two nights in the South Yarra offices, Lester's premises had rooms on the top deck that catered for overnight accommodation, a cross between a motel and a fortress. A couple of his men occupied a room at the head of the stairs. Lester had words with me before I left for Tullamarine airport with Tiny early the next morning.

'When you reach London, you'll be picked up by Rod Fillery, he runs a security outfit similar to ours here. Tiny will identify him to you and you to him. This is a photo of Rod, I know him well as we were both in the Metropolitan Police together. When you're under his care, do exactly what he says...got that?'

I nodded, so did Tiny. Lester held out his hand and gave me a firm handshake.

'OK!' he said. 'Best of luck, but I think you'll be all right. In the meantime, remember Tiny is in charge, he knows the drill. Do as he says...right?'

'Right!' I responded.

*

We reached the airport, Lester and his men spread around the lounge and departure bays. Some of the counter staff on the departure bays seemed to know Lester, I was through easily and into the departure area. Tiny never left my side, he followed me onto the aircraft and sat me by the window, planting himself stolidly in the centre seat. The gangway seat was unoccupied all the way to Sydney, so was the gangway seat from Sydney to Auckland and then to Hawaii. All the way Tiny never left my side and always had the appearance of instance readiness. Whether he was ex-cop or ex-boxer I never found out, but in a physical scrap either would be acceptable, you'd want him watching your back.

His conversation was frequent but limited, most of it revolved around Australian Rules Football and cricket, but he had a winning manner and succeeded in making me laugh once or twice despite my tensions and the knowledge that with each minute we travelled Jane was slipping further and further away from me.

We touched down at Los Angeles and were whisked away to a hotel in the city off Wilshire Boulevard. My experience of the city was limited to peering through the hotel room window, I was fascinated by the brown haze that lay on the horizon and appeared to surround the city.

'That's the LA smog,' grunted Tiny. 'Imagine what a shit state your lungs would be in breathing in that stuff all your life.'

'Lucky we're only here one night then,' I said and Tiny agreed.

We caught a cab back to LA International Airport the next morning, Tiny checked all around as we exited the hotel, taking no risks. He even gave the cab the once over, we were travelling light but he insisted on what gear we did have being placed in the boot. He wanted to check it was empty.

'Airport,' he announced laconically to the driver as we took off from the hotel.

At the airport he didn't relax, anyone who came close received the once over, and he was still on the alert when we joined the queue to board the flight. The flight was from Los Angeles to New York, we were changing flights there so this time we didn't need to leave the confines of the airport in New York. There was an item of interest at Los Angeles as we boarded, apparently one of the Major League Baseball teams was also on the flight, they were due to play one of the New York teams the following day in the end of season play-offs.

'I wouldn't have minded seeing that,' I remarked to Tiny.

'Me too,' he said. 'I've seen a few games in my time when I've been in the States. I've followed Cleveland for years, don't ask me why. Maybe we'll see some baseball on the way back, eh?'

We reached New York without mishap, the baseball players were besieged by autograph hunters as we disembarked, I queried the number of people who would be following them across the width of the United States, about 3,000 miles.

'They're the Los Angeles Dodgers,' said Tiny. 'They used to be the Brooklyn Dodgers many years ago. They still have a large following in New York.'

'Why did they go west?' I asked.

'Money!' answered Tiny. 'The New York Giants pulled out as well, I guess not even New York could support three baseball clubs with the wages the players get these days.'

When we touched down at London Airport Tiny became restless, we went through Customs with the rest of the passengers and passed through into the main Arrivals area.

'Come on.'

Tiny led the way into the club lounge where we had a cup of coffee and sat with our backs to the wall. A drinks waiter came over and we ordered. Then three men entered through the main door and I was aware Tiny had tensed. They spread out and seemed to be looking for somebody, for one awful moment I thought these were Laurie Fisher's men and it had all been for nothing. One detached himself from the rest and came over. Tiny rose to his feet, still looking guarded, but the other made a placatory gesture with his hands.

'Rory Ferguson?' he asked. 'I'm Rod Fillery.'

'Hold on,' Tiny reached into his top pocket and produced a laminated photograph. He held it up, examined it then eyed the newcomer. He studied both carefully then nodded.

'Are you from Ludlow Tours?' he asked.

'Sure thing, you wanted to go on the London Wheel?'

Tiny smiled and held out his hand.

'I'm Rory Ferguson...call me Tiny' he said.

'Good. And you'll be Phil Meredith.'

'I am,' I replied as we shook hands.

'All right. Let's go, quickly.'

'What was all that about?' I asked Tiny as we exited the airport building.

'Can't be too careful.' said Tiny. 'Jack and Rod Fillery worked out a sequence of recognition patter, plus the photo. Recognition signals are usually a load of unrelated bullshit. You don't want a response that could be assumed from the question.'

There was a lot of milling around in the car park area, I was placed in one car but as we moved through the car park, I was exchanged into another. All the time Fillery was talking on a mobile phone or radio transmitter, giving instructions.

We headed into the city of London with one car preceding us and another following; it was like a military operation or Presidential cavalcade although we made full use of side streets. Fillery was receiving information all the time presumably giving details of traffic blockages and how to avoid them. Finally, we drew up in an imposing street in the commercial centre of the city, as I looked through the window it seemed to be the haven for solicitors, accountants, a few insurance companies, stock brokers and banks.

The other two vehicles pulled up around us and their occupants spilled out onto the carriageway and pavement, one of them superintending and checking all around. They spread themselves up and around the steps, the leader waved to Fillery who turned to me.

'OK!' he said. 'Out quickly and into that doorway there.

You'll find someone waiting for you, he'll take you straight to Matthew Pelham. Now go!'

CHAPTER 25

The ball swung late as it descended, curled off the fairway and headed for a knot of trees. It vanished into the undergrowth, but before Gilmore had time to bemoan his luck it reappeared above the leaves and bounced out onto the edge of the fairway.

'Lucky' I commented. 'Must have hit a tree.'

'After that triple bogey on the 12th I deserved a break.'

We walked down the fairway pulling our buggies behind us, Gilmore took one-handed slashes at the daisies that were rife along the edges.

'This fairway needs mowing,' he grumbled. 'So, what are you going to do now?'

'Leave the Jupiter for a start and take a long holiday,' I replied. 'After that I'll probably go to Europe for a couple of months and see a bit of culture.'

'Are you getting married first?'

'You bet!' I said. 'As soon as I got back to Australia I asked

Jane to marry me. She accepted, on condition I told her and the police immediately if anyone else took a shot at me.'

'When's the happy day?'

'In a couple of months, we've booked a reception centre in Stawell.'

'Who's your best man?'

'Bill Otway, I think he's forgiven me for the scare I gave him.'

'What about his girl-friend?'

'Marlene gave me some stick, she came round eventually, after we'd both promised there's be no more Boy Scout camping expeditions. She's OK now.'

'Groomsmen?'

'That's being fixed, you'll be one of them. But for Heaven's Sake don't turn up wearing golfing gear and don't bring your clubs.'

'Why not? I haven't got anything else.'

I addressed my ball and lofted it onto the green before we headed for Gilmore's ball.

'Guess you'll be living a life of luxury and idleness from now on?'

'No!' I said. 'I've given it a lot of thought since I've claimed that inheritance and the idea of doing nothing doesn't attract. I've seen what happens to large winners on Tatts Lotto and the football pools, they either gamble the lot away for excitement's sake or take to drink. But having said that, there is a problem... the sum of money is far too much.'

'So I repeat...what now? Charity?'

'No. Too much money can be frittered away by some of these charitable organisations, not enough of it goes to those who need it and too much of it goes to administration and expenses. I'm equally cynical about overseas good causes. In many cases the money goes into the wrong hands - poor people in rich countries contribute money that finishes up in the pockets of the rich people in poor countries...although cancer research will benefit, I have decided on that.'

I watched as Gilmore selected a club and began addressing his ball.

'I've decided, as it was family money, Bromyard that is, that other members of the Bromyard family should benefit as well. I believe that's what John Brodie Matthews really wanted. he rushed into that eccentric clause on his will because he wanted to keep Laurie Fisher out, but at that stage he didn't know where the living members of his proper family were, even though he'd been carrying out research and found some of them. What he had found was that the Bromyard family members seemed to attract bullets, bombs or torpedoes whenever a war started.'

'Did you find out where they are...living ones that is?'

'Well, apparently John Bromyard, he's the one Laurie Fisher's men got to, had a wife and daughter and I consider the daughter, being a Bromyard, is entitled to a share of the proceeds especially as her father was a victim. The same applies to John Bromyard's widow. He had just walked out and left her; he seems to have been a ratbag of the first order. Six further living male Bromyards descended from Nathaniel Bromyard were found, although it seems I was the senior one as far as blood lines and the family tree was concerned.'

'Has you had any more strife since then?'

'No, after I presented myself to the lawyers in London and claimed the legacy, Fisher was stymied. If anything had happened to me after that, he would never have been in the running. After I inherited, if I was killed the money would have gone into my estate which then would have gone to *my* next of kin, it would have gone to my sister Mary and if he'd attacked her it would have got him nowhere, it would have gone further away from him to *her* next of kin. For him it would have been like chasing last night's dream as the more people he eliminated the further away it would get. After I'd inherited it, the money took off in a different direction as far as he was concerned.'

We walked towards the green where Gilmore's shot had landed a metre off the flag. I walked to my ball and took the putt.

'Good shot.' said Gilmore but my ball teetered on the edge, then decided to stay on the lip of the hole. 'I spoke too soon, but now you're there you may as well finish it off.'

'Good idea,' I tapped it in.

'So you're giving the whole lot away?' he asked as I retrieved my ball from the hole.

'No. I'm not that altruistic, I deserve something for what Brodie Matthews put me through, he couldn't have foreseen what did happen although what he did do probably made it inevitable, Fisher being what he is. There was about thirty million plus, in pounds sterling, after the lawyers and the research charities had their share. Then after I'd kept what I wanted and taken care of my sister, I split it amongst the other seven living Bromyards who could be traced, there's two in Australia, two in England and three in Canada. I'm keeping about half of it, which will be more than enough for a good house and maybe enable me to set up an insurance brokerage somewhere around here.'

'Seven Bromyards - I thought you said there were six.'

'I'm counting John Bromyard's widow.'

'She'll be happy then, despite the sad loss of her husband.'

'Pigs arse! He was no damned use to her at all. I've met her since I got back, she's a nice woman but he treated her appallingly. He finally abandoned her and went to live with some bird in St Kilda and refused to pay any maintenance. But at least now the daughter will get some decent schooling. Further, nobody knows yet what I'm doing, you're the first apart from my lawyer and a genealogical researcher who found the other Bromyards. He's done all right as well with all the work I've given him.'

'What happened about the shooting?'

'Shooting? Oh Halls Gap you mean? Well, that wasn't so good, I had a very unpleasant interview with the police, I've had my gun licence suspended pending investigation and they took away my gun and Bill Otway's. On the other hand, they're not pressing charges, their forensic boys found plenty of bullets during their search, but no .22. The rest were 9mm.'

'You didn't fire any?'

'The rifle wasn't loaded, Bill didn't know it was in the Land Rover until we arrived at our camp. It was a new one, he'd just got rid of his old one, it had never been fired. They finally believed me when I told them I was an innocent party and that bloody general store owner was talking bullshit. Plus the CCTV confirmed it.'

'What about the bloke you clobbered on the mountain?'

'Initially that was a worry, I must admit,' I conceded. 'It was in the back of my mind all the time I was on the run with Shaw, I was fully expecting to be arrested for assault if not murder if I was arrested'.

'So, what happened to him?'

'He was one of the bastards in the pub in Melbourne, I'd just given him a headache for several days.'

'What happened after that?'

'There was an Inspector Parrett from somewhere around Horsham or Ararat, he was Ramsey's boss. He examined the area and located our meat safe, it was still hanging from the tree, we'd forgotten about it in all the excitement, I think Parrett must have tracked it by sense of smell! His forensic squad went all over that area and they found score marks on trees and dug out some 9mm bullets. They accounted for at least four shots fired at me.'

I reached into my golf bag, took out my water bottle and took a swig.

'Funny thing, I had a call from Ramsey, he dropped in at my apartment. Gave me all the information; told me they were suspending my licence and then the bugger confiscated my rifle, which surprised me, my gun hadn't been involved in that fracas at all.'

'I suppose the bastard made a meal of it.'

'No, he didn't,' I shook my head. 'Believe it or not, I had some empathy and sympathy from him. We actually struck a rapport and we've even arranged a round of golf. He knew I'd been shot at before with that business when I'd been chased all over that wood near Ararat.'

'Well if you do have a round with him, don't take too long over your shots. He might fine you for loitering. What happened to the blokes who were after you?'

'Ramsey told me the police arrested three of them in that Melbourne pub. They are still in custody, they haven't been bailed, they're awaiting trial I think, they've been charged with using unlicenced firearms and they're being investigated for the murder of John Bromyard, including the bloke I clobbered on the mountain. Ramsey said Scotland Yard were interested in all of them, they all have records as long as your arm!'

'When are you leaving the Jupiter?' asked Gilmore as we left the just completed hole and pushed our buggies towards the 14th tee.

'In about a month, when I've cleared up all the loose ends and everything is settled, after that I'll be off. When I'm broking I should see much more of you, professionally that is, I'll expect a lunch every week.'

'No harm in expecting!' said Gilmore. 'What will you call yourself, Stawell Insurance Brokers, Meredith Insurance Brokers, thought of any names?'

'I've thought of that, but it won't be Meredith. I'm changing my name to Bromyard, I owe that much to John Brodie-Matthews, and to Graeme Shaw I guess.'

'That'll be a blow won't it, Meredith is part of you.'

'It still will be, I'm just changing the names round, so I'll be Philip Samuel Meredith Bromyard. That was Brodie-Matthews' requirement, that it went to the closest and senior male relative bearing the name Bromyard. He stipulated that in the will, and I inherited because I'm a direct descendant of the Bromyard Line and I bore the name even though it was a double-barrelled version. It should be my real surname anyway as it turned out.'

'Well, it'll take some time for me to get used to that.'

'No it won't, you'll still refer to me as 'that stingy miserable old bastard' so it changes nothing!'

Gilmore grinned and spread out his hands in acknowledgement. He left his buggy by the side of the next tee and reached for his No. 1 iron. He squinted down the fairway and then to the right. It was the 14th fairway, the same dog leg hole we had been negotiating weeks before when we had attracted rifle fire.

'Now, what are we doing here, Mr Bromyard? The usual? I take it we're going straight over those trees are we, and cutting the corner?'

I glanced up the fairway at the dog leg with the clump of trees on the right-hand side of the fairway.

'Suit yourself' I said, 'Hold on . . .! There's somebody in the trees up there.'

Gilmore rested on his club and scratched his head.

'That's odd. Yes, you're right. It's probably only tramps. We'd better go straight up the fairway and shoot round the bend. But that's strange, it looks to me as if they're hiding in there.'

'It looks as if...what? As if they're hiding...!' I peered closely at the trees in the distance and then picked up my ball and rammed my No 1 wood back into the bag. 'Oh bloody hell! Look, I've had enough for today, let's go for a beer. We'll do the back nine tomorrow.'